TABLE OF

C000120610

CLIFFORD'S WAR

PALMETTO
PUBLISHING

Charleston, SC
www.PalmettoPublishing.com

Clifford's War: Without End
Copyright © 2022 by J. Denison Reed

First Edition

Hardcover ISBN: 978-1-73716-405-0
Paperback ISBN: 978-1-73716-404-3
eBook ISBN: 978-1-73716-403-6

CLIFFORD'S WAR

WITHOUT END

CHAPTER ONE

The scorching late summer sun reflects off the windshield as a car skids around a bend. The rubber of the tires vibrates as they bounce, screaming across the sizzling pavement. Loose gravel is kicked up and tossed across the road, striking other cars as Sara slides around the turn.

"MOVE IT!" Clifford loudly bellows, just before grasping his side, grimacing in pain.

"We're almost there! Just hold on!" Sara says, concerned for her friend. She fishtails around another bend, spraying a thick cloud of dust and debris into the air. She accelerates and dodges the other drivers.

"Excuse me! Sorry!" Sara exclaims, as they blare on their horns and extend their middle fingers while driving on the double-lane highway. Clifford wails in pain as he grasps his side again. "Oh, God! C'mon, HURRY!" he cries.

"Just another minute!" Sara quickly exclaims back. She swerves, finds a wide-open lane, and punches the gas. She swiftly takes an exit and speeds down the ramp to a side street near the urgent care facility, which is conveniently tucked into a shopping center with a large grocery store lot.

She cruises into the parking lot, dodges a pedestrian, and swoops into a parking space.

"Hang on, we're here!" she says to Clifford, who's moaning in pain.

"Have someone come get me! I'm in too much pain to move!" Clifford says in a pained voice.

"Okay, sit tight. I'll get someone," Sara calmly says as she throws the car in park. She swings the car door open, slams it shut, and bolts through the parking lot, into the office of the small urgent care facility. The light breeze through the trees and bushes blowing into the car window offers Clifford no comfort as he doubles over in the passenger seat in great pain. Strangers shoot him a concerned look as they walk past with shopping carts while he lets out several painful cries.

Clifford sits up, looks over, and can see Sara talking with the staff of the urgent care center. Through the large front window, he watches as she shifts her weight from her toes to her heels and runs her hand through her hair. Clifford closes his eyes and groans as another painful wave hits him. He is filled with extreme nausea from the pain, but he grunts and continues to apply pressure to his side.

He opens his eyes again and watches as she jogs toward the car with a slight smile on her face.

"What's going on?" Clifford grunts.

Sara smiles again, "Okay, they can't see you. We have to go to the ER."

"WHAT?! WHY?" Clifford cries in shock. "I'm fucking DYING!"

"I'm sorry, Dee, it's only a few blocks away. You'll be okay," Sara says calmly as she starts the car.

She pulls out of the parking lot and takes a side street toward the hospital. A woman jogging up the sidewalk starts to head toward the crosswalk, and Sara slows and waves her across.

"WHAT THE FUCK ARE YOU DOING?" Clifford cries. "GO!"

"There's someone in the crosswalk, Dee," Sara explains.

"I DON'T CARE, JUST GO!" Clifford cries again.

"Calm down. That isn't helping," Sara says.

"SHIT, I'M GOING TO DIE!" Clifford yells back at her wavering, much calmer demeanor. Sara, concentrating on the road, quickly passes a car.

"You're gonna be okay. You're not going to die. So, just shut up!" Clifford smacks the side of the car and grimaces in pain.

"You know, we could be on route seven. The traffic really sucks today!" Sara says, trying to make casual chit-chat while hastily maneuvering around more cars.

"Just fucking GO!" Clifford says through his teeth and closes his eyes while clenching his fists in pain.

The car comes to a slow stop and Clifford opens his eyes. "WHY? Stopping?" He begins to question. "NO STOPPING! Why? Why are we STOPPING?!" Clifford cries while looking around.

Sara sighs, "We're at a red light. I can see the hospital. It's another block away."

"RUN THE LIGHT!" Clifford yells, still in excruciating pain. "RUN THE LIGHT!"

"No!" Sara says calmly. "Jesus! You're going to be alright. Two more minutes. Okay? Unless you want to walk the rest of the way."

Clifford, now sweating from the pain, starts grunting and dry heaving violently.

"Don't you dare throw up in my car!" Sara says as she starts to drive through the intersection. Clifford starts to cry as he grabs his lower abdomen and leans up to put his head out the window. Sara quickly pulls up to the front door of the ER and the car comes to a jolting stop, tossing Clifford back into the seat.

"Here! Let's go!" Sara says as she swings open her door. Clifford wastes no time. Clawing desperately at the door handle, he shoves the car door open and stumbles out of the car, falling to the ground. Sara jogs over, pulls him to his feet, and Clifford starts to stumble away into the hospital. She stops and fixes the seat belt hanging out so she can shut the car door.

Clifford begins to dry heave again, and this time it produces. He vomits from the pain and it splatters across the hospital floor violently. The world around Clifford starts to close in and his vision goes dark. He falls to the floor with a loud thud. The sound of the hospital staff rushing toward him is the last thing he could hear as his vision completely faded to black.

* * *

The rhythmic beeping and sounds of the hospital machines have become a familiarity to Clifford as it's the first thing he keys in on as he begins to regain consciousness. A blurry Sara comes into focus. "What happened?" He asks in a daze.

"You passed out. You're in the hospital. Just rest," she says, trying to keep him calm.

A doctor shuffles into the room, reading a medical chart.

"Yep, kidney stone," she says, looking at the ultrasound. "Four millimeters looks like."

"Is it big?" Clifford asks. Sara lets out a slight chuckle, "Is that what you ask all the ladies?"

The doctor, trying to remain professional, can't help but look over at Sara with a snarky grin on her face.

"Ha-ha, funny," Clifford mocks. "I'm just trying to get perspective. Is that average or bigger?" he continues to ask. The doctor smirks, trying to hold back from laughing. Sara, however, laughs.

"Oh my God. Seriously you two!" Clifford exclaimed, starting to get annoyed.

The doctor quickly regains composure and says, "Yes, Mr. Dee, that is above average. If it were a little bigger, we would consider trying to break it up via sonic waves, but It should pass naturally. A fair comparison would be like pushing a golf ball through a garden hose if that helps?"

Clifford snips, "Not really. Sounds like it won't fit to me."

She continues, "Well, luckily your garden hose stretches. I'm going to prescribe you some pain medicine, ureter muscle relaxers to help make the passing easier, lots of fluids, and rest."

"Am I going home?" Clifford asks.

"We don't usually keep patients here for this sort of thing unless surgery is required, and that's not the case here," she says, handing the prescriptions to Sara.

Clifford adjusts himself, sitting further up in the bed, "How long until I pass this thing?"

The doctor says, "That is all up to you and your body, lots and lots of fluids. The more you pee, the faster it comes out. Could be a day, could be four. Just keep drinking."

Clifford smiles and says, "Okay sure, I'll load up on drinks."

As the doctor heads out of the room, she turns and says, "One more thing. You are on some pain meds that should last only a few more hours. Just make sure you fill these right away."

Sara smiles, "I like her!"

Clifford begins to sit up, "You like all the girls."

Sara shrugs and nods in agreement.

*   *   *

After parking out front of his place, Sara helps Clifford walk to his condo. With the remaining Tye Brothers money he stashed away, he was able to purchase four units outright in a brand-new neighborhood for himself and his other three teammates. Because of the timing of the neighborhood's construction, they were able to ask for a few accommodations before the units were finished, but unfortunately, couldn't get all four of the units together. Clifford chose a lower-level entry condo. Bailey also chose the lower-level entry but had a custom elevator put in on the wall he shares with Clifford.

Clifford, being in a corner unit, was able to choose a wrap-around style balcony from his bedroom to his kitchen area. He had access to it from the kitchen, living room, and his bedroom, which gave him an ideal one-hundred-and-eighty-degree view of his surroundings.

Sara and Daniel both chose the upper-level entry models for added privacy. They share a wall, and their entrances are across from each other. A small well landscaped picnic area separates them from Clifford and Bailey. The condos were surrounded by a nature preserve with walking trails and dense trees. It offers privacy and a woodsy ambiance, which is something that everyone loves.

Sara helps Clifford inside and walks with him over to a chair. He plops down and lets out a huge sigh. Sara walks up to his kitchen area and gets him a lukewarm glass of water from the tap. She returns to where Clifford is lounging and hands him the water with two of the painkillers.

"Take this," Sara demands.

"But I'm not really in pain anymore," Clifford argues.

Sara sighs, "Yeah, but remember, the doctor said that you need to start this right away because the pain-block she put you on will only last a few more hours. So, take it!"

"Yeah, fine," Clifford says. "You know I hate taking pills."

"Get used to it. You have like five you need to take every few hours," Sara orders bluntly. Clifford gives her a sarcastic smile before taking a huge swig of water.

"Get some rest, I'm gonna go to the store and pick up some jugs of water for you. You need to up the fluids to push that stone out."

"Okay, would you get something that has a flavor in it?" Clifford asks.

"I'll get a bunch of stuff," Sara yells back as she shuts the door.

Pushing up from his chair, Clifford lets out a huge sigh.

He can tell, even with the painkillers in his system, that his body is angry with him. He heads upstairs, walking past a framed newspaper article calling Martin DiPietro a hero for his actions during the police station bombing. He glances at it and proceeds to walk into the kitchen and opens his fridge. Inside, next to the beer, is a bottle of lemonade. He grabs it and pours it into his glass and chugs it in two gulps. He repeats this process until the bottle is gone.

He remembers how Martin used to chug lemonade when he got stones. He never looked it up for himself but recalls how he told him that the lemon would help dissolve the calcium in the stone and make it easier to pass.

Clifford never admitted how hurt he was when Martin was killed. He considered him a good friend.

Clifford grabs the TV remote and clicks it on. - The local news is on. The anchor, Angie, was talking to her co-host Marina about the uptick in traffic over the last year. Clifford scoffs, "Tell me about it," he says to the news story.

He usually hates the news. He hates being reminded of how terrible the world is continuing to get. It seems like all the hard work he put in as a combat soldier was not making a difference.

The news, especially in the Washington D.C. area, was always very political. With so much spin, it's hard to keep facts straight.

He shakes his head as the news story changes abruptly to cover an update on a string of local robberies, so he changes the channel to cartoons. He tosses the empty bottle of lemonade in with the recycling and sips the remaining of it in the last glass he poured himself.

He sits in a recliner and can start to feel the meds kicking in. Feeling a bit woozy, he sets the drink down on an end table and passes out in his chair. Being asleep only felt like seconds, but Sara was shopping for almost an hour. She returns to find Clifford passed out in the chair upstairs.

Clifford opens his eyes to the sound of her voice. "Hey, sleepy," she says gently, nudging his arm.

"Oh, Jesus!" Clifford says, seeing her face.

Sara chuckles, "Once again, I'm Sara. If you could stop calling me 'Jesus,' that'd be great!"

Clifford scoffs, "It's just that every time I wake up, I'm seeing your face. I mean, you're pretty, but..."

Sara narrows her eyes and says, "Um, thanks?" She grabs his arm and helps him out of the chair. "Let's get you to bed." Clifford pushes out of the chair and walks on his own towards his room.

"What kinda goodies did you get me?" he asks. Sara starts rattling off a list of flavored waters and sports drinks.

"Did you get lemonade?" Clifford asks.

"No... wait, was I supposed to?" Sara asks back.

"Nah, it's okay. I just heard it was good for kidney stones." Clifford says while rustling his hair. Sara continues to help him to his room and puts him to bed.

"Okay," she starts, "You need sleep. I'm going back to my place and if you need anything, call!" She continues as she places his cell phone on his nightstand.

"Oh, shit!" Clifford says, coming to a realization.

"What?" Sara asks.

Clifford sits up in his bed. "I have a stakeout tonight with Daniel."

"Uh, not anymore. You're resting until you pass that stone." Sara pats his leg and motions him to lay back down.

"If he needs company that bad, I'll do it with him," Sara continues.

"Okay, I guess that works," Clifford says, still woozy. "Just make sure you brush up on the case. The file is on my desk."

Sara turns out the light and says, "Sure, no problem. Call if you need anything. We got you."

Clifford grumbles as he drifts off to sleep.

CHAPTER TWO

Exhausted, Sara finally gets back to her condo. Daniel is sitting on the front steps.

"Hey!" he says with a nod. Sara waves and heads over towards him.

"So, how's he doin'?" Daniel asks.

"Kidney stone," she says with a smirk.

"Oof!" Daniel says in sympathy with a pained look on his face.

Nodding, Sara says, "Yeah, he's going to be out of commission for a few.

Oh, and it looks like I'll be with you tonight for the stakeout."

Daniel slowly smirks. "This is going to be fun."

A devious smile crosses Sara's face. "I know right?" Sara continues, "Where's Bailey? I tried calling and knocked on his door but he didn't answer."

Daniel shook his head. "C'mon, it's Sunday. You know where he is."

Sara cocks her head to the side, "He's still doing Basketball?"

* * *

The sound of chairs clashing together fills the court. Bailey slaps at the ball and steals it from his opponent. He breaks away from the crowd and dribbles the ball with one hand and wheels swiftly away from the group with his other. He switches hands as an opponent comes up on his right side. Bailey twists away from him. He wheels a bit closer and with a swooping hook shot he sinks the rock right in the center, nothing but net.

"Yeah! That's it, boys! Right there! All fabric on that shot!!"

His opponent shakes his head as he wheels away toward mid-court. Bailey continues his trash talk, "Don't be mad. It's all skill, baby! I've been out here for years!"

He wheels over toward his teammates and high-fives before the next play starts.

After the game Bailey chats with his teammates and exchanges good-byes before looking at his phone. He notices a few missed calls from Sara.

He returns her call.

"What's going on, baby girl?" he says as she picks up the phone. After a minute of intently listening, Bailey shakes his head at the news of Clifford. "No shit? Kidney stones? That's what he gets from eating all those almonds on those stakeouts. I told him too much of that shit wasn't good for him." Bailey continues. "Yeah, okay. I'll be home in twenty or so. I'll check up on him. You have fun with Daniel tonight." Bailey hangs up the phone and shoves it in the side pocket of his chair and continues on.

* * *

The evening turns to dusk while Sara and Daniel sit in the back of a van with hidden cameras pointing toward a window in an upscale D.C. apartment building. Sara, still in awe of how luxurious the back of the van is, says, "You know, now I see why you and Clifford always want to do these stakeouts. This is noice!"

Daniel lounges back on the small couch in the back and lets out a sigh. "Yeah, it's alright," he says as he stretches out.

"But seriously, I set up motion alerts and sound alerts so if something distracts us, we can go back and look at recordings and still catch what's going on."

Sara nods, "Cool. What does that mean?"

Daniel says, "We don't have to stare at the window the entire night."

"Okay, cool," Sara says.

Daniel looks around and says, "Sooooooo... Mario Kart?"

"Hell yeah! Toss that controller over here." Sara says excitedly.

* * *

Several hours pass and Sara is beating the snot out of Daniel in video games.

"How are you this good?" Daniel asks.

"Practice my young grasshopper!" Sara says in an over-the-top accent.

"Terrible," Daniel says.

Sara shrugs "What's terrible?"

"Your accent was really bad," Daniel says, laughing. The motion sensor lights up and they begin to hear a series of beeps.

"That's the motion alarm," Daniel says, reaching for the remote control. He changes the screen to the camera recording the window. They hear people walking into the room, but the video isn't coming up. He continues to mash buttons and gets an infrared video of two heat signatures in the shapes of bodies walking into the room.

"Shit, how do you switch it to regular video?" Daniel asks himself.

Sara shrugs and says, "I dunno, but I think they're talking. Let me get the headphones."

* * *

Clifford jolts awake in pain. The nausea the kidney stone created was too intense to fight. He jumps from his bed and rushes toward the bathroom in a hurry. Nearly missing, he throws open the toilet seat and begins violently throwing up. He can hear Bailey calling from downstairs.

"Yo, Dee! You okay?"

Clifford wipes some vomit from his lip. "Yeah, peachy."

"That sounds more like pea soup," Bailey shouts.

"Looks like it, too," Clifford yells back.

"So, uh, do you need me to come up there? I can, but it will be a few minutes."

"No, I'm good! I just need to get through this real quick and take my pain meds. I'll call you if I need you," Clifford says, knowing Bailey has his back.

"Okay. I, uh, I'm going to stay down here a little bit. Watch some TV, just to be sure. Cool?" Bailey says, being a concerned friend.

After another violent heave, Clifford blurts out, "Sure, make yourself at home."

Bailey wheels over toward the coffee table and grabs the remote. He flips it to ESPN and starts watching basketball highlights. A few minutes later, Clifford slowly makes his way down the staircase. Bailey rolls over toward him and asks, "How's it goin'?"

Clifford shoots a half-smile and slides his feet across the wood floor over to the counter that has his pain meds on it. He grabs the bottle, opens it, and shakes two pills out. He opens the fridge and sees it stocked with Gatorade and flavored waters. There is a note: *Drink the Gatorade, not the beer.*

Clifford smiles at Sara's note and turns toward Bailey. "Beer?"

"Nah, I'm good," Bailey answers back.

Clifford grabs a Gatorade and shuts the door. He cracks it open and chugs it after taking the two pain pills. He walks over to a chair in the TV room next to Bailey and plops down.

Bailey looks over, "You okay?"

"Not really. Shit hurts."

"I bet."

Clifford rubs sweat from his brow, "I've been tortured before."

"Me too," Bailey said firmly.

"Yeah, I know. I remember what, that fucker, Stacey did to you. But, this is as bad, or even worse than torture."

"No shit?" Bailey says in shock.

Clifford asks, "Not really, but close. Heard from Daniel and Sara at all?"

Bailey says, "Yeah, Sara told me she's having a blast. They're playing video games."

Clifford smiles, "Figures Daniel would have brought it."

* * *

Daniel and Sara are both listening intently as they try to get a visual of the two people in the room. "I almost got video up, just another minute," Daniel says.

"Shh, it's hard enough to hear." Sara quips back. Daniel, trying to be silent, goes back to messing with a circuit board, trying to fix the video when he hears a pop and fizz sound. The video comes on, but no audio. The circuit board lets out a puff of smoke and is charred black.

"Oh, fuck!" Daniel says, worried. "This isn't good."

Sara, now laser-focused on the video, waves Daniel away.

"Sara!" Daniel says, trying to get her attention.

"Stop, I got this," she says. "Get me a notepad and pencil."

"What?" Daniel asks.

"Hurry, I'm reading their lips," Sara says.

"You can read lips?" Daniel asks.

"Yeah, but I'm not going to remember what they're saying," Sara replies.

Daniel checks that the video is recording and turns to Sara, "We're recording."

"Oh, good, because I already forgot most of what they were talking about." Sara says. They both go back to watching. The woman in the video walks behind the man, draping her hand over his shoulder and down the small of his back. He turns to face her as he removes his jacket and slowly starts to unbutton his dress shirt. The woman slips one shoulder out of her dress, then the other.

The dress falls to the floor.

"Ooh, close your eyes," Sara says to Daniel.

Daniel lets out a light chuckle. "I've seen boobs before."

"Me too, and those are nice ones," Sara replies.

"Uh, maybe YOU should close YOUR eyes," Daniels mocks back.

"Not a chance in hell. This is getting good. Popcorn?" Sara asks, handing Daniel a bag of store-bought white cheddar popcorn.

"I'm good," he says.

In an embrace, the couple is pressing up against each other while kissing passionately.

The woman leans away and the two begin talking. The man walks over to the counter and grabs the two wine glasses, handing her one. He knocks back the wine in one fell swoop. She sets hers down and walks to the bathroom. A moment later she returns and wraps her arms around him.

He pushes the woman down on a couch out of the frame of the camera. The man walks toward her and can be seen lifting her hips and removing her panties.

She reaches up and pulls the man down by his unbuttoned pants. She returns to a standing position and starts removing his clothing. After tossing his underwear toward the bed, she turns and walks away, toward a chair on the other side of the room. She picks up her purse and pulls out a tube of lipstick. She presses the tube against her lips and slowly and very seductively puts the lipstick on.

She tosses the tube of lipstick onto the bed. She leans down, placing her hand behind his head and begins to press her face against his, but then backs off. She stands up and bends over to grab the man's shirt. She rubs the lipstick on his collar and begins collecting her clothing. The man is still grasping the back of the couch and struggles to stand up. He makes his way to his feet, and she pushes him back onto the couch, violently.

She grabs her purse and walks over to the kitchenette. Pulling a vial out, she gets some tissues from the box, pours the liquid from the vial onto them and uses it to remove the rest of her lipstick.

The man makes his way back to his feet, takes two steps toward her, and crumbles to the floor.

"Holy shit!" Daniel says. "What just happened?"

"Uh," Sara whispers to herself. "I think that was a murder."

Daniel looks over at her, "Should we do something?"

"No, I don't…" Sara pauses. "I don't know. Maybe we should call 911."

"Maybe we can save him?" Daniel says.

"We can't," Sara says. "We can't get involved."

CHAPTER THREE

The next morning Bailey can be heard yelling at Daniel.

"How did you fry the circuit board!?" Daniel shrugs.

"C'mon man! I spent weeks perfecting the van. Wha'dja do to it?"

"The video wasn't coming on! I thought there was a loose connection or something."

Bailey shakes his head and with an eye roll, he rolls away from Daniel and the van.

Daniel shrugs it off and shouts over to Bailey, "I'm going to take this over to the office in a few, will someone come pick me up?" Bailey ignores him and keeps rolling. Daniel continues, "Is someone going to pick me up?"

* * *

Wincing in pain, Clifford is talking with Sara, "So any ideas why the Senator was murdered?"

Sara looks over in awe, "HE WAS A SENATOR?"

"Yeah," Clifford says while biting his lip and wiping sweat from his brow. "A junior Senator, Jason Reeves, married, one kid. From Wiscons— didn't you read the file I gave you?"

Sara looks away in denial, "I skimmed it."

Clifford narrows his eyes, "It was the first page."

"Mmhmm." Sara says, still denying that she didn't even crack it open.

Clifford starts to stand up. "Are you okay?" Sara asks.

"Yeah. I gotta pee." He says grunting and groaning in pain.

"Are you taking the pain meds?" Sara asks.

"Yeah, but they only stop so much pain." Clifford replies as he walks into the powder room and flips on the light.

Sara yells over to Clifford in the bathroom, "What about those urethral muscle-thing pills? Are you taking those?"

Clifford ignores her and just shuts the door a little louder than normal. Sara jolts and blinks to herself at his reaction. Bailey glides into the room and says, "So what'd Clifford have to say about the Senator?"

"You knew he was a Senator?" Sara asks.

"Yeah, it was on the first page of the report. Didn't you read it?" He asks.

Sara narrows her eyes, "Shuddup. Did you take it easy on Daniel?"

Bailey smiles, "Nope. But seriously, it's not a hard fix, I just gotta swap out the circuit board. I just wanted him to feel bad for messing with my van."

"When are you going to get the hand controls working so you can drive it?" Sara asks.

Bailey scoffs, "That's easy, I've been procrastinating on that because I have to get it inspected and get my license, too. I'll get it done eventually."

"Mmmhhhmmm," Sara says, raising her eyebrow.

"I will!" Bailey returns.

"Sure," Sara replies. Bailey tuts and cuts his eyes at her reluctance to believe him. Sara says back, "Don't you suck your teeth at me."

Bailey tuts again.

Clifford can be heard letting out a painful groan from the bathroom. Bailey and Sara look at each other with a pained, awkward smile. Sara lets out a sigh and shakes her head. "Well, on that note, I'm going to go follow Daniel to the office. He's going to need a lift back."

Bailey looks over as she starts to walk out, "Tell him not to break anything else on the way there."

* * *

Clifford returns from the bathroom, wiping his face and drenched in sweat. "I need to pass this thing."

Bailey nods, "It should be soon. Once the pain hits, it's typically the next day."

Clifford shrugs, "Well, any minute now, I guess."

"Just keep up the fluids," Bailey says as he turns toward the door.

"Yeah," Clifford says, "We should meet up tonight to talk about this case."

"You should rest." Bailey quips back.

"Yeah, I know," Clifford says, "but we really need to get things straight before we talk with the cops. The longer we wait, the worse it will be for us."

"True," Bailey says. "I'll have Sara and Daniel write up a report and we can go over it tonight."

* * *

Later that evening Sara heads over to Clifford's. She knocks once, opens the door, and lets herself in. She rounds the corner and Clifford is sitting across from a much older gray-haired man in conversation.

"Oh, so sorry! I'm interrupting, aren't I?" she asks as the men look over.

"It's okay. Daniel is upstairs watching football," Clifford says, motioning for her to go up.

Sara looks over at Clifford and sees that he is looking better than earlier.

"You feelin' better?" She asks.

Clifford smiles, "I am. I passed it a couple of hours ago. Thank you for asking."

"Perfect," Sara says and then turns toward his guest, "Oh, you're Mr. Hamilton, right? You work with Clifford on the government cases."

"Yes, that's right, but you can call me Doyle," he says with a smile.

"Or Badger!" Clifford says with a chuckle.

"Badger! Ha!" Doyle says with a lighthearted laugh. "Only my old Army buddies call me Badger."

Sara smiles and walks over to him with an extended hand. "I want to thank you for bringing us here and giving Clifford the amazing job he has now. I loved Kentucky, but we had to get out of there and if it wasn't for you, I'd— We'd—" Sara starts to fumble over words as she's talking.

"It's okay, dear. Dee and I go way back. If there's anything I could do to help you guys out, I will."

Sara smiles after hearing him refer to Clifford as Dee. She nods and says, "Thank you, Doyle."

After a slight pause she blurts out the question, "Can I call you Badger, too?"

Doyle chuckles, "Sure, Badger it is!"

Sara smiles and lets out a slight squeal as she turns to head upstairs. Clifford shakes his head and lets out a slight laugh.

"She's a special character," he says to Badger.

"She seems like a sweet girl," he says back to Clifford.

* * *

Sara bounces into the room and plops down next to Daniel. "Go team! Kick a field basket!" she blurts out, mocking Daniel's beloved football.

"That didn't even make sense, Girly-girl!" Daniel says, not even diverting his attention from the TV. He leans forward in anticipation of the field goal attempt. "Gaaaaahhh!" he erupts as it drifts wide left.

"Did he miss?" Sara says with a smile.

"Yeah…He missed the field basket," Daniel said with a glare.

"You know," Sara starts.

"What do you want?" Daniel asks, cutting her off.

"I want to offer you some culture!" Sara returns.

"Culture?"

"Yeah, Culture!"

"Like what?" Daniel asks

"Welp," Sara says, "I just started this painting class"

Daniel cuts her off, "Nope, painting is boring."

Sara continues, "And there is something I think you would really like."

Daniel cuts her off again, "Boring!"

Sara keeps talking, "...and I think you might meet someone."

Daniel pauses, "Wait. Meet someone?"

Sara stops for a second. "What?"

Daniel asks, "Are you trying to hook me up?" Sara knows that Daniel has been in a dating rut for the last few months. His last girlfriend crushed him, and that is the reason he has been hitting the gym hard, working on his physique.

"Well..." Sara says.

"'Well, what?" Daniel asks.

"I can't guarantee that you will meet someone, but we were asked if someone knew someone who knew someone who wanted to model."

Daniel shakes his head in disbelief. "Model?"

Sara smiles, "Yeah, for the class to paint."

"Oh, so you're asking me to model for your class?"

Sara nods slowly, "Yeah."

After a slight pause, "Hell yeah!" Daniel says with a slight smirk. "I will totally do that!"

"Really?!" Sara says with excitement.

"Yeah, I think I will! That could be fun," Daniel says as he is posing dramatically.

"Okay, but this is for painting, so you have to sit still for a while."

Not really paying attention, Daniel nods and says, "Yeah, sure"

"Like really still," Sara continues.

"What?' Daniel asks.

"You have to sit still for a long time. It's painting, so you can't move... for like an hour," Sara says.

"Oh." Daniel pauses for a moment causing an awkward silence between them. "You know what. Yeah, I can do this," Daniel reaffirms.

Sara smiles and clenches her fists in excitement. "The class is next Friday!"

"Okay, I'm wide open!" Daniel says. "This is perfect! Wait!" He pauses. "Am I getting paid to do this?"

Sara bites her lip, "I think so, but I didn't ask."

"Really?" Daniel slightly frowns in disappointment.

"I mean, probably!" she says in an optimistic tone.

"You know what?" Daniels asks, "I'll still do it! But if anyone offers money, I'm taking it."

Sara nods, "Totally. I'm gonna text Paul, he's gonna be so excited!"

"Who's Paul?" Daniel asks.

"Paul Michaels. He's the owner and runs the class. Don't worry, he's cool."

Daniel nods, "Okay. Cool."

* * *

Clifford breaks up the duo, "Hey, Bailey's here. Let's chat downstairs."

Daniel looks over at the TV, "But the game?"

Clifford cocks his head to the side, "You weren't even watching the game. You were chatting about becoming the next Naomi Campbell."

Daniel with a loss of words just fumbles some vowels before saying, "Yeah, okay."

"Is Badger gone?" Sara asks.

"Yeah, He has a big announcement to make in the morning," Clifford says.

"Sounds exciting!" Sara says as they start toward the stairs

"Who's Badger? And who's Naomi Campbell?" Daniel asks, following the two toward the stairs.

The team congregates with Bailey in the sitting room where Clifford and Badger were just talking. Bailey starts the topic of conversation, "Alright guys, so I put together the footage that our trusty Sara and Daniel shot and came up with this," he says as he displays some still shots of the infrared video. He switches the pictures to a clear motion of the woman pushing the senator down onto the chaise and leaning in to kiss him.

"Unfortunately, this is the only clear shot we got of her. There is no audio and we can barely see her full face. You can make out that she says something to him, but we can't hear it."

He plays a loop of video that was focused on her lips but it's too blurry to distinctly make out what she's saying.

"This is because of Molly," Sara says.

"What?" Clifford asks

"She is saying, 'this is because of Molly.' At least I think," Sara confirms.

"How can you tell? It's way too distorted," Clifford replies.

"Yeah, my little sister is deaf and we learned to read lips while we learned sign language."

Clifford looks over in awe, "What? You never told me that."

Sara smiles and says, "You never asked."

Bailey looks over at Daniel, "Did you know she had a little sister?"

Daniel just shakes his head.

Clifford breathes deeply in frustration, "Okay, we can share our family details in a bit, let's focus on whoever this Molly person is, and who she is to the Senator."

CHAPTER FOUR

It's a cool morning with a crisp breeze in the air. Clifford spots Sara and Daniel walking together. He calls over, "Hey, you guys going to that paint class?"

Sara nods, "Yep!"

Clifford gives a huge smile, "You two have fun. I gotta go into the city and meet up with the FBI. I called them and told them we had info on the Senator's death, and I need to turn in the videos and brief them with our findings."

With a look of pity, Sara says "Well, that's no fun for a Friday."

"Yeah," Clifford says, "I'll trade you."

They both shake their heads no and start to walk away.

Daniel looks back and says, "See ya."

Clifford lets out a slight laugh, "Be safe!"

* * *

Going into the district is always a chore. The traffic is terrible, and the D.C. city driving is always a challenge. Clifford pulls up to the FBI building parking garage when he is stopped by a guard.

"Where's your pass?"

Clifford replies, "I'm here to see Agent Sims, he called me in."

The guard shakes his head. "Staff only parking. You gotta turn around and go a block up. That's the visitor parking. On the left."

Clifford finds his way back to the entrance of the FBI building after fighting the city traffic, searching for a parking spot, and walking up to the visitor entrance. He checks in and gets a message handed to him from the desk.

"This is from Agent Sims," the clerk says. As Clifford is putting his visitor pass on this shirt pocket, he says, "It took me nearly a half-hour to drive up to your visitor parking and walk back. I think I got the last spot."

With nearly no facial expression the clerk says, "Welcome to D.C."

Clifford shakes his head at her comment and opens the note to read that Agent Sims was called away.

"Sims is out, is there someone I can just give this to on his behalf?" Clifford asks the lady behind the desk.

"What do I know?" She quips, "I just process the visitor badges. I ain't no special agent."

Clifford wipes his brow in frustration, "Right, sorry."

Feeling a bit sympathetic, she replies, "Look, these guys are really busy and sometimes they have to follow leads unexpectedly. Keep the pass, it's good for 24 hours. There's a breakfast place a block over that has the best bagels and lox in town. Come back and check in after you eat."

"Thanks," Clifford says as he starts to turn away.

He heads down the block and spots a shop with a huge sign that reads, "Lox of Love."

Clifford chuckles to himself and walks into the bagel shop and orders. A few minutes later he steps out back to a seating area in an open garden between the buildings and sits at a round metal table. He faces the street and sees a park area in front of another building. Clifford takes a bite of his bagel, sets his coffee down, and then pulls out his phone to check the time.

In fairness to Agent Sims, he was thirty minutes late for his meeting with him. He tosses the phone down on the metal lattice table and it lets out a light clang sound. He looks over after noticing the sound disturbed a man reading while enjoying his own breakfast. Clifford nods in apologies, takes another bite, and gazes into the park across the street.

He lets his mind wander a bit until he spots a gardening truck pull up. The name on the side reads "Herndon Leaf, Garden, and Gutter."

He wonders for a moment why they would hire a landscaping company from so far out in Herndon. He takes another bite of his bagel and then thinks that it's just a name, they could have expanded into the city.

A man in thick tan pants, brown boots, and a tan button-down gardening shirt jumps out of the truck and heads toward the back of it. He pulls out a leaf blower backpack and straps it on. He walks toward the front of the park, nearest where Clifford is sitting, and starts blowing the leaves from the street into a pile in the park. Clifford watches as the leaves dance across the ground, blowing in waves from the leaf blowers' powerful wind.

Three men in expensive suits walk from the tall building across the street on the other side of the park. Clifford notices because this seemingly gained the attention of the landscaper as he suddenly changes direction and heads toward the gentleman.

The three men stand on the corner for a minute when a dark town car pulls up and they pile in. The landscaper stops following and watches as the car drives off. He turns off his blower and heads back toward the truck. He locks eyes with Clifford who instantly looks away, knowing he was caught looking.

Clifford looks back up toward the landscaper who has reached the back of his truck. He places the leaf blower pack into the back and locks eyes with Clifford one more time, making it obvious he knew he was watching. He walks to the driver's seat of the truck, still maintaining his eye contact with Clifford, and jumps in the driver's seat, slamming the door shut.

He starts the truck and drives off.

Clifford shakes the thoughts of malice from his head. The landscaper's behavior seemed strange, but it was probably nothing. He finishes his bagel in between sips of his coffee and heads back toward the FBI building.

Walking up toward the building he spots a few men in suits also walking up to the front of the FBI headquarters. Their FBI badges are hanging from their chests, ready to show the guards at the door. He glances over at one of them and sees the name: T. Sims.

"Agent Sims?" Clifford asks.

Agent Sims looks over at Clifford and says, "Yeah, that's me."

Clifford extends his hand to shake, "Clifford Dee. I was supposed to meet you about an hour ago. Traffic."

Sims lets out a light smile, "There's always traffic in the district, even when you plan for it. Let's go up to my office. I have a bunch of questions for you."

* * *

Just outside P. Michaels Studio of Art, Sara breaks the news to Daniel that he is going to be a nude model.

"A what?" Daniel says.

"Well, I was hoping I could just assume you understood that you were gonna be, um, disrobed," Sara explains.

"I don't even know how to begin to argue that logic and besides, I don't want you looking at me that way," Daniel says.

"Uh, I'm more into tacos than I am sausage, buddy. Besides, your parts will be covered. Paul will pose you behind a sheet, then he'll drop it so the students can paint you, respectable-like. No one will see your twinkie."

Daniel scoffs, "Twinkie? You were closer with sausage."

"You know, I regret using food analogies." Sara says, "It's starting to ruin two foods I like," she continues as she walks into the studio.

"So which do you like more, Twinkies or sausage?" Daniel asks as he begins to follow her inside.

Sara yells back toward Daniel, "If you ruin snack cakes for me, I swear!"

Daniel laughs to himself as he follows her inside.

Daniel is instantly greeted by the studio owner and art director, Paul Michaels.

"Oh. My. God. Is this Daniel?" Paul asks in pure excitement.

Sara smiles, "Mr. Michaels, this is Daniel. Daniel, this is Paul Michaels."

"Mr. Michaels is my father who went out for a pack of smokes when I came out of the closet and never came back. Please call me Paul," he says.

"I'm Daniel, and I'm sorry about your dad?" he says in a question.

"Don't worry about it, that's his loss. I was an absolutely amazing child," Paul says in a flourish.

Daniel laughs nervously, "I'm sure you were."

Paul motions for Daniel to follow him and then points toward Sara. "Oh, Sare-bear, be a dear and go set up the supplies and set the chairs up. The class should be here any minute now."

Daniel follows Paul into a room. He closes the door behind them and turns toward Daniel.

"Okay sir, I give this little speech to everyone. We are all human and alive. Breathing is okay, scratching your nose is okay as long as you move your hand back to the exact location I put it in. Do not change your pose. You will be sitting. You will be completely naked. Your privates will not be on display. I will pose you in a way that no one in the class will see your private areas. I will probably see you while I am positioning you, are you comfortable with that?"

Daniel was nervous. Sara was his only gay friend and he didn't know any gay men. Growing up, being "gay" was an insult. He remembers kids on the playground or in class would call each other an array of homophobic slurs to insult each other. Daniel thinks for a moment and knows that he has grown past such immaturity from his childhood, so he swallows hard and says, "Yes, I'm okay with that."

* * *

Sara is in the other room setting up the chairs when she hears the door open. She looks over and a few members of the class are coming in. She finishes setting up the work areas and she spots Daniel and Paul walking out of the room. Daniel, in a robe, walks behind the white curtain. His shadow can be seen through the curtain and she can tell that he dropped his robe.

She hears Paul gasp. "Oh my! Was your father a horse?" Paul blurts out. Sara fumbles with the painting supplies as she was setting them out for the class.

"Everything okay?" she yells out to Paul and Daniel.

Paul stammers, "Everything is hmm…" Paul stops to collect himself. "Fine. Everything is fine."

CHAPTER FIVE

Clifford steps out of Agent Sims office looking stressed and runs his hands through his hair. He spent the last hour talking about why he had a team outside the Senator's window. He didn't legally need to disclose that it was the Senator's wife that hired him because she suspected an affair, and he didn't.

Clifford wouldn't disclose that information as he was really big on the privacy of his clients. It didn't stop Sims from pressing him, but Clifford wouldn't budge. He starts to make his way to the elevator when he hears Agent Sims calling out for him.

"Dee," he says, "One more thing."

Clifford turns to see him in a light jog to catch up.

"I just wanted to say that I read about what you went through in Kentucky. It made national news."

Clifford didn't look surprised. "Oh?" he questions.

"Yeah," Sims says, "I just wanted to say that I respect that you're keeping your client's privacy and I know from what I read that you're an honorable guy who wants to do the right thing. It's just -"

Clifford cuts him off, "You have no leads?"

Sims nods, "A few, but not many. No good ones, really. Anything you got would be a huge help."

Clifford nods and says, "This is probably nothing, but maybe check to see if he has an acquaintance or knew someone named Molly."

Sims narrows his eyes. "Molly?"

Clifford nods, "A team member read the killers lips and thought she said the name Molly. If I get anything else, I will let you know."

Sims pats his arm, "Thank you. Here's my card." Agent Sims hands Clifford his card and turns away toward his office. He glances back and says, "Sorry if I drilled you in there, It's just my job."

Clifford smiles, "I get it, I'm used to it."

* * *

Sitting still was easy for Daniel. What was difficult was knowing that everyone was staring at his naked body. He felt awkward being on display, but he held composure for the entire hour, although it seemed like an entire afternoon.

Just like that, Paul walks up and raises the curtain.

"Okay folks, that's all the time we have today."

Paul escorts Daniel to the back room and thanks him.

"Get dressed and come back out to the stage to be recognized. We like to do this for our models," Paul says as he shuts the door. Daniel hurries to get dressed.

A few minutes later, he pops his head out of the room and Sara waves him out. Paul turns around and says, "Oh my God, here he is! Our glorious model, Daniel. Please everyone, a round of applause."

Daniel steps out onto the stage, this time fully clothed as the room, standing, applauds him. He waves awkwardly and then gives a little bow. He blushes and waves again and starts to walk down from the stage to meet with Sara.

Sara hugs him. "That was so awesome of you to do this," she says.

Two men walk over and one of them says, "Hey Sara, who's your friend?"

Sara smirks and says, "Daniel, but you're not his type. He's straight."

The man continues, "Well, if you ever want to switch teams, give me a call."

Paul turns to the men and says, "Okay, you two, break it up. Besides, if he does, I have dibs."

He turns toward Daniel and says, "I'm kidding."

He then turns toward Sara and mouths the words 'I'm not kidding' while rolling his eyes.

Sara laughs and Daniel looks over and asks, "What'd I miss?"

"Nothing, Baby Bear. Let's get you home before more poachers come over." Daniel lets out a nervous laugh and agrees.

*   *   *

Clifford finds his way out of the city. He likes everything about his new hometown, except for the polarizing politics and the traffic. The traffic is almost the worst of the two. When Clifford hit Route 66, everything slowed down to a crawl. A few more miles down the road, it became a standstill. After a few minutes of sitting in the same spot, Clifford jumps out of his car and heads toward the median to see if he can view the chokepoint.

The backup looked to go on for miles.

He rolls his eyes and lets out a grunt of disgust. He sees a big transport truck up ahead and walks over. The trucker spots him approaching his rig from the side and opens the door.

"Hey there!" the trucker says to Clifford as he is walking up.

"Hey!" Clifford says back. "I was just curious if you heard anything across your radio."

"You betcha," he says, "There was a pretty gruesome car crash up there. A truck up there pretty much has a birds-eye and he said there was a car flipped and caught fire with a bunch of guys in it. Probably all dead."

"Yikes, sounds bad," Clifford replies.

"Yeah, poor souls, said it looked like four guys."

Clifford shook his head, "Yeah, terrible. Thanks for the info."

"You betcha. We're probably in for a long wait so I hope you got snacks."

Clifford heads back to his spot in the jam and others are starting to pop out of their cars. He looks over to a few people staring at him in curiosity about what is going on and he shouts out, "Bad car accident. Looks like people died."

One guy shakes his head and says, "Jesus Christ these shitty drivers," as he was getting back in his car, clearly more frustrated about being inconvenienced rather than the people who lost their lives.

As Clifford reaches his car, he glances over toward the opposing traffic, driving smoothly when he spots a truck that reads, 'Herndon Leaf, Garden, and Gutter' on the side.

He thought to himself that it was strange that he saw that truck twice in the same day, but in the same instant, thought that the company probably had a fleet of trucks. He still couldn't shake it, because his gut was rarely wrong.

Clifford jumps back into his car and calls Bailey to tell him he was going to be late getting back to town.

CHAPTER SIX

It was closing in on 6 p.m. when Clifford made his way back to the neighborhood. He pulls into his spot and steps out of the car and starts up the path toward his condo.

Across the hall, Bailey's door opens.

Sara pops her head out and says, "Hey stranger, over here." Clifford turns around and sees her standing with a drink in hand, ready to hand it over to him.

"What's this?" Clifford asks.

"We saw the news about the big backup and knew that you'd be grumpy, so we decided to make dinner," she replies. Clifford shoots her a sweet smile.

He shoves his keys back into his pocket and walks over to Bailey's condo and steps inside. Sara hands him the drink and they both walk into the living room. Around the corner was the kitchen and off to the side, on the wall that he shares with Clifford, was a custom elevator which Bailey was just rolling out of.

"Hey, buddy. I called the gang over. Figured we could do dinner since you were stuck in that mess. It's all over the news."

Clifford looks over at the TV where they were replaying the traffic report. "Is that it?" Clifford asks.

"Yep. Apparently, there were three important men killed in that crash. Big time money type of guys. They also said they were government lobbyists too, so you got the conspiracy nuts on this one as well," Bailey continues.

"Lobbyists?" Clifford asks.

"Yeah, you know, the guys that grease palms to help get bills signed that benefit big corporations by screwing the little guys," Bailey replies.

Clifford scoffs, "I know what lobbyists are."

"Oh, why'd you ask, then?" Bailey questioned

Clifford shakes his head. "It's nothing."

Bailey says, "Nah man, it's something. I can tell when you have something. What is it?"

Clifford thinks back to his morning in the city. "I was having breakfast and I saw this lawn care guy in this park across the street. He walked over toward the building where three men were and they jumped into a car."

Bailey stops him for a second, "Like a black town car?" and points toward the TV. Clifford looks over at the news reporting the vehicle was from a local transportation service.

"Exactly. Then, he packed up quickly and drove off... Oh my God, that was a hit!" Clifford exclaims.

Bailey raises his clasped hands above his head. "First a Senator and now three lobbyists? What is this?"

Daniel walks into the room and interrupts the two. "Hey, mind if I put this on ESPN?" he asks, unaware of the conversation.

Clifford looks over toward Daniel, "Not now, I think we have a case."

* * *

Minutes turn to hours as Daniel sits on the couch with a beer in his hand watching basketball highlights. Sara finishes up her last drink. Clifford and Bailey are still talking shop about the Senator and the lobbyists being linked and trying to come up with a lead.

On his laptop, Bailey types away and says, "Look, see the Herndon Leaf, Garden, and Gutter, LLC, is a legit business. Here is its SCC file for the state of Virginia. It has a webpage. It even has a tax ID."

Clifford says, "He probably stole the truck."

Bailey shakes his head, "Nah man. If he stole the truck, there would be a police report. That's bad juju for a hitman."

"Good point," Clifford says.

Bailey, perusing their website, says, "Hey! It looks like they only have vans."

"Huh?" Clifford questions

"The company doesn't use pickup trucks. You said it was a truck," Bailey tries to confirm.

Clifford nods, "Yeah a white Silverado, in fact."

"Look," Bailey says as he turns his laptop toward Clifford. The picture of their fleet showed all-white panel vans and some vans with trailers attached.

Clifford says, "They use vans." He then scans more of the webpage and notices a banner that says, "Serving the Herndon and Sterling areas." Clifford's phone begins to vibrate on the marble counter across the room. It startles them as it breaks the silence in the room.

Clifford jolts up and grabs the phone. "Hey, it's Marlon."

The entire room perks up.

Sara jumps up and stumbles a bit before gaining her composure. "Hey, put that sucka on speaker."

Clifford obliges and sets the phone on a table as the group gathers.

"Hey, Marlon! We're all here," Clifford says.

Before anyone could say anything else, Sara blurts out, "Hey bitch!" with a very drunken slur.

Marlon addresses her first with a quick, "Hey slut!"

Sara smiles, "Woot!"

Marlon laughs and says, "Sounds like you guys are having a good time. What's the occasion?"

Daniel laughs and says, "Dee got stuck in traffic."

Marlon responds, "Well shit, that's a perfectly normal thing to celebrate."

Clifford laughs and says, "Yeah, they all felt bad because I was stuck behind a big accident for about seven hours. They sprung for some drinks and dinner."

"Seven hours! Holy shit!" Marlon says.

"Yeah, four people died and there's a criminal investigation going on. We're starting to dig into it, too," Clifford responds.

"I bet!" Marlon says. "What else is new?"

Daniel jumps into the conversation. "I posed as a nude model today!"

"Like in front of people?" Marlon asks.

"Yeah, it's a painting class that Sara's in. They painted me."

The others are trying to hold back from snickering.

"Reealllly?" Marlon asks. "Well, I always had high hopes for ya, kid!"

"What's up, man?" Bailey asks.

"Your cousin wants me to take a vacation," Marlon says.

"You do something?" Bailey inquires boldly.

"Nah, man, we're good. It's just that she feels I've been working too hard." Marlon continues, "Another club popped up last year and started recruiting some of my girls. I've been spending a lot of time tryin' to get more dancers, come up with more shows, the whole nine yards," Marlon explains.

"Ah, got it." Clifford says.

"Yeah, so I figured I could take a break and get my mind right. I can come out your way and see some of the sights."

Sara excitedly says, "Yes! There is so much we can do and see!"

"I'm not sitting in your class!" Marlon says. The group starts laughing.

Clifford asks, "When are you thinking?"

"In a couple weeks. I have to make sure that Josh is good to go with the opening and closing procedures."

Clifford, surprised, asks, "Josh? What happened to Vince?"

Marlon laughs, "He's managing that new place now. Those dumbass fuckers. They've got no idea how terrible he was at the money. I promoted Josh to manager."

Clifford smiles, "Good for Josh."

Marlon says, "Yeah, he's doing okay. So how's mid-September for everyone?"

Bailey says, "Perfect, you can bunk with me if you like."

"Sure thing. I have to run, so let's go over the details later," Marlon says.

Bailey says, "Yes sir! I got two rooms I'm not using, so you have your choice. Oh, and tell my cousin she better call me. I haven't heard from her in months."

"Sounds good," Marlon says, "and don't worry, I'll give her shit for you."

Bailey laughs, "You better."

After the call, Clifford turns to Sara and says, "Hey, we're sorry we got a bit carried away with our theories. Do you two have any thoughts on this?"

Sara says, "Nah, it's okay. I was just listening. But I think I need to call it a night." Bailey looks over at Daniel and nods toward Sara. Daniel picks up on the gesture and says, "Hey Sara, I'll walk with you."

After the two leave, Bailey and Clifford continue to poke and prod at the case.

CHAPTER SEVEN

The next morning Sara wakes with a terrible hangover. She stumbles out of bed and slides across her wood floor in her socks toward the living room. She sees the lights of an emergency vehicle strobing across the room. She shakes the sleep from her eyes and walks toward the window. Her blurred vision becomes focused and she can see two police cars in the parking lot.

"What's this shit?" she asks herself.

She walks downstairs and pokes her head out of the door. The chilly morning air meets her face. Sara walks back upstairs and grabs her phone from the nightstand and unlocks it to see a text from Dee that read: *Stay inside!*

Sara responds: *What's going on?*

The text was left unread for several minutes, which felt like an eternity for Sara. She decides to call, but there is no answer. She calls Bailey, also with no answer. Sara tries Daniel and finally someone picks up. With sleep in his voice Daniel answers, "Hello?"

Sara in a panic says, "Tell me you know what's going on?"

Confused, Daniel says, "What? Going on about what?"

Sara says, "Look out your window!"

Daniel responds, "I just see trees!"

"THE OTHER SIDE!" Sara yells into the phone

Daniel grunts, "Okay, fine. Hold on," he says getting out of bed. "Holy shit! What's going on?" he asks Sara once he peeks out the window facing the parking lot.

"Goddammit! I'm coming over!" Sara exclaims as she hangs up the phone. She grabs a jacket and slides her feet into slippers and heads down to the door. She opens the door a crack and looks over toward Daniel's condo. She can see him open the door so she sneaks out and rushes over toward him.

He swings open the door and says, "I got this from Dee."

He shows her the same text and Sara replies, "That's a group text, he sent it to all of us."

Sara's phone begins to ring. "It's Dee!" she says in worry.

She puts it on speaker. "Hey Dee, I'm over at Daniel's."

Clifford responds, "Good, stay there."

Sara asks, "What's going on?"

Clifford sighs, "Everyone is okay. There was an active shooter. My bedroom window was shot out."

*   *   *

Hours go by and the cops have left. Clifford walks over to Daniel's condo and knocks on the door.

Daniel opens the door and Sara is laying on the couch with frozen peas on her head. She slowly opens her eyes and gets a peek of Clifford and jolts up. "Dee, what happened?"

Clifford says, "It's okay to go out now. The cops still haven't found the shooter, but they think they're long gone."

Clifford notices that Sara is still in her pajamas and says, "You know what, you two get dressed and meet me at my place in thirty. I have to start cleaning the glass off my bedroom floor." Sara meets up with Daniel a little more than a half hour later and they walk over together.

They walk up to Clifford's and knock on his door. Clifford opens up Bailey's door from across the hall and says, "Hey, I'm over here." They turn and walk over inside.

Clifford closes the door behind them and says, "I got most of the glass up, but I just need to wrap the window to keep the air conditioning in. It's supposed to get hot today."

Sara folds her arms and says, "You know, we still don't know what happened. Ya care to enlighten us?"

"Right, sorry," Clifford replies. "Have a seat."

Clifford sits down and starts in on a story. "Last night after the two of you left, Bailey and I continued pulling at the strings with that landscaper. We figured out that the truck was a fake because the business only had vans and used trailers. Bailey then had the idea to hack into the traffic cameras and try to see if we could follow the truck out of town. Well, he couldn't."

Bailey jumped in, "Not that I couldn't. I can. I just couldn't do it from my house without my IP being logged, so I stopped."

Clifford nodded, "Right, whatever he said. Anyway, we abandoned that idea and decided to pick back up in the afternoon. At this time, it was already after 4 a.m."

Sara questions, "4 a.m.? We left at, what, 10? 11?"

Clifford nodded, "Something like that, yeah. We were digging for a while."

Daniel confirms, "Sounds like it."

"Anyway," Clifford says, trying to continue, "I left Bailey's and saw a note taped on my door. I took it off and opened it. It was just a white card that someone kissed with lipstick. I thought that was weird, so I walked around the front of the condo to see if I could spot anyone walking about, and that's when I heard the shots. I dove into the bushes and low-crawled around the corner. There were more shots, I could hear the bullets ricocheting off the brick just above the window and then the glass broke above me."

Sara stops Clifford for a moment, "Wait, you crawled TOWARD the gunfire?"

Clifford nods, "Yeah, Why?"

"Are you a crazy person?" Sara asks.

Clifford says in a serious tone, "I've been shot at a lot in my life, I'm at the point where I want to know who's shooting at me."

Sara just nods in agreement. "Fair."

Clifford continues, "So, I couldn't spot where the shots were coming from so I backed out and headed to Bailey's. He was already at the door. We figured someone would have called the cops after the shots rang out, and they did. It was really quiet for several minutes until we could hear the sirens. I met with the cops and they told me to get back inside."

Bailey snips, "I stayed inside. If the cops saw a brotha out there, they'd shoot first and ask questions second."

"After the police did a sweep they knocked on my door. I opened Bailey's and invited them in."

Bailey snips again, "Against my wishes."

Clifford replies, "We had to give our statement."

Bailey shrugs, "Whatever."

"We talked with the cops for about an hour and they did another sweep before they told us it was okay to go outside. Hence my texts."

Sara leans back in her chair, "Woah. Crazy Saturday morning."

Clifford responds, "Yeah tell me about it."

Sara sits in thought for a moment.

Clifford keys in on her face and asks, "What?"

Sara looks over at Clifford and says, "I'm just thinking about something you said."

"What?" Clifford asks again

Sara's eyebrow raises as she thinks. "You said there was a note with lipstick on it?"

"Yeah, super weird, right?" Clifford says.

Sara asks, "Did you show it to the cops?"

"Pfff. No. I honestly forgot about it after the shooting started. But they probably would dismiss it anyway."

"Uh, yeah, probably. But you know, it kinda sounds like a calling card," Sara says.

Clifford scoffs, "Like in the movies?"

"Huh?" Sara questions

Clifford explains. "People don't leave evidence willingly. That's purely a Hollywood fantasy."

Sara, frustrated, says, "Just let me see the lipstick print."

Clifford rolls his eyes and leaves the room to get the note that was left on his door.

Sara says, "Where are you going?"

Clifford shouts behind him, "To get your evidence."

Bailey looks over toward Sara and Daniel, "So, you're thinking this thing was planned?" Sara shrugs and walks away toward the kitchen.

Bailey shouts, "Hey, don't go raiding my fridge like you did yesterday."

Sara shouts back, "Oh, c'mon. Like your fridge had anything worth raiding."

Bailey says under his breath, "Says the chick who was eating all my cheese last night."

Sara shouts back, "I heard that! And that is exactly what I was looking for. That blueberry Havarti was amazing."

Bailey looks over at Daniel, "White girls and their cheese, amirite?"

Daniel asks, "Yeah, why do they like cheese so much?"

Clifford walks back into the room with a small envelope in his hand.

"Okay," he says, handing the envelope to Sara.

Sara jumps as if she was jolted by an electric shock and snatches the envelope from his hand. She sits down at the island bar as everyone starts to crowd around.

"Let's see!" she says as she opens the envelope and pulls out the lipstick note. She pauses for just a moment just before she slams it down onto the island counter.

"As I suspected!" she bursts out. Clifford looks confused.

"What did you suspect?" he asks.

Sara picks up the note and flops it in her hand. "This is the exact same lipstick that the hooker assassin lady put on before she killed that senator dude."

Clifford scoffs in disbelief, "What? You saw that on a video, you can't possibly know what shade it is."

Sara says in a flourish, "Oh, no, no-no. It has nothing to do with the shade. This lipstick is 'Cher Sans Raison' from Jacques Francois. The cheapest I've seen is five hundred dollars a tube. This lipstick is on my wishlist. I just can't convince myself to pull the trigger on it yet. That kiss on the paper is probably worth like ten or twenty dollars."

Clifford raises his hands in objection, "Wait, wait, wait. You wanna pay that much for colored wax?"

Sara rolls her eyes, "It has a velvet finish." Clifford looks over toward the other men in the room, who shrug as they are just as confused as he is.

Bailey smiles, "Okay, bougie."

Daniel chimes in, "Why is it so expensive?"

Sara looks over, "Because it's Jacques Francois."

Daniel shrugs, "I don't know what that means."

Cocky, Bailey says, "No one knows what that means."

Sara purses her lips and says, "It's like why Bailey buys two-hundred-dollar Jordans when his legs don't work." Daniel slowly looks over with his mouth agape.

Bailey cocks his head to the side, gives Sara a little side eye, and says, "I'ma get mad at you later for that one, but that's a fair point."

She continues, "Yeah, I know you will, but guys, you're missing the point. Whoever shot at you killed the Senator. That is what I am trying to tell you."

Clifford looks over to Bailey, "She's right. We should put a pin in the landscaper and focus on the one who is shooting at us." Sara begins to speak again but is interrupted by a loud knock on the door. Clifford, the closest to the door, walks over and opens it.

Agent Sims, holding his badge, eyes up Clifford and says, "Mr. Dee, we need a moment of your time." Clifford pushes the door open and let's Sims and another agent walk in.

As they enter the kitchen, Bailey looks over and says, "Ah, hell naw! Dee! Why you lettin' the Feds in my house?"

Clifford raises his hand in pause, "Hey Bailey, this is Agent Sims, and Agent-"

"Hibbard," the other agent says bluntly.

Clifford nods and begins to introduce everyone in the room when Sims stops him.

"It's okay, we know who you all are."

Bailey scoffs, "Shit. On the Feds' radar now."

Sims looks over at Bailey, "It's not like that. No need to worry. At least not yet." Bailey just rolls his eyes and purses his lips.

Clifford asks, "So how did you know we were all over here at Baileys? I only gave you my information."

Sims shoots a slight smile, "You do know the last letter in our acronym stands for Investigation, right?"

Clifford raises a brow and cocks his head, "Touché." Sims and his partner walk about the kitchen looking around at the decor.

"You two," he says pointing toward Sara and Daniel. "You were home asleep, I'm assuming, when the shots were fired."

Sara nods. "Didn't hear a thing," she says. Daniel doesn't say a word.

Agent Sims looks over toward Clifford and Bailey, "Why were you two up so late? Working on something?"

Clifford starts in, "Bailey and I were working a lead on those lobbyis—"

Bailey cuts in, "Dee and I are running with a theory, really."

Sims looks over, "Is it a theory or a lead?"

Clifford glances over to Bailey and back to Agent Sims, "He's right, it's a theory."

He continues, "We think that the lobbyists were assassinated."

Sims perks up, "Really, why?"

Clifford pauses for a moment, "Like I said, just a theory, but…"

"But?" Sims asks.

"But," Clifford says, "I have a hunch."

"Oh, a hunch, huh?"

Clifford smiles and politely continues, "When I came to see you the other day. I noticed a landscaper over in one of the parks. He seemed a bit shady. He was paying more attention to the building across the street than he was to the park. That's when those three lobbyists came out and he sprung over toward them, but just missed them because they got into that town car."

Sims nods and says, "Interesting. So, then what happened?" Clifford continues, "He double-timed back to his truck and took off. I took note of the company so I could look it up later. While sitting in traffic due to the fatal accident of said lobbyists, I noticed the same truck driving in the area."

Sims rubs his chin, "I see. So that's why it's a theory." Clifford nods. Sims turns away and walks about the room for a moment.

He turns back and says, "I heard about the shooting on the way here. That's not why I came. I wanted to talk to Sara and Daniel about what they saw the night you were watching the Senator."

Clifford narrows his eyes, "So you don't even care about the lobbyists or the person who took a shot at me?"

Sims quickly retorts, "Not my case. Not my problem. I'm investigating the Senator."

"What if they're related?" Clifford asks.

Sims smiles, "I doubt they are." Clifford feels a vibration coming from his pocket. He pulls out his phone and sees the caller ID. Doyle Hamilton, it reads.

Clifford looks over at Sims, "I have to take this."

"Sure," Sims says back with a slight tone of annoyance in his voice.

"Hey, Badger," Clifford says to his former Army Commander as he steps into the foyer.

"Dee, I have some news, but I'd rather tell you in person. Are you home?"

Clifford paused for a moment, "Actually we are all over at Bailey's place right now."

"Great!" Badger says with excitement. There was a brief pause before there was a loud knock on the door.

"Ah, hold on a second sir, someone's at the door."

Clifford opens the door to see Badger standing there with the phone in his hand. "You can hang up now, Dee," he said with a smile.

"That was quick," Dee says.

"I was in the neighborhood," Badger says as he steps inside the condo.

The two walk through the foyer and back into the kitchen area where Sims was beginning to question Sara and Daniel.

Sims turns around and eyes up Badger. "Who are you? You look familiar."

Badger just smiles and says, "Doyle Hamilton."

        instead of trying to find who killed the Senator?"

Sims stumbles on a few words when Badger continues, "I know you're trying to do your job, but I would hate to see Sorren get upset when he finds out that a lot of time was wasted by you questioning a team that has already given you their official statements."

Sims nods, "You know what, I see your point." He turns toward Sara and Daniel, "If I have any further questions, I will schedule a time to chat."

Badger smiles, "That's a good idea."

Sims and his silent partner head toward the door. Sims opens it and walks out. His partner turns around and says, "Thank you all for your time," as he slinks out behind Sims.

Clifford lets out a sigh. Bailey wheels over toward Badger and says, "That was gang shit, man. I love how you handled that guy."

Badger nods, "Glad you approve."

Badger takes a deep breath and clasps his hands together. "Well, that was exciting, and I'm about to add to the excitement."

Clifford perks up, "Yeah, you said you wanted to break some news."

"I do." Badger says, continuing, "As it turns out, Senator Reeves was a representative of Wisconsin, my home state, and I was asked by the Local Democrat Election committee if I were to run in the special election for his seat."

The group collectively begins to congratulate him when he continues. "Now don't get too excited just yet. Reeves was a Republican and the GOP is trying to lobby the Governor to appoint another Republican, but the DNC was granted a special election if the Governor feels they are submitting a qualified candidate. They chose me."

Daniel smiles, "That's awesome."

Clifford asks, "When will we know if they decide to appoint or hold an election?"

"We should know this week. They have until tomorrow to submit and my name was submitted this morning," Badger replies.

"Congratulations, boss!" Clifford says.

"Let's hold on to the congrats. I want to wait until they make a decision. I should know next week for sure," Badger replies, trying to reign in the excitement. "I just wanted you to be the first to know."

Bailey's smile started to fade when he realized no one asked the obvious question. "So, Badge, when you get accepted, 'cause we all know you will, who's taking your spot at the agency? Who's going to be our new lead for government cases?"

Badger let out a sigh, "That's up in the air at the moment. Dee, I'm sure you remember First Sergeant Kevin Burr?"

Clifford smiles, "Yeah, I remember he was a jerk."

"Yeah, you remember him." Badger scoffs. "Well, he became my deputy after I retired from the military and took a government job. He was promoted and took a position with the CIA. I'm offering him my position."

Clifford shakes his head, "No way sir! He was a loose cannon in Afghanistan. I don't think-"

Badger held out his hand to stop Clifford, "Stop right there, Dee. I know you two never saw eye to eye. Burr grew out of his pettiness and has led three different departments for the government. He's the most experienced and the best choice. If I didn't recommend him, someone else would have. Trust me, he's changed since you two last knew each other. He and I have become like you and Mr. Bailey."

Clifford bites his lip and nods, "I understand. Maybe I should reach out to him."

Badger smiles, "How about brunch, all of us, next week. My treat?"

CHAPTER EIGHT

Mid-morning is particularly chilly for this time of year. Clifford parks the van and walks over toward the passenger side where Bailey is exiting from the mechanical ramp and helps him out of the van. The two men travel toward the entrance of Clyde's restaurant and meet with Sara and Daniel.

This is the first time that any of them have been to this particular restaurant. The decor could be described as "country chic." The building was an old farmhouse with an attached barn. It was very classy, but in a very rural theme. They had rustic displays of roosters, ice-cold water served from old antique steel pitchers, and farm-themed knick knacks on the walls and ceiling moldings. The lobby had a huge roaring fireplace next to a winding staircase. In front of the fire were old couches and chairs on top of an antique-style rug where people would sit and wait for their reserved tables.

Clifford approaches the hostess stand, "We're here for the Hamilton brunch."

"Yes sir, let me just check the reservations," the hostess says while looking at the computer. "Ah, yes, right this way." She escorts the team to a private room that was blocked off exclusively for the brunch. She opens the door and Clifford can already see Badger sitting across from Kevin Burr.

A sinking feeling enters his gut as his mind slips back to First Sergeant Burr screaming at him, blaming him for being caught prisoner in Afghanistan. He knows for sure that it was Badger's call to rescue him, because Burr would have left him in the Taliban prison to die.

Kevin glances over and notices Clifford walking toward the table. He proceeds to stand and step out from his chair. With a huge smile on his face, he extends his hand. Clifford winces for a moment and then proceeds to shake his hand. "First Sergeant Burr! It's been a very long time," Clifford says.

"Oh wow! It hasn't been First Sergeant Burr in a very long time. Please, Kevin," he insists.

Clifford nods, "Kevin. Sure."

Kevin turns toward the table and asks everyone to sit. The group filters in. Clifford and Sara are on either side of Badger, Daniel sits next to Kevin, and Bailey is at the head of the table.

Badger starts the conversation, "As you guys already know, the special election was granted and I am officially running for Senate. I wanted to hold this brunch to reacquaint you, Dee, with Kevin. Kevin will be taking over my position with the Agency and effectively be your official government contact and customer for those pesky government cases. Kevin, this is Dee's team. Bailey is pretty good with computers. Sara and Daniel are both apprentices under Dee, who help dig up information on things and people that, let's just say, are out of our government jurisdictional reach."

Kevin shoots Badger a confused look. "What do you mean?"

Clifford jumps in, "Well, as a hired contractor, we can do things faster without approval."

Badger cuts him off, "Partly right, Dee. The government still needs approval. It's just that a contractor can act while the approval is pending. They just can't release the information to us if the request is denied. We can go into more detail in private. Let's just say, Dee and his team have been a very big asset to our operations."

Kevin nods, "I see. That's good to know."

Badger smiles, "Let's focus on the menu and we can discuss business later."

After the meal, the group was still having idle chit chat and Clifford is starting to feel a bit better about Kevin. He never mentioned the past, and Kevin seemed to treat it as if it never happened. Clifford was beginning to think that he forgot about it. In that same thought it just slips out, "Kevin, about Afghanistan," Clifford says with a pause.

Kevin's eyes widened, "Oh Dee, man I haven't thought about Afghanistan in a long time. I know that I said a few things that were, uh, unprofessional, at the time and I can't even begin to apologize for it."

A slight hint of a smile brushes across Clifford's face, "Yeah, it hit me hard for a while and I just wanted to clear the air about it."

Kevin nods, "For sure, I get it. Can we consider it water under the bridge?" Clifford doesn't think this is a great apology, but it was probably the best he was going to get. "Sure," he says to end the painful conversation.

Badger clasps his hands together, "Okay gang, let's adjourn this meeting. I got the check, so feel free to head out. I know Kevin and I have a lot to talk about. Thank you all so much for joining me."

* * *

A few weeks after the brunch, Clifford hasn't picked up any new government cases. Badger has been in full campaign mode and Kevin has yet to be in contact. He was announced as interim chief, so Clifford believes it's only a matter of time before they get the call to be put on a case. Clifford finishes up an email sent to Kevin about the weekly teleconferences that he used to have with Badger and asks to pick them back up again. He doesn't want to get too far behind, or even worse, out of the work scope.

After sending the email, Clifford walks to his kitchen to get himself a glass of juice. Bailey calls him on the phone and asks him to come over and see something that he discovered.

A few minutes later, Clifford knocks on Bailey's door.

Bailey pulls open the door, "Hey, come in. I've been working on this music piracy case for J-Rock studios. They thought that someone was stealing some of their music."

Clifford cuts him off. "Yeah, I remember. This is that rap thing, right? It's literally the only thing paying the bills right now."

Bailey scoffs, "Have you heard from Kevin yet?"

"Nope, hopefully soon. It would be nice to get back on that payroll." Clifford says.

Bailey continues, "Yeah, it would. It's like sixty percent of our income. So anyway, check this out. You remember that J-Rock studios had me looking into the music of Jimmi from Philly, right?"

Clifford sighs, "Yes, you keep mentioning how you were going to rap with him. What was your handle again? CrippleKing?"

Bailey gets serious, "What's wrong with my handle, Dee?"

Clifford stumbles over his words, "Nothin'. It's great."

"That's what I thought! Anyway, JFP thinks that this other group..."

Clifford cut him off, "Wait, JFP?"

Bailey lets out a sigh, "Keep up. Jimmi from Philly, otherwise known as JFP, had his music stolen, right?"

Clifford confirms, "Yes. Tracking."

Bailey continues, "So, his manager, Ray, asked me to dig into this other artist, Dark Fenix. You know Dark Fenix?"

"Nope!" Clifford says.

Bailey laughs, "I didn't think so. Dark Fenix had some mild success over the last four years or so, but he does more branding than music. He has his own clothing line. He does hats, shirts, jeans... Even his own energy drink, right?"

"Still tracking," Clifford says.

"Okay, so like every other year, or so, Fenix will release a new album and do a huge YouTube release, followed by a short US tour, then an international tour."

"Okay, so?" Clifford says.

Bailey gets quiet for a second. "Dark Fenix has been stealing music from unknown local artists." Clifford remains quiet and blinks a few times.

Bailey asks, "You heard me, right?"

Clifford says, "Yeah, but this doesn't sound very Earth-shattering. What's the big deal?"

"Okay, I'm gettin' there," Bailey continues. "Dark Fenix stole music from JFP. JFP is getting more popular and wants to prove, beyond reasonable doubt, that he had his music stolen. I was able to hack into the servers from Dark Fenix and pull a bunch of files. I found original tracks from JFP."

Clifford says, "That's great."

Bailey continues, "That's not all I found. There was one file location that was double encrypted. I was able to run that de-encryption program I was working on and it worked like a charm. I downloaded it and opened it." Bailey says as he turns the computer towards Clifford's sightline.

Clifford's face changes as he is starting to comprehend the file he is looking at. "This is not music."

Bailey smiles. "Nope," he says as he clicks on a new file.

Clifford squints, "That folder right there. Click on that one. What is that?"

Bailey opens the new folder.

"Oh my God!" Clifford says as the folder contains dozens of files. "These files are names of weapons. Are they smuggling guns?"

"Looks that way to me," Bailey says.

"Open one of those files."

Bailey clicks a file but it opens to a garbled mess of numbers, letters, and special characters.

"The contents are also encrypted, and we don't got the key to unencrypt it," Bailey says.

"Shit!" Clifford says. "Of course, it's encrypted. Can't you run that program on it again?"

Bailey shakes his head, "Nope. I tried it. It don't work. This uses a different type of encryption key that the program doesn't recognize."

He sits for a moment to think.

"Where's The Dark Fenix's studio located?" Clifford asks.

Bailey shakes his head, "Wow, he ain't a superhero! It's Dark Fenix, or just say Fenix. They're local to D.C. That's why J-Rock studios reached out to us."

Clifford's mind is racing. He knows this is big, but with Badger focusing on his campaign and Kevin not answering calls and emails, he isn't sure where to go with this information.

"Okay, make a copy of the encrypted folders for us. Take the copyright infringement info to Johnny from Philly."

"Jimmi." Bailey corrects.

"What?" Clifford asks.

"It's Jimmi from Philly. Just say JFP."

Clifford sighs, "Okay, JFP. Send them the information regarding the copyright and close the case. Make sure they do not disclose where they got the information. We can't tip our hand that we got whatever this weapons information is, or whatever it leads to."

Bailey nods, "Got it. I'll tell them to mention they got the info from an insider. We don't want them looking externally. I will also do my best to hide my tracks."

"Hide them well. This could get really bad." Clifford says.

CHAPTER NINE

Later that afternoon Bailey drops off a thumb drive to Clifford with all of the information regarding the files they found. Clifford palms the thumb drive and asks, "Did you find any more information?"

Bailey replies, "Everything I got is on there. There's a lot of stuff that didn't make sense, so you might want to take a look to see if you can understand it."

Clifford begins to turn away when Bailey grabs his attention. "Hey!"

Clifford looks back, "Yeah?"

"One more thing," Bailey says and continues with an audible, "Uhh…"

"What, man? Just tell me." Clifford says.

Bailey lets out a sigh with a little half-smile. "We gotta deliver the files to JFP's manager in person."

"What?! Why?" Clifford asks.

"It's about digital signatures on the file," Bailey explains.

"Come again?" Clifford asks in confusion.

Bailey tries to dumb it down, "I know you ain't a tech guy, but it's like this. If we transfer the file to JFP, there will be two digital receipts attached to it. Ours and theirs. If they hand over the file to prove copyright, they'll be able to tell who downloaded it. If we load it onto a thumb drive, we can remove ours so it's completely anonymous. Now, the digital receipt for Dark Fenix's servers is still on there, so they can tell that is where it came from, proving the copyright fraud. Now, we normally don't care if people know they got the information from us because coming across information is not illegal and they cannot prove how we got it. But in this case," Bailey paused for a moment when Clifford connected the dots.

"Yeah, we don't want them to know what else we found on their servers," Clifford says.

"Exactly."

Clifford thinks for a moment, "We can have Sara and Daniel drive up tomorrow…"

Bailey squirms for a moment before cutting Clifford off. "Well, Dee, I thought I could go up with Sara. I think it would be best…"

Clifford cuts Bailey off, "You want to meet JFP," Clifford says with a smile.

Bailey shoots a smile, "Yeah, I do. But there are other reasons."

"Uh-huh, sure. Like what?," Clifford says.

"Reasons!" he replies. A few silent seconds pass before Bailey pleads, "C'mon."

"Yeah, you take Sara up there and Daniel and I can hold down the fort."

"My man!" Bailey says excitedly.

Clifford smiles and says, "Be careful and please be professional."

"Always!" Bailey confirms with a straight face.

Clifford shakes his head and walks away. Bailey smiles and wheels back toward his condo.

* * *

Later that evening, Clifford heads over to Daniel's place and spots him walking out.   "Hey, Dan!" he shouts to get his attention.

Daniel waves and starts a slight jog toward him. "What's up?"

"You and I have a date with a Senator-to-be," Clifford says.

"Huh? What's that?" Daniel asks.

"We're going to go visit Badger," Clifford responds. "Tomorrow, Sara and Bailey are going on a road trip to Philly, and you and I are going to meet up with Badger. He's only in town until Tuesday so we need to catch him before he flies back to Wisconsin."

Daniel nods, "Okay. Cool. I was about to go for a jog, wanna come with?"

Clifford smiles, "I really should, but I'm not dressed for it."

Daniel smiles back. "K, old man," he says and starts to jog off.

Clifford scoffs and yells at the back of Daniel as he is jogging away. "I'm only like twenty-two, uh, three years older than you!"

Daniel shouts back, "I know, I'm just messin!"

Under his breath Clifford muttered "That fucking kid."

Sara walks up behind Clifford as he is beginning to turn away. "Hey old man," she says with a chuckle.

Clifford looks unamused, "Yeah, you and I are even closer in age."

Sara laughs, "C'mon, that's his way of cutting loose with you. You remember twenty-one, right?"

Clifford scoffed, "My twenty-one and his twenty-one are way different. I was dumping sand out of my boots after being shot at when I was twenty-one. He sits on his front step picking gravel out of his sneaker tread after going for a light run at twenty-one. It's not the same."

Sara sticks out her lip, "Aww, baby. Yeah, and I was closing the club trying to dodge creepy sex offenders at twenty-one. Bailey was probably running from the law after stealing a car at twenty-one. We all lived different lives."

Clifford looks at Sara, "Yeah, I get it. I didn't let you make me hire him so he could poke jabs at me."

Sara puts on her serious face, "No, you hired him because he had no one in his life. You hired him because he would have been selling drugs and getting shot at if you didn't. His twenty-one exists because of you."

Clifford nods his head at the truth that Sara laid on him. "Yeah. You're right. I really do get it. Trust me." Clifford says.

Sara smiles and says, "Now, let the kid riff on you and take it like the father figure you are." Clifford shakes his head and lets out a small laugh.

Sara starts to sing a botched version of a song, *"You can be his father figure."*

"Oh, no. Stop that right now!" Clifford says as Sara continues. Clifford covers his ears and says, "They're bleeding now. Please! The agony!"

Sara laughs as she drapes her arm around Clifford.

He turns to her and says, "You know I love you right?"

She tilts her head away, "Don't you get all mushy on me, Papa Bear!"

Clifford smiles, "Like a little sister, you brat!"

She laughs, "Yeah, I know. Just messin' with ya, old man."

Clifford says, "Okay, enough with this old man thing."

* * *

The next morning, before the sun crested the hills, Clifford walks out and spots Sara climbing into the driver's seat of the van. He walks over and leans in the passenger window. "You guys be safe," he says.

Sara looks back at Bailey who is tinkering with the onboard computer system in the back. She looks back toward Clifford and says, "He's occupied and I have my music up here. We'll be okay. Tell Badger I said, 'Hi'."

Clifford nods, "I will."

Sara asks, "What time are you going to meet up with him?"

"Well, it's another brunch, and meet-up is really a loose term," Clifford says.

Sara shakes her head. "He doesn't know you're coming, does he?"

"Not exactly, I figured this was one of those, 'ask for forgiveness instead of permission,' types of situations,' Clifford says.

Sara shakes her head, "I hope you know what you're doing."

"Me too. Get to Philly safe!" Clifford slaps the side of the van like a cheesy used car dealer and Sara drives off. He watches as Sara rounds the corner of the parking lot and then behind the condos.

He turns to see Daniel walking up behind him. "What's up?"

Daniel says, "Nothing, I was about to go for a jog. Did I miss them?"

Clifford nods, "Yeah, they just drove off."

Daniel asks, "What time are we heading out?"

Clifford smiles, "Go for your run. I'll come by and pick you up."

Later in the morning, Clifford puts on his sunglasses and roars up to Daniel's condo in his brand-new Mustang GT. A few seconds later he spots Daniel poking his head out of the door. Clifford waves for him to come on and honks the horn.

"Oh, hey! You finally picked up your Mustang! Can I drive?" Daniel asks nervously, expecting a hard no.

Clifford smiles, "Tell you what, you can drive back."

"Promise?"

Clifford smiles, "Yeah. Promise!"

* * *

Badger is in the restaurant sitting with a group of his government colleagues when the host arrives at the table.

"Mr. Hamilton, a Mr. Dee is here to speak with you. He says it's urgent."

Kevin, who is sitting beside Badger, scoffs and says, "Who does he think he is? Can you tell him to go?"

Badger smiles, "Kevin, it's okay, but shouldn't he be contacting you?"

Kevin smirks, "Should he?" he smugly asks.

"Excuse me, this should only take a moment," Badger says as he pushes away from the table.

Kevin looks around and says, "I guess this would be a good time to use the restroom. Pardon."

Kevin walks a step behind Badger as he approaches Clifford and Daniel in the lobby.

Clifford says, "Great! I got you both."

Kevin sneers and continues walking, "I'm headed to the men's room," he says, continuing past them.

Clifford rolls his eyes and looks back at Badger, "See what I am dealing with?"

Badger looks sternly at Clifford, "What are you doing here, Dee?" he asks.

"I wouldn't be here if Kevin would answer his phone or return my calls. I stumbled onto something that your department needs to see."

Badger shakes his head, "You need to work with Kevin. That isn't my department anymore. It's his."

Clifford leaned in closer, "We found a file while working a case. It has a listing of a lot of military weaponry. I think someone is using a rap artist to smuggle weapons out of the country. We could really use government resources to investigate this," he says in a whisper.

"Guns?" Badger says loudly in shock.

Clifford motions to quiet him.

"Do you have proof of this?" Badger asks.

Clifford nods, "Sorta. We found files with the names of weapons, but the contents are all encrypted. We found logs that were sent to another server but it's on a different domain. We couldn't identify who owned it, but we are still looking into it."

Badger lets out a huge sigh, "Can you send them to me?"

Clifford hands over a thumb drive. "I have a copy for you here."

Badger takes the drive and shoves it into his pocket.

Clifford continues, "There is something else. We found another file that had what we think are code names for something in it."

Badger looks confused. "What? Codenames for what?"

"There was a text file among the weapons files. This one said Landscaper, Tofana, and Dorothy. Each had a monetary value next to it."

Badger asks, "What the hell do you think that means?"

Clifford says quietly, "I'm not completely sure, but bear with me. I think they might be code names for assassinations."

"What in the world makes you think that?!" Badger exclaims.

Clifford pulls him closer and starts to whisper, "Senator Reeves had a garden club that he was known for. I think they used the codename Landscaper for him."

Badger begins to look worried, "And the other two?"

Clifford sighs, "They are feminine, so I am thinking Senator Christianna Laurence and Senator Phyllis Cummings."

Badger's eyes begin to widen. "Oh my, they were all on the same committee. Do you really think someone would put a hit on the Senate majority and minority leaders? This is huge!"

Clifford nods, "Yeah, Reeves was a hit, that I know. I just can't prove this yet."

Badger says, "You need to turn all of this over to that FBI Agent, Sims. You need to call him right now."

Clifford shakes his head, "I don't know if I can trust him."

Badger nods, "You can and you will. You have to."

Kevin approaches the group and sighs, "The food is getting cold."

Badger nods, "Yeah, I'm sorry Dee, I can't help. You have to talk to Sims."

Kevin looks over to Badger, "Who's Sims?"

Badger shakes his head. "Don't worry about it. Go eat your soup before it gets too cold."

Kevin looks over toward Clifford and says, "Well, bye. Thanks for your visit," and proceeds to walk off.

Clifford looks at Badger and points toward Kevin. "He's still shows me his ass. You see that, right?"

Badger shakes his head, "I'm sorry, Dee. You'll have to make it work somehow."

Badger turns and walks back toward his table.

Clifford runs his hand through his hair and looks over at Daniel.

"Sorry, man." Daniel says at a completely dismissed Clifford.

Clifford shrugs and says, "That didn't go the way I expected it to go."

"Maybe we should reach out to that FBI guy. It makes sense," Daniel says.

Clifford looks over and says, "Yeah, it does, but first," he pauses, "Pull the car around," Clifford says, tossing the keys to Daniel.

"Awesome!" Daniel says with a smile and jogs out the door.

Clifford looks toward the area where Badger and Kevin walked and spotted Kevin walking away from the table on his phone. He turns and spots Clifford looking at him. Kevin waves goodbye, gesturing to Clifford to leave.

Clifford rolls his eyes and waves back. Under his breath, Clifford says, "God damned jerk."

The host walks up to Clifford and says, "He is totally a piece of shit. You can just tell."

Clifford looks over, "He's always been like that."

The host says, "Work in food service long enough and you can tell who will leave under ten percent or over fifteen percent as soon as they walk in."

Clifford laughs, "And him?"

The host smirked, "He's an under five percent kinda guy."

Clifford smiles, "Two percent, if you're lucky."

The host smiles back. "Have a good day."

"You too," Clifford says as he walks out the door and jumps into the passenger side of his Mustang.

CHAPTER TEN

Sara and Bailey are reaching the outer city limits of Philadelphia.
Bailey shouts from the back, "Hey baby girl, we're getting close. We just got to Wilmington, Delaware."

Sara shouts back, "Yeah, I got it on GPS up here. I know where I'm going."

"Okay, cool," Bailey shouts back. He spots a road sign for a town in New Jersey and shouts, "JJ told me we got a cousin that moved to Penn's Grove."

"Where's that?"

Bailey shouts back, "Penn's Grove. It's in New Jersey."

Sara winces, "Who would want to live in New Jersey?"

"Oh, c'mon, I'm sure it aint so bad." Bailey says back, "But, I think they are expanding over there."

A half-hour later Sara pulls up to a building that looks like a brick warehouse with lights. A huge sign out front reads "J-Rock Studio & Sound."

Sara looks back and says, "I think this is it."

Bailey's eyes widen and a smile slowly streams across his face. Sara parks in a handicap spot and steps out of the van. She walks toward the side where Bailey was already prepped on the mechanical lift. The lift touches down and Bailey rolls off quickly. "Let's go!" he says in a hurry.

"Dude, I gotta lock up the van," she says as she hits the button to engage the lift. She locks the van by remote as the lift closes and slams the sliding door shut. She shoots Clifford a quick text letting him know they made it and jogs up toward the door where Bailey was already waiting.

Her jog slows down to a walk as she catches up to Bailey. "Dude, slow your roll. Literally," she says as she reaches the door.

Bailey narrows his eyes and tuts, "Was that a cripple joke?"

"Yes," Sara says in exasperation.

Bailey nods, "Legit."

Sara opens the door and holds it for Bailey. He rolls in and heads toward the reception counter. The receptionist holds up a finger as she talks with someone over a headset. After a minute she clicks a button to end the call and looks over toward Sara and Bailey.

Sara begins to talk but Bailey cuts her off, "We're here to see Ray and JFP."

The receptionist points over toward a seating area and says, "They're in the recording studio guys, it'll be a minute."

The two head over to the chairs. Sara sits and Bailey wheels up to a magazine rack and grabs an old issue of Vibe magazine and rolls back toward Sara. After what seemed like a small eternity, which was really closer to about fifteen minutes, Ray walks out into the waiting room.

"James Bailey?" he asks.

Bailey looks up from his magazine, "Yeah, that's me."

Ray looks over and says, "Oh, I didn't realize you were..."

Bailey cuts him off, "In a wheelchair?"

"Yeah," Ray says.

"Yeah, it's hard to tell from my accent," Bailey says.

Ray smiles and says, "That's a good one."

Ray motions for the two to follow. "Jimmi's recording in the booth right now so we will go into the sound studio and watch."

They head into the recording studio and Bailey's eyes light up when he sees JFP from behind the glass. He starts nodding his head with the beat and lets out a huge smile. After a few minutes the operator turns on the mic and says, "Alright Jimmi that was perfect. Let's take five and continue in a bit."

Ray leans over and turns another mic on and says, "Hey, Jimmi come in here, I got someone who wants to meet you." He looks over toward Bailey and winks. JFP walks into the studio with a bottle of over-priced high-end water in his hand.

"What's up?" Jimmi says.

Bailey smiles, "Yo, JFP. What up, my man?!" he asks, unable to hide his excitement.

Sara looks over at Bailey, "What's going on? Who are you right now?" she demands.

"Hey Dawg!" Jimmi says, greeting Bailey. "I heard you were the one that cracked my case."

"Yeah, man," Bailey said, "Just doing my thing, keepin' it real, you know?"

Jimmi nods, "Yeah, I feel ya. How'd you get in that chair? Drive-by?" Jimmi asks.

Sara leans in and sarcastically quips, "Gruesome dolphin attack. SeaWorld..."

Bailey glares over at Sara.

"For real?" Jimmi asks.

Bailey shakes his head, "Na, she trippin'. I was boostin' cars as a teen. Owner got a shot off, hit me in the back."

Jimmi nods, "Deadass, man? That sucks."

Jimmi points at his water, "You want one of these jawns? They good. The only water I drink now."

Bailey smiles, "Nah, I'm good!"

Sara whispers to Bailey, "What's a 'jawn'?"

Bailey smiles and whispers back, "Not sure, just go with it."

Ray claps his hands. "Okay, now that we're all acquainted, let's get down to business. My office," he says as he turns to walk out of the recording studio.

The three follow him as he walks down the hall and into a huge room with two couches and a large desk. Behind the desk are posters of stars he managed and records on the wall of awards he won. Ray sits on the edge of his desk and hits a button that lowers a large projector screen.

"You said you have a thumb drive?" Ray asks.

Bailey wheels over and hands him the drive. Ray takes it and plugs it into a USB port on his computer. He picks up a tablet and projects his screen. He opens the file and sees sheet music and lyrics for two of JFPs songs.

"Amazing, these were recorded but never released," he says.

Bailey explains, "If you look at the file here, and go into the file settings, you can see that they were downloaded three years ago. Over there on the side is the MAC address of their studio's server. This can prove that they were poached from your servers and loaded onto theirs."

Jimmi looks over at Bailey, "You a smart mutherfucka."

Bailey laughs, "I got into tech after my accident."

Jimmi smiles, "Respect."

* * *

After their closed-door meeting, Sara and Bailey head out of the office. Jimmi follows behind while Ray picks up a phone to call Dark Fenix's manager.

"Yo, that was some smooth-ass techy shit, man!" Jimmi says.

"Thanks, man. If you ever need someone to sing backup or want a track to sing over, lemme know," Bailey says in a not-so-subtle ask.

Jimmi smiles, "I got guys for that, but I will give you a shout out in my next title. Good?"

Bailey smiles, "Deadass?"

Jimmi nods, "For real, deadass."

Bailey fist-bumps Jimmi, "Bet!"

Jimmi opens the door to the waiting room and holds it for Bailey and Sara. "Thank you guys," he says as Bailey rolls through. Sara looks back and smiles. "I like how unique, but simple your rap name is," she says.

Jimmi smiles, "Thanks, I wanted to keep it real, but using my true last name, Goldman, probably wouldn't sell many records."

Bailey says, "I dunno, Beasties did pretty well."

"Yeah, that's true. But I'm mixed. I don't know if that would have made a difference. It's all marketing."

Sara nods and says, "Yeah, but that shouldn't make a difference, you know."

Jimmi nods in agreement. "Oh fo-sho! But sadly, it does."

Sara pats him on his arm and smiles. "We should probably get going. Hey B- wanna get cheesesteaks?"

Bailey looks back, "Heck yeah, let's go."

Jimmi laughs, "Bye, y'all."

CHAPTER ELEVEN

Clifford jumps in the passenger seat and pulls out his phone to check traffic.

"Hey, I-95 is slammed, let's take the back roads," he says to Daniel.

Daniel smiles, "Sure thing."

Daniel slowly drives through the parking lot and pulls up to the road. He checks both ways and rips out of the lot and onto the road in a roar.

Clifford jolts and turns toward Daniel, "NO!" He shouts, "Take it easy!"

Daniel's smile fades. "Aww, c'mon!" he says as the car throttles down.

Clifford shakes his head. "I get it, but it's still new. I don't want anything happen to it."

Daniel smiles, "Understood."

Clifford sits in silence for a moment as he remembers what it was like when he got his first Mustang. He drove it up from Florida to Kentucky, hitting every back road, and ripped down every straightaway. He was a few years older than Daniel is now. Clifford sees a sign for an old backroad up ahead. He remembers it being hilly and fun to drive down. He turns to Daniel and says, "Hey, hang your next right."

Daniel slows the car and puts the blinker on. He carefully turns onto the road and slowly picks up speed.

Clifford smiles and says, "Hey, this is a fairly straight road, not many cars, and a little diner about three miles or so on the left. Let's see how fast you can get us there."

Daniel does a double take toward Clifford. "Really?"

Clifford smiles, "Really!"

With that, Daniel mashes the gas and takes off. The slight hills are no challenge for the Mustang as it slightly vaults over them. Their bodies feel weightless for a split second. Daniel lets out a loud, verbal "Wooooo!" as the car's wheels touch asphalt again.

Clifford's smile couldn't be bigger. He turns and says, "Come on man, drive it like you stole it!"

Daniel presses harder on the gas and the Mustang jolts forward in a thrust.

Clifford smiles again. After a few minutes, he says, "Okay, speed racer, take it down a notch. We're getting close to that diner."

Daniel eases off and the car slows quickly. He gets back down to normal speed and turns toward Clifford. "Thank you. That was really fun," he says.

Clifford nods, "Yeah, I know. I haven't been letting you guys let loose in a while. Seemed like it was time."

Daniel spots the diner and asks, "Are we stopping?"

Clifford nods, "We skipped breakfast so I figured we could at least get some eggs or something."

* * *

The waitress sets down the scrambled eggs in front of Clifford and the steak and sunny side up eggs in front of Daniel.

Clifford shakes his head. "Lots of protein," he says at Daniel's plate.

Daniel smiles, "Fuel for the muscles."

Clifford nods and asks, "How much bigger are you trying to get?"

Daniel perks up and says, "Actually, I'm trying to slim down and get cut. But, I do want to gain about five pounds of muscle and shred fat so I look lean."

"Huh, okay," Clifford says, pretending that he understood it.

Daniel continues, "It's hard, actually. Lots of math, macros, knowing what's what when it comes to food. It takes a lot of effort."

"I bet," Clifford says.

Clifford looks down at a text message on his phone and says, "Oh good, they made it to Philly."

Daniel smiles, "I can't wait to hear what Sara says about Bailey meeting JFP."

Clifford laughs, "Is he really *that* big a fan?"

"Oh yeah," Daniel says, "I caught him rapping to himself one day. He said something like, JFP and me gonna take it easy, smoke some wheezy."

Clifford tilted his head back and let out a loud laugh. "Oh, man! I had no idea he was a fangirl."

Daniel says, "Oh, legit fangirl!"

The two continue to eat and laugh. Clifford can't help but think that this is probably one of the few times they were able to bond since they met. It's all been just a professional relationship since. He started to realize Sara was right. Daniel didn't have a father figure in his life and Clifford was the closest thing to it.

After a few more bites, Clifford looks over at the Mustang. "We should get going soon," he says.

Daniel nods. "Yeah. Can I still drive?" he asks.

"Absolutely!" Clifford says with a smile.

Clifford tosses a fifty-dollar bill on the table and they head back toward the car.

Daniel looks over and says, "Dude that's over a fifty percent tip."

Clifford smiles and says, "They work hard. They deserve it."

Climbing into the passenger seat, Clifford glares out the window and down the road. He's watching the Autumn leaves fall from the trees and float aimlessly toward the ground. The sound of Daniel starting the engine jolts Clifford from his daze.

"You okay, boss?" Daniel asks.

"Yeah, I'm good," Clifford says as he shakes the trance from his head.

Daniel slowly pulls out of the diner's lot and Clifford continues to stare out the window. He glances into the side mirror and spots a white truck with wording on the side.

"Stop," Clifford says instinctively.

Daniel jolts the car to a complete stop before pulling out onto the road.

Clifford glares at the truck and the driver inside. His eyes trail downward to the wording on the side. "Herndon Leaf, Garden, and Gutter," it reads.

Clifford's eyes widened. "Daniel, GO!" he exclaims.

Daniel steps on the gas and flies out of the lot onto the road.

The truck quickly follows.

Daniel looks panicked. "What is it?"

Clifford, looking back as they are speeding away, says, "Remember that Herndon landscaper? The one I thought was responsible for the death of the lobbyists?"

Daniel glances in the rearview, spotting the truck. "Is that him?" he asks.

"Yep!" Clifford says, "We have to lose him."

Daniel asks, "Why is he here?"

Clifford glances back, "My guess? He's involved with the gunrunning. Someone was tipped off that we found their information."

Daniel asks, "How?"

"I don't know. Maybe there was something on the file that Bailey had. Maybe something he didn't notice," Clifford replies.

Clifford looks back to see the truck gaining ground.

"You have to go faster, Dan," Clifford says,

Daniel shakes his head, "I can't on these back roads."

Clifford looks back again to see a pistol sticking out of the driver's window.

"DOWN!" Clifford shouts.

Several pops ring out as Daniel and Clifford both duck their heads. Bullets from the gun dance across the driver's side and back of the car, luckily missing the tires.

The driver pulls the gun back into the window. After a minute, he trains it back on the Mustang through the window and fires again, shattering the back windshield.

Clifford pulls a revolver from the glove box and points it through the back of the car. He fires two shots into the front of the truck. A puff of white smoke begins to billow out the front of the truck and it begins to rapidly slow. The Mustang pulls away quickly as the landscaper points the gun out of the window again. A few loud bangs ring out and Clifford can hear the bullets land across the roof of the car and one rips through the leather seats in the back.

The truck, about fifty yards back, is still losing ground, but Clifford knows that he will make that up when they hit the town in a few miles. Clifford turns back around and sees a sign that says, 'Hill ahead, blocks view of road.'

Clifford looks over at Daniel, "Speed up and when you hit that hill, slam on the brakes and cut the wheel to your right."

Daniel looks at Clifford. "Are you sure?"

"Do it! NOW!" Clifford demanded.

Daniel crests the hill and does just as Clifford told him to do. He stomps on the brakes, slowing the car as it descends the hill. He cuts the wheel, putting Clifford front and center toward the oncoming truck. Clifford takes aim out of the passenger side window just as the truck was beginning to rise over the hill.

Clifford squeezes the trigger several times and sends a slew of rounds into the windshield. He could see one of the rounds hit the driver. Clifford aims for the tire. He squeezes off one more round and it strikes the passenger side tire, causing the truck to veer off the road.

The truck drives into a small drainage ditch on the side of the road at around forty miles per hour, sending it spiraling in a barrel roll, through some brush, and into a small clearing. Still moving forward while rolling, it strikes a tree and comes to a jolting stop upside down.

"Holy shit!" Daniel yells out in shock.

Clifford exhales sharply after holding his breath in order to get those clean shots.

"Pull off to the side," he says to Daniel.

The Mustang creaks as Daniel pulls it closer to the soft shoulder and ditch on the side. Clifford opens the door and leaps over the shallow ditch and muddied tire tracks of the truck. He glances at his weapon and counts only two rounds left inside. Keeping it at the ready position as he is walking, Clifford is prepared to fire if necessary.

He circles around toward the back of the car and notices that the driver's side door is open. Slowly approaching, he glances inside to see the cab empty.

He looks back toward Daniel and shouts, "He's gone."

"Gone?" Daniel questions.

"Yeah," Clifford shouts back, "Gone!"

Daniel looks around. "Maybe he was thrown from the car."

Clifford steps a bit closer and looks inside the cab and spots blood on the seat and dash.

The bullet that hit the driver went clean through him and out the back of the seat.

Clifford circles the truck and looks around at the surrounding trees and brush. He spots some that appear to be disturbed, but not by the accident.

"No, it doesn't look like it. We should get out of here," Clifford says as he backs away toward Daniel and the road.

CHAPTER TWELVE

A few hours later, Clifford and Daniel pull into the parking lot of their condos. Daniel turns down the street and Clifford, seeing Marlon leaning against a car with his arms folded, turns to Daniel and says, "Shit! I forgot he was coming today."

Daniel looks over at Clifford and asks, "He was?"

Clifford nods slowly as they approach. "Yeah, and I think I was supposed to pick him up from the airport, too."

Marlon, clearly looking upset, walks slowly up to the Mustang and leans in the passenger window. "Where the fuck..." He pauses as he notices the damage to the car and redirects his question. "What the fuck happened to your car?" he asks instead.

Clifford takes this opportunity to use it as an excuse. "We ran into a snag."

Marlon looks around at the bullet holes in the side, "I'd say so."

Clifford looks over at Daniel and says, "Go park it and meet us inside," as he starts to get out of the car.

Marlon wraps his arm around Clifford's shoulder and says, "Let's get you a drink, you clearly need one."

Daniel walks in while Clifford pours some rum over ice for Marlon.

"This all you got?" Marlon asks.

Clifford smirks, "I can pour that back into the bottle."

Marlon, remembering the first drink they shared, laughs, "It's fine."

Clifford continues, "I'm not much of a hard liquor drinker. You know this."

"Yeah, yeah. I'm just messing with you," he says.

Marlon looks over at Daniel, "You drinkin'?"

Daniel shakes his head, "Nah, I'm dieting, and alcohol kills the fat burning process."

Mocking his voice, Marlon says, "Ah, kills the fat burning process." He then turns to Clifford and says, "More for me then!" Marlon takes a swig of the rum and sets the glass down.

"So, what's the plan? Where's Sara and Bailey? Off getting my welcome gifts?"

Clifford laughs and says, "They had to run up to Philly, they should be back soon."

Marlon nods. "Sure, sure."

Clifford continues, "Everyone has a spare room, so you have your choice of places to stay."

Marlon takes another swig of rum. "Yeah, I'm pretty sure Bailey said I could crash at his place, but we can talk about that when they get here."

Daniel chimes in, "That's a good idea, but you can always stay at my place if you need to."

Marlon nods. "Thanks buddy!" he quips back at Daniel before turning his attention back toward Clifford. "So, are you going to tell me what happened to your car out there or what?" he asks again.

Clifford, about to take a sip, says "Well, we had to go see a friend about an incident. A case we're working on, rather. On the way back in town we ran into a guy that didn't want us to remain among the living."

Marlon's eyes widened. "And he shot up your car? How do you always find trouble like this, Dee?"

Clifford smirks, "Apparently, it's my superpower. So, anyway, we fired back and he veered off the road."

"Did you kill him?" Marlon asks.

"I don't think so," Clifford tells him.

"Welp, I ain't staying with you, then, good buddy," Marlon says with a laugh.

Daniel again says, "You can stay with me, Marlon."

"You were with him, he's coming for both of y'all," Marlon jokes .

Clifford looks over at Daniel and mouths, "No he isn't," then turns toward Marlon with a glare.

"What?" Marlon asks jokingly.

Clifford shakes his head and then continues with the story. "So, after we left the scene of the accident, we called the police and the FBI."

Marlon stops the conversation. "FBI? Why the feds?"

"I'm getting there," Clifford says, continuing. "We found some info about gun smuggling. We think that's why the guy was chasing and shooting at us. We have to meet up with a special agent tomorrow in D.C. to hand over the information."

"Cool," Marlon says, taking another swig of his drink. "Can I come with you to D.C.? I've always wanted to see the monuments and shit."

"Yeah, of course," Clifford says. "We can go in the morning and I can skate off to the meeting with the FBI and we'll meet back up."

Marlon raises his glass and says, "Perfect."

Clifford picks up his glass, clinks Marlon's, and both men take a swig.

Daniel looks out the window and says, "Hey, looks like Sara and Bailey are back."

The three men walk outside and watch as Sara is helping Bailey out of the van and closing it up. She turns and says, "Hey guys," then does a double take when she sees Marlon. "OH! Hey, stranger!" She says as she starts a slight jog up toward Marlon and throws her arms around him.

"What's up, girl?" Marlon says with a huge bear hug, lifting Sara off the ground.

Bailey rolls up and greets Marlon. "Long time, no see," he says looking up at him.

Marlon lets out a huge sigh, "Yeah, it's good to see the gang again."

Clifford looks around and says, "Let's go in, we have a lot to talk about."

The group walks into Clifford's condo and starts to sit. Sara sees that Clifford and Marlon had drinks poured and says, "Ooh, drinks!" and makes her way over to the bottle.

"Oh, I love Bumbu!" She says with excitement as she begins to pour.

Marlon takes a swig, "It gets the job done."

Clifford asks the group, "So we need to go over sleeping arrangements. Who is taking in Marlon?"

Bailey chimes in, "Oh, he's staying with me. I insist."

"Insist?" Clifford asks.

"Yeah, Marlon is family, and JJ asked me to take care of him while he's here," Bailey explains.

Marlon looks over at Bailey, "Thanks fam. And that's a relief because I don't want to be in Dee's place when that guy comes to finish him off."

Both Sara and Bailey perk up. Sara puts her glass down. "Wait, what?" she asks.

Clifford shakes his head. "It's nothing. Daniel and I had an altercation with someone. He shot up the Mustang."

"Holy shit, for real?" Bailey asks as Sara heads toward the window.

"For real," Clifford says.

Sara, looking around the parking lot, spots the Mustang. "Nuh-uh!" she exclaims as she spots the car with bullet holes scattered across the side. "I didn't even notice that." Sara returns from the window as Clifford begins to explain to her what happened. She sits at the counter island and grabs her drink with both hands and sips as Clifford talks about how Daniel did a great job of defensive driving and was able to get him a clean shot of the truck.

Her eyes light up in excitement as Clifford talks about the truck doing a barrel roll off the road and into the brush.

Bailey chimes in, "So he isn't dead after all that?"

Clifford shakes his head. "Nope. You'd think so, but he ran off into the woods."

Clifford pauses for a moment to reflect and continues, "Anyway, So when I got a few bars on the phone, I called the local police to report the accident and told them what happened. I then called the FBI and talked to Sims. He wants to meet with me tomorrow. I'm planning on taking Marlon into the city with me so he can do some sightseeing while I meet with the Feds."

Sara chimes in, "Ooh, can I come too? I haven't been to D.C. to sightsee in... since forever."

"Cool, anyone else?" Clifford asks.

Daniel says, "I can't. I have a class in the gym early tomorrow."

Bailey looks up at Clifford and asks, "How early are we talkin'?"

Clifford says, "I'm thinking we leave around six am. I have to meet with Sims at nine-thirty."

Bailey shakes his head. "Nah, I can't, not that early. Not two days in a row, military man"

Clifford nods, "Okay cool. So, Marlon and Sara, meet me here before six?"

Sara scoffs, "That's really early."

"So, do you still want to go?" Clifford asks.

Sara nods. "Yeah, it's still early though."

"Sorry, but I want to beat the traffic into D.C. and make that nine thirty meeting."

Sara nods and rolls her eyes as she sips on her rum.

CHAPTER THIRTEEN

The early birds have yet to even think about the worm when there is a knock at Clifford's door. With a fresh cup of coffee in his hand and his hazel eyes still partially asleep, he walks out of the kitchen, down the hall, and opens the door.

Marlon looks at him and says, "What if I was that killer?"

Clifford lazily points to a camera in the corner of the hall between his and Bailey's condos.

"Had them installed a few weeks ago. I can see who is at my door from anywhere," he says as he points at his smartwatch. "Besides," he continues, "I seriously doubt the guy would simply knock on my door."

"Cool. So are you still doing everything out of your house like you were doing back in Kentucky?" Marlon asks.

"Well, yes and no. We have an office where we keep our records, but we do everything online. Schedule meetings and communicate with clients via phone calls or video conferencing. We rarely need to go into the office."

Marlon asks, "Why even have an office?"

Clifford smiles, "It's a write-off. Plus, everyone's buying business property out here. I own the building and the two acres it's on. I'm hoping that in five to ten years, I can sell it for a small fortune and just retire on a small island somewhere."

Marlon laughs, "Like you'd retire?"

"I just might one day," Clifford says.

"Yeah, okay," Marlon scoffs.

Sara shuffles out from the picnic area, across the parking lot, and toward Clifford and Marlon. "I'm so tired," she says with her sleepiest of faces.

Marlon laughs and says, "Sleep in the car you big baby."

"I can't. I won't fall asleep when I'm moving. It's a thing," she says.

Clifford nods and says, "Well, we should probably get going."

He throws the rest of the coffee down the back of his throat and walks inside his condo. He sets the mug down in the kitchen, grabs his keys and wallet, shoves the USB for Sims into his pocket, and takes his jacket off the hook in the hall. He sees the gun he shot the driver of the landscaping truck with, sitting on a table. He walks to get it, but then hesitates for a moment, knowing the gun laws in D.C. are much more strict. Since he will be using public parking and visiting the FBI and federal memorials, he decides to leave it behind. The last thing he needs is a weapons charge because he's not registered to carry in D.C. He makes a mental note, as he takes it back up to his room and places it in a drawer, to clean it and put it away properly when he gets back later.

Clifford throws on his jacket and heads out the door.

Traffic into the city was smoother than normal for a Friday morning. Clifford finds all-day street parking in the middle of downtown. He glances at his watch and pulls out his phone.

"Wow, we made good time. I can walk with you to one of the memorials, but I gotta head over to the FBI to meet with Sims. I'll call you when I'm done," Clifford says to Sara as they are getting out of the car.

Sara lets out a huge yawn. "Yeah, I guess." She shuffles her feet over to a bench and sits down.

Marlon stretches his arms over his head. With a yawn, he asks, "Which memorial you guys want to go to first?"

Clifford looks at his phone and says, "Well, the World War II memorial is on the way. We can hit that and walk up toward the Washington Monument, and we can part ways at the Smithsonian."

Sara stands up and bends over, starting to stretch. Clifford and Marlon look over at her with an odd look. She then stands up straight and pulls her leg up behind her to stretch her quads. She notices the men oddly looking at her.

"What? It's a lot of walking!" she says.

Clifford shakes his head, "Let's go."

* * *

After visiting the memorials, the group makes their way up toward the museum. Clifford glances at his watch. "Shit, I gotta go. My meeting's in twenty." He starts in with a light jog and turns and says, "Have fun, I'll call when I'm out!"

Sara shouts back, "We know!"

Clifford continues to jog up the street and turns down 10th avenue and heads toward the security office at the FBI. A bit winded, he stops to catch his breath before he enters the building.

Stepping inside the office he walks up toward the lady behind the counter. "I'm here to see Agent Sims." She passes a form under the glass and says, "Please fill this out. If you have any devices that can connect to the internet, they need to be put in those lockers."

She points over to small cubbies with removable keys on the wall.

Familiar with the procedure, Clifford smiles and starts to fill out the form. When finished, he heads over to the wall and takes off his watch and grabs his phone. He sets them inside the locker, locks it, and pockets the key.

The woman behind the desk takes the form from Clifford and points him toward the guard by the metal detectors. Clifford smiles and heads over.

The guard asks, "Any phones, smartwatches, and/or weapons of any kind?"

"Nope, it's all in the locker," Clifford responds.

"Okay, empty your pockets in the bin and step through," he says pointing to the little bin waiting to go through the x-ray.

* * *

Marlon and Sara head up the steps of the museum and realize that it doesn't open for another hour. Sara looks at the sign and says, "Well shit!"

Marlon's stomach lets out a slight growl. "Since we got some time, how about we get something to eat."

Sara smiles and says, "I could eat." She pulls up a map on her phone and says, "There is a breakfast spot two blocks, next to the metro station. Maybe a fifteen-minute walk."

"Perfect!" Marlon says.

After a little walk, the two enjoy a quick bite to eat at the cafe on the corner. Sara pays the check and meets Marlon outside.

"We should head back, the museum opens soon," she says.

They begin to walk back and as Sara rounds the corner, she runs into a man clutching a bible. She looks at him as if there is something slightly familiar about him. "Hey," she says, trying to get his attention.

He snarls back at her, "Hey yourself, watch where you're going! Fucking tourist."

Marlon jogs over and reaches out to grab him, "Hey, buddy!" Marlon says. The man pushes him away and yells, "Get off me," and starts a slight jog away.

Sara shakes her head. "What an asshole!" she says as she glares at him. "Wait a second." She says, coming to a realization. "That's Kevin."

Marlon looks over. "Kevin? Well. Kevin's an asshole," he says.

"Kevin is Clifford's new boss," Sara explains

Marlon shakes his head, "Still an asshole." He looks back at Sara who is in deep thought. "What are you thinkin'?" Marlon asks.

"His office is on the other side of the city. He must have got off the metro. I'm going to follow him to see what he's up to," Sara says.

"Bad idea," Marlon retorts.

Sara starts to walk away. "I need to find out. You head over to the museum, and I'll meet up with you. I just want to see where he's off to, in such a hurry."

Marlon shakes his head. "Whatever! Just be careful." he says.

Sara starts a slight jog and rounds the next block. She slows and watches Kevin from about twenty yards behind. He crosses the street and heads toward a historic church.

Sara follows him across the street and watches as Kevin enters the church.

She pulls out her phone and calls Clifford, but it goes to his voicemail. She ends the call and continues into the church. She steps inside the sanctuary and looks around briefly. She spots Kevin sitting in a pew next to the confessional.

Sara sits down in the back and starts to send Clifford a text. The sound of the buttons on her phone is amplified in the silence of the church. She stops and switches her phone to silent. She continues her text message to Clifford.

"Ran into Kevin. Literally. Didn't recognize me. Followed him to a church. Something's up."

She looks up and sees someone leave the confessional. Kevin stands up, still holding the bible as he begins to stroke the gold-colored ribbon bookmark sticking out from between the pages. She aims her cellphone camera and snags a photo as he opens the confessional door and steps inside. She sends the photo to Clifford.

* * *

Back at the FBI headquarters, Sims enters the conference room where Clifford is waiting.

"So, you flee the scene of a traffic accident and call me for a meeting. Why?"

Clifford scoffs. "There is a bit more to it than that. My car is in the middle of thousands of dollars' worth of bodywork after all the holes he shot into it. Besides, I drove to the local sheriff's department to report the incident."

Sims sits down across from him. "Yeah, so I heard. But why would someone chase you down to send you to the morgue?"

Clifford pulls the USB from his pocket, "To get this."

Sims reaches over and takes the USB from his hand. "What's this?"

Clifford says, "Well, why don't we take a look?"

Sims raises his eyebrow and looks back at the USB as he twirls it through his fingers.

* * *

Marlon heads into the museum and enters a huge hall. He starts looking around and walks over toward a large elephant in the room. "That's a big fucking elephant," he says to himself.

A woman glares at him after hearing his choice of words.

"What?" Marlon asks, addressing her glare. "Talk about the elephant in the room," he continues to himself, but loud enough for her to hear.

She shakes her head in disgust and walks away.

Marlon shrugs and continues on looking at the exhibits.

* * *

Sara waits and watches as Kevin is inside the confessional. A few minutes later he opens the door and begins to walk toward the main entrance of the church to leave. She snags another picture and sends it to Clifford.

As he steps past her aisle, Sara waits a few seconds and then begins to stand up. Kevin quickly heads out of the church. Sara awkwardly steps out of the pew as she notices a woman a few aisles in front of her, watching as Kevin leaves.

This woman stands up and walks toward the confessional and enters.

Sara decides to sit back down and wait.

The woman didn't stay long. The door of the confessional swung back open. Sara points her cellphone up and snags a photo of the woman as she's walking out.

Sara notices that there was something in her hand she didn't have before. She continues to watch as the woman grows closer and can see clearly that she is holding the same bible that Kevin walked in with. The gold ribbon bookmark shimmers as she walks past the lit prayer candles. The woman stops and opens her bag, shoves the bible inside, and closes it. She continues toward the entrance of the church and leaves.

Sara stands up and continues to shimmy out of the pew.

She steps outside the church and looks to her left to see Kevin walking away. She looks right and spots the woman walking toward the metro station.

* * *

Clifford steps outside the security office of the FBI as he was putting his watch back on his wrist. He looks at his phone, which says that he has four messages from Sara.

He opens the phone and starts going through the messages.

Sara's phone vibrates. It's Clifford.

She answers the phone, "Hey, Dee!"

"Where are you?" Clifford urgently asks.

"Did you get my messages?" she asks.

"Yeah, where are you?" he responds.

Sara, a bit out of breath, says, "I'm following that woman."

"Where?" Clifford says, aggravated.

"To the metro," Sara says as her tone of voice instantly changes, "And tell dad that I will be home soon."

"What?!" Clifford asks, confused.

"Yep, bye," Sara says as she ends the call.

Sara receives a text from Clifford.

Dee: *"WTF? Call me back!"*

Sara: *"She's right here. Can't talk. On Silverline."*

Dee: *"Get off next stop. I'll pick you up."*
Sara: *"K"*

Clifford picks up the pace, getting back to the car as quickly as possible. He reaches into his pocket and fumbles with the rental car keys. He clicks the remote to unlock the door, whips it open, and jumps in.

He pauses for a moment and takes a breath. "Everyone is okay!" Clifford says to himself.

He starts the car and quickly pulls out of the spot and proceeds to make his way out of the city.

* * *

Marlon exits the museum and looks at his phone. No texts from Sara or Clifford. He shrugs and says to himself, "I'm sure they're okay."

He starts a group message with them and texts them.

"Just finished the museum. Going to check out the Linc-mem."

He locks his phone but does not notice the error that said: Not sent.

* * *

At a stoplight, Clifford picks his phone up and sends a quick text.

Dee: *"Where are you now?"*
Sara: *"Tysons. She's not getting off."*
Dee: *"You guys should get off at Dulles."*

Sara reads the text and says, "What?" out loud to herself.

The woman turns around. "Excuse me?" she asks.

Sara shoves her phone into her pocket and says, "Sorry. My brother sent me a text that made no sense."

The woman narrows her eyes, nods, and turns back around.

She pulls out her phone and starts texting someone.

Sara tries to peek over her shoulder but can't see the phone. She starts to push past the woman to try to get a glance at her phone.

"Excuse me," Sara says as she purposely bumps into her to look at her phone.

She got a clear view.

She was in mid text with someone titled "KB2D2".

It was clearly a code name for anonymity.

The previous text was cut off, but it was clear it was from Kevin because it mentioned meeting at the church at the same time Kevin was there. The current text was partially completed.

"I need pics of eve-"

Sara read as she glanced down at the woman's phone. As Sara glances up at her, the woman is staring her in the eyes.

"It's rude to read others' text messages," she said with a death glare.

Sara's eyes widened. "Sorry! I didn't mean to," she says as she continues past.

* * *

Marlon reaches the Lincoln Memorial and starts up the stairs. He stops and turns around and pulls out his phone. Still no new messages. Again, he shrugs and opens his camera app and takes a selfie with the memorial in the background.

"Oh, that's a good one!" he says.

He shoves the phone back into his pocket and continues up the stairs to the monument.

* * *

Sara moves toward the door of the train to posture that she is ready to leave.

The woman, finished with her text, puts her phone into her purse and looks directly at Sara, and smiles.

Sara sends a text to Clifford.

Sara: "F'd up. She saw me looking at her phone."

After a few minutes, she gets his response.

Dee: "OFF AT NEXT STOP!"

The woman turns away from Sara and finds a seat. She sits down and picks up a newspaper that was sitting on the seat next to her, crosses her legs, and starts to read.

Sara texts Clifford back.

Sara: "Next stop is Reston, TC. Getting off there."

Clifford races through Reston and pulls up to the metro station. He spots Sara sitting on a bench alone.

"What the fuck?" Clifford asks himself, confused about why she is alone.

He pulls up next to her. She stands up and walks toward the car.

"Where's Marlon?" Clifford asks.

* * *

Marlon checks his phone again - no new notifications.

"Fuck it!" he says to himself, "I'm having fun."

He continues toward the Korean and Vietnam war memorials, reading the names on the wall. "Ooh, that guy was a Marlon, too!" he says out loud. "MARLON'S OF THE WORLD!" He boasts to himself in jest.

* * *

Sara's eyes open as wide as dinner plates. "OH SHIT!!" She exclaims, realizing she forgot to tell Clifford that Marlon went back to the museum. She picks up her phone and sends Marlon a message.

Sara: "Hey...We left. Sorry. Emergency. Call me!"

She climbs into the car and says, "We need to go back to D.C. I left Marlon at the museum."

A look of panic crosses Clifford's face.

"You followed her ALONE?" he questions in disbelief. "I thought you were together!"

Sara bites her lip.

"Sorry, Dee. We really gotta go get Marlon!"

* * *

Marlon leaves the war memorials and heads toward the MLK statue. Upon approaching, he pulls out his phone and turns on the camera and snaps a few pictures. He turns around and takes another selfie with the marble statue, then looks on in amazement at the American icon, nodding in approval.

He glances at the phone again and still not seeing any new notifications starts to worry a bit. He puts the phone back into his pocket and decides to head closer toward where they parked earlier that morning.

* * *

Clifford and Sara pull back into the parking lot and spot Marlon walking toward them.

Sara jumps out of the car and raises her hands in question.

"What the fuck bro, can't you answer a text?" she yells across the parking lot.

Confused, Marlon asks, "Wait, you texted me?"

Sara responds, "Like four times!"

Marlon, still walking toward them, pulls out his phone and starts to look closer at it.

He stops in his tracks and lets out a huge laugh. "Son of a bitch! I still had it on airplane mode!"

Clifford slaps his forehead. "Jesus, man. We were worried."

Marlon reaches the car and says, "My bad. Had fun without you fuckers, though."

CHAPTER FOURTEEN

Clifford walks towards Sara, who is slightly irritated sitting with her arms crossed at the counter-island, as Bailey and Daniel listen to Marlon tell his story about being in D.C. with his phone on airplane mode wondering where they were.

"Hey," Clifford softly says to Sara.

Sara just shakes her head, then eventually looks over at him.

"Why are you even mad? You're the one who left him," Clifford says.

"Don't," Sara says.

Clifford puts on a sympathetic face. "Don't what?" he asks.

"Don't you dare put this on me. He got me worried and just brushed it off."

Clifford puts his arm around her and says, "Look. No one got hurt. Marlon's a big boy and can take care of himself. Trust me. I've seen it."

Sara relaxes a bit and turns toward Clifford and says, "Okay, fine! I'm more mad at myself because I made a mistake and forgot about him. Is that what you want to hear?"

Clifford smiles and says, "It's okay. I've made mistakes like that. Forget about it and let's try to figure out where our mystery lady went."

He pulls a rolled-up sheet of paper from his back pocket and gives it a little wave.

Sara perks up, "What's that?"

"The Silver line map," Clifford says with a wink.

Sara smiles as Clifford turns toward the rest of the group.

With gusto, to break up Marlon's intriguing story, Clifford says, "Okay ladies, listen up!"

He unrolls the map and sets it on the counter-island. He grabs the salt and pepper shakers and uses them as weights to keep the rolled map in place on the island.

The other three gather around the island next to Clifford and Sara.

Marlon looks over toward Bailey, being lower than the counter, and says, "I don't think he can..."

Bailey taps Marlon's leg to stop him from talking.

"Hey, check it." he says quickly.

Bailey presses a button on the side that starts a hydraulic motor, raising the back of the wheelchair so he is almost in a standing position.

Marlon looks dumbfounded. "Damn! You're like Iron man or some shit!"

Bailey smiles. "Designed it myself."

Clifford looks at the two. "Yes we're very proud, now onto my thing."

Bailey tuts and his smile turns to a frown at Clifford's dismissive comment.

Clifford smooths out the map and adjusts the shakers to keep it down. He points at the stop where he picked up Sara.

"Okay, this is where I met Sara and there are only five more stops where the woman could have gotten off," Clifford says.

Instantly Bailey, Marlon, and Daniel collectively say, "The airport."

Clifford looks over, "Why the airport? It could have been any stop."

Bailey says, "Dude, she was in D.C., she got on a train and was texting someone. She's most likely picking someone up or meeting them at the airport. It's the most logical thing."

Clifford scratches his head, "Yeah, I guess. But I don't know."

Daniel says, "I was thinking she might have gotten a rental from the airport or she drove there to park and take the train into the city."

Marlon chimes in, "You know, her being on the train doesn't mean she was traveling home. She could have been meeting someone. All we know for sure is that she's in the metro area."

Clifford clenches his fist in frustration, "Yeah, you're right. She could be going anywhere. I hate dead ends."

Sara shakes her head, "I'm sorry guys, I got spooked. I should have stayed on the train."

"Absolutely not. I am glad you got off when you did. No need to put yourself in danger," Clifford says.

Sara smiles. "What about the text to KB2D2? Do you think that was a code for Kevin?"

Clifford shakes his head, "Again, we can't be sure. We can't even be sure that they were secretly meeting. Are you sure she picked up the same bible Kevin had?"

Sara nods, "Oh, one hundred percent it was the same."

Clifford strokes the stubble on his chin. "Okay. We still don't have enough information. We'll have to sit on this for a bit. I'm not sure where else we can look."

* * *

The next morning, Clifford knocks on Daniel's door.

After about a minute he answers. "What up, Dee? I'm 'bout to hit the gym."

Clifford, still shaking some sleep from his eyes, asks, "Have you seen my gun? The one from the car chase the other day?"

Daniel shakes his head. "Nah. You can't find it? Maybe you left it in the car."

With a worried look on his face, Clifford says, "It's missing and I am sure I brought it inside the house. Especially since the car is in the shop."

Clifford starts to lose his balance and catches himself.

Daniel asks, "Whoa, buddy, you okay?"

Clifford shakes his head, "I woke up suddenly and in a daze. I feel like I have a hangover."

Daniel nods and starts to look concerned as Clifford continues.

"Yeah, so I had this weird dream that someone was in my house and I was trying to fight him off. He grabbed my gun and pushed me. He pointed the gun at my face and then without a word, ran off."

"That's a crazy dream, and you probably should have called me," Daniel says.

Clifford runs his hand through his hair, "Yeah, weird. And now I can't find that gun. I know I put it in my side drawer. It's not there. Oh, and my phone's messed up."

"Messed up? Missing your gun? Are you sure it was a dream?"

Clifford shakes the thought from his head, "Yeah, I mean. It's crazy right? Yeah, it had to have been."

Daniel steps out of his condo, "I'm gonna help you look for the gun."

Clifford shakes his head. "No. It's okay. Go to the gym. I just need a coffee or something. I probably put it somewhere else. I'll find it."

Daniel drapes his arm around Clifford and says, "The gym isn't going anywhere. Let's go take a look."

Clifford lets out a worried half-smile. "I don't want to put you out. Do you think Sara's up?"

Daniel, walking further out from his door, says, "She's doing another art thing this morning, and I think Bailey and Marlon are over at the center playing ball."

Clifford nods and says, "Okay, cool. I'll just keep looking."

Daniel says, "Dee, you're not yourself right now. Let's look for that gun. That's more important."

Daniel helps Clifford back to his condo. As Clifford heads inside, Daniel notices that the red light on the security camera is out. Clifford walks up to the coffee maker and starts to make a pot of coffee.

"I just can't seem to wake up," Clifford says.

Daniel starts digging through the closet in the hall and shouts, "Did you check your security camera yet? Maybe you could see someone come in."

Clifford replies, "My phone wouldn't work. I guess I can check my laptop."

He shuffles over toward the counter island where his laptop was sitting.

Daniel yells over to Clifford in the kitchen, "So this dream? Were you in bed when it started? I just think it's a bit weird."

A sudden, loud thud startles Daniel and he runs, full sprint, down the hall and into the kitchen.

On the floor next to the island, Clifford lays on the floor.

"Shit!" Daniel exclaims and runs to his side. He rolls him onto his back and checks to see that he is breathing while feeling for a pulse.

He finds it.

"Okay, okay, okay..." he repeats to himself as he fumbles with his phone to call 911.

* * *

Sara sits on the patio of the Blend Coffee Bar sipping her hot coffee while her friends are talking. Her mind is wandering about the recent events with the lady on the train. She regrets letting the fear get in her head and leaving the train. This was a huge lead in the case and Sara cannot help but think that she let it slip away because she was afraid.

Her friend, Denise, notices that Sara is putting on a bit of a fake smile and that her mind was elsewhere.

"Hey, girl, where you at right now?" Denise asks, tapping Sara on her arm.

Sara jolts and her attention snaps back to her friends at the table.

"Oh, god, I'm so sorry!" she says, rubbing her face with both hands, "I've been thinking of this other thing for a while. It's nothing. Work stuff."

Denise pats her hand. "Don't let that negative stuff take up space in your mind."

Sara smiles. "Yeah, you're right. Thanks."

She looks around and realizes that all three ladies at the table were looking at her.

She instantly apologizes, "Sorry, ladies. What were you talking about?"

Tianni says, "Only that I am just a bit devastated right now. You know that Rodney Brown was traded to L.A., right?"

Sara shakes her head. "What? Who?"

"Uh, that's the basketball player Danica married."

Sara's eyes get huge.

Danica is the mononym of a local celebrity who is huge in the arts. She donates and supports the local art programs and even sponsored exhibits all over the metro area.

"What? She's staying here, right?!" Sara exclaims.

Tianni shakes her head, "Girl, no. They're selling their beautiful house."

"No! Oh, NO!" Sara says. "I love Danica."

Brianne nods and says, "That's why we were talking about it. You're over there daydreaming."

Denise swats at Brianne and says, "Leave her be."

Sara dumps her head into her hands. "Is she still going to do the spring art festival next year?"

Tianni says, "I have no idea. I haven't heard anything about it, but I hope so."

Sara shakes her head. "Are you sure they're moving?"

Brianne chimes in, "Yeah, Tianni just said she found their place on the market." She opens an app on her phone, sets it on the table, and pushes it over to Sara.

The phone app was for multi-million-dollar homes on the market. Sara starts swiping through the pictures. Each picture of the home was grander and more extravagant than the last.

"Are you sure this is Danica's house?" Sara asks as she is gawking at the photos.

Denise, looking over her shoulder, says, "Oh yeah, look at those murals. That's totally her work."

The other three ladies continue to chatter about the house and how upset they are about their favorite local celeb leaving town as Sara is stuck in a glare at the last page of the album, which had the real estate agent's information with a picture of the woman selling the home.

Brianne looks over and says, "Why are you glaring at it? You gonna buy it or something?"

Sara, in a locking stare with the picture, is peering at the face of the woman from the metro. She slowly looks up at Brianne and says, "Maybe I will. Text me that listing."

Brianne scoffs and says, "Yeah okay," as she grabs her phone back.

Sara refuses to let go of the phone. "Send me the listing!" She insists.

Brianne muscles the phone from Sara's grip, "Okay, fine! I will. Jeez," she says in a semi concerned tone.

* * *

Later that afternoon, Clifford awakens in the hospital. Daniel is sitting in a chair on the other side of the bed.

"Martin?" Clifford questions.

Daniel looks over at him and stands up. "Hey, it's me, Daniel"

Clifford shakes the image of his old, deceased friend from his mind. "Oh, Dan. Sorry. What happened?"

Daniel says, "Dude, you just passed out. They have you on a drip and ran a tox screen. I told them that you were not feeling yourself and had a weird dream last night."

Clifford tries to shake the slight headache and sits up.

"Have they found anything from the screening?" Clifford asks.

"Results aren't in yet."

The doctor walks in and promptly says, "Results are in gentlemen. You have gamma hydroxybutyric acid in your system."

With a confused look, Clifford asks, "What?"

"G.H.B. is a date rape drug. You have the classic symptoms. Confusion, forgetfulness, bodily weakness, and a bad headache."

Daniel smiles. "Did you get date raped last night?" he jokingly asks with a growing smirk.

The doctor looks over. "It's really no joking matter. He had a major reaction to the drug. It slowed his heart which is probably the reason he passed out this morning."

The smirk quickly left and a serious look drew on Daniel's face.

Clifford adjusts himself and asks, "How would I have been drugged?"

The doctor looks over at Clifford and says, "My bet, you were injected while you were sleeping. It would have reacted faster in your system than taking it orally and the side effects would be much stronger."

Clifford scoffs, "I think I would have known if someone injected me with something."

The doctor points at a light bruise on his arm. "You sure? That looks like an injection site to me."

Clifford looks down in disbelief.

The doctor continues, "Someone wanted you incapacitated for some reason. We typically consult the police when women have this in their system, but we haven't called yet."

Clifford perked up, "Please don't."

"It's standard procedure when someone has G.H.B. in their system. They typically just ask a few questions and let you go. We can only assume there was no rape in your case, but it is still criminal to drug someone against their will."

Clifford shakes his head, "I don't need to file a report. I'm good."

The doctor shakes his head, "Okay, it's up to you. I want you to stay for another hour or two before I discharge you just to make sure the drug is completely out of your system."

The doctor leaves the room to check on other patients.

Daniel looks over at Clifford and says, "Why don't you want the police involved?"

Clifford shakes his head. "Not yet at least. I want to know more about what happened to me first."

Hours later Daniel pulls into the parking lot of the condos where his concerned friends sit waiting. Clifford gets out of the car and Marlon looks over and asks, "Hey man. How's your butthole?"

Whipping his head toward Marlon, Daniel exclaims, "DUDE!"

Sara shouts, "FOR FUCKS SAKE, MARLON!"

Clifford looks over toward Daniel, "You told 'em I was roofied?"

Daniel awkwardly smiles.

Sara walks up to Marlon in haste, "You work with almost all women. Would you say that to them? What if JJ heard that comment?"

Bailey chimes in, "JJ'd kick your ass for that one. For sure."

Marlon sulks, "Yeah, okay. My bad."

Clifford looks over, "Yeah man, it's a touchy subject."

A smirk starts to grow on Marlons face as he start saying, "That's what Sh-"

Sara whips her hand quickly across Marlon's shoulder, "GUPPY, NO!"

Marlon lets out a verbal "Ouch" as he grasps where she struck him. "Ok, fine. No jokes."

"Clifford shakes his head and says, "I know you like being an asshole, but this is no joke."

Bailey asks, "You file a report yet?"

Clifford shakes his head, "No, not yet."

Bailey smiles. "I didn't think so."

Daniel, looking confused, asks, "Why aren't we calling the cops?"

The three look over toward Daniel.

Marlon says, "Have you met Clifford Dee? He's an investigator that don't like the cops in his business. Clifford, Daniel - Daniel, Clifford. He goes by Dee."

Clifford shakes his head. "It's not that. I just want more facts before I have the officials looking into our affairs. I will call them soon. Promise."

Sara smiles and says, "Oh I have some information for you."

Clifford says, "Let's go inside and talk."

The crew heads into Clifford's condo and a brief flash of the dream comes back to his mind.

Clifford says, "I think it was the landscaper."

Bailey looks over, "What?"

Daniel grabs Clifford by his shoulder. "The landscaper you shot? The one that was shooting at us?"

"Well, maybe not. I don't know. I don't think-," Clifford stammers. "It could have just been a dream anyway."

Sara shakes her head, "Dee, that dream you're talking about probably really happened."

Daniel with a worried look says, "We definitely need to call the cops, Dee!"

Clifford again shakes his head, "N-not yet. If we had a friend, like Martin, then sure. But we don't know anyone and they'll probably just laugh us out of the station. I mean, look how my own friend greeted me."

Marlon rolls his eyes.

Sara leans against the counter and says, "Okay, now my thing. Dee, remember that lady from the metro?"

Clifford looks over, "Yes, dear. I remember all about that, it was yesterday."

Sara smirks, "I don't know what that roofie did to you."

Clifford closes his eyes for a moment and looks back at Sara, "Go on. You were talking about the woman you let get away."

Sara scoffs in disgust, "Yeah, you do remember. So anyway, the woman is a real estate agent!" She opens her phone and hands it to Clifford.

Clifford looks at the listing and looks at her picture. With an unimpressed look on his face, he says, "You sure this is her?"

Sara perked up, "Oh, I am certain it's her."

Clifford hands the phone back to Sara with an unsure look on his face. "What?" Sara asks.

Clifford shakes his head, "It's not making any sense."

Sara leans forward on her toes, "Who cares if it makes sense, it's her!"

"I don't know," Clifford says, crossing his arms in thought.

"Dee, that's the woman from the metro!" Sara says confidently.

Clifford, still looking confused asks "Why would Kevin have a secret meeting with a real estate agent?"

Sara throws her arms up, "I don't know! But it's her!"

Clifford nods, "Okay, I believe you. I just don't understand it."

Marlon looks over to Clifford and says, "So this gun you dreamt was stolen, where did you keep it?"

"Bedroom. Why?"

Marlon looking over at Clifford's desk says, "There's a gun over here, is this it?"

Clifford walks over toward the desk, "Yeah. It is. But I don't remember putting it there."

Next to the desk was a blood-stained black hoodie sitting in a wire trash can.

Marlon points at it, "Dee. Look."

Clifford looks down and says, "That is not mine. What the fuck is going on?"

Bailey wheels over and says, "Maybe it's time to make a call to the cops."

A loud knock on the door breaks the tension.

Clifford looks over to the group as he walks toward the door, "Yeah, let's call them."

Daniel, who was looking out the window, says "Dee, the cops are already here."

Clifford swings open the door to find the local police.

The police, with a warrant in hand to search the premises are waiting for them on the other side of the door. Clifford asks, "What's going on?"

The cop hands him the warrant and says, "Clifford Dee, you are under arrest for the murder of Doyle Hamilton."

Sara, with a concerned look, questions, "Badger?"

CHAPTER FIFTEEN

The room was dimly lit with a two-way mirror and a table bolted to the floor. Clifford sits with thoughts racing wildly with his head resting on his clasped hands.

Who would kill Badger? He was a kind man. Everyone loved him and he was commanding, but with a gentle passion, which everyone respected and adored.

It must have been political. He was in an impressive lead in the polls for the senate special election.

Clifford has been questioned by the police before but never for a murder. Since Martin's death he found it difficult to become close enough to a member of law enforcement to consider a friend, and now he feels like he has no one he can trust.

Now he sits in wait.

After a few minutes, the door swings open and a detective walks inside.

"Mr. Dee, can I get you something? Coffee?" she asks.

Clifford shakes his head.

She continues, "I'm looking through your record here and I must say, you are impressive. Army Ranger, Congressional Medal of Honor, medically discharged... You became an investigator for hire in Kentucky, then moved here to Northern Virginia. Why did you move?"

Clifford drops his hands and looks at the detective. She was light skinned with beautiful curls in her hair. She had soft brown eyes and looked compassionate.

She is the 'Good Cop.' Clifford thinks to himself.

With a lump in his throat, Clifford speaks, "Badger asked me to join his team. He was my commanding officer just before I was discharged and he wanted me to come work for him."

"Hmm, Badger? Is that what you call Mr. Hamilton? Was that a nickname or something?"

Clifford nods, "Yeah, or something."

She nods as she scribbles into her notebook.

"I see. When did he ask you to join the team?"

"A little over two years ago," Clifford says.

She continues to write in the notebook and then suddenly closes it.

She leans in and asks Clifford, "Why didn't you get rid of the gun and hoodie after killing him?"

Clifford leans back into his chair. He came to the realization that she really thinks he killed him. This isn't going to be a good cop/bad cop situation. She's both.

"Wow. Sweet and to the point," Clifford says.

She sits in silence, staring at Clifford, waiting for him to answer.

Clifford leans back in. "I did not kill my friend," he says in a matter-of-fact manner.

The detective leans back in her chair and eventually stands, taking a position of authority. "Mr. Dee, we found the murder weapon in your home. It had recently been fired by you. Oh, and blood-stained clothing that matches the eye-witness descriptions."

Clifford's voice raises, "This is obviously a frame job! Check the hospital records for Christ's sake! I was admitted. I couldn't have been in the hospital and killing someone at the same time."

She places one hand on the table. "Yes, Mr. Dee. We're aware that you were in the hospital. My guys are speaking to the doctor right now. What

I'm thinking is that you drugged yourself to alibi out. But you weren't planning on being so weak so you couldn't get rid of the evidence in time."

Clifford shakes his head. "You cannot seriously be considering that I did this! That would be a terrible plan to murder someone!"

"So, you had a better plan? What was it?" she asks.

"What?" Clifford says, confused.

He starts to realize that she is trying to get him emotional and uncomfortable. He takes a deep breath and calms himself.

"I didn't kill Doyle Hamilton. He was my friend and I liked and respected him like a father. However, I will find out who killed him. I promise you."

She smiles at Clifford and says, "Cute. It's going to be difficult to do your sleuthing behind bars."

Clifford can hear some commotion from behind the door. Suddenly it opens.

An officer pokes his head into the room and motions for the detective. She sets her notebook and file on the table and walks to the door. The two are whispering, but Clifford can make out, "FBI."

She pulls the door wide open and says, "I guess I'm getting some coffee."

Just outside, Agent Sims looks on with his arms folded. She closes the door behind her, leaving Clifford alone in the room.

A few moments later the door opens and Sims walks in. "Hey, buddy. Looks like you're coming with me. FBI is taking jurisdiction on this case due to Mr. Hamilton being a high-profile person in an election. They're signing the prisoner transfer paperwork now."

The door swings open again.

A squirrely looking man with a cheap suit and briefcase walks in. "No more questions," he demands.

Clifford looks over, "Wait, are you my attorney?"

The man nods. "Yeah, sorry I'm late."

Clifford shakes his head. "Where's Keith?"

The man continues, "Mr. Thompson is in the Bahamas with his wife. At least, I think it's his wife. But anyway, they sent me in his place. I'm Barry Lipschitz."

Sims holds his hand out. "No, no, no, no, he's being transferred to my custody and we're going down to FBI Headquarters to sort a few things out."

Barry looks up. "Who are you?"

"Agent Sims, FBI."

Barry nods. "Great, the Feds! Look. My client has answered enough questions already. Get the CliffsNotes from the police. Oh! CliffsNotes! Did you see what I did there? CliffsNotes. I gotta tell my brother that one."

Clifford turns and looks over at Sims who's shaking his head at the terrible pun.

Sims sighs and places his hand on the table. "Mr. Lipschitz, your client has been formally charged for a crime. The booking agents are signing him over to me, so I hold the right to question Mr. Dee over the next 24 hours. You can follow me to headquarters if you wish and file the paperwork for his release there."

Barry adjusts his glasses and says, "Okay, fine. Take Mr. Dee, but you're not taking the kid. He hasn't been charged with anything. Daniel is coming with me."

Clifford turns in his chair. "Dan's here?"

Barry looks over. "Yeah, they brought him in for questions, too, after he said he was with you before your hospital stay. They haven't charged him with anything. I'll process his release and take him home. I'm gonna be down in D.C. for you tomorrow."

Clifford nods. "Sounds good."

"You need anything, Cliff?" Barry asks.

Clifford shakes his head and looks over at Sims. "No, I think I'll be okay."

* * *

Clifford sits in the back of the FBI van that was transporting him to D.C. The rhythmic sounds of the road lull him to sleep. In his dreams he can see someone in his home.

He lies in bed watching as they swiftly move like a breeze, across the room. He clutches his comforter, pulling it tight, as the figure waltzes into the bedroom with a syringe. Watching while frozen with fear, the gloved hand injects his arm with the toxin.

He looks up at a masked face as it begins to blur and change into a monster. The figure backs away and begins to dance across the room like a ballerina. The figure shifts from a hooded man into a woman in a red dress and slowly, methodically goes through his drawers. They find the gun in the nightstand drawer where Clifford left it. Helplessly he cries out, "No!"

The red dress-wearing ballerina morphs back into the masked figure in a black hoodie and walks up to him. He grabs the figure and pulls them close, feeling the sleek and slender arms under the thick hoodie. Clifford's pushed back down onto the bed and his gun is now shoved in his face.

The car comes to a sudden stop at the FBI headquarters, jolting Clifford awake. He shakes the sleep from his head but holds onto the dream.

CHAPTER SIXTEEN

Daniel knocks on Sara's door. She opens the door and throws her arms around him.

"What happened? Where's Dee?"

Daniel shakes his head. "FBI has him. He was transferred."

"Shit! No, this is bad!" Sara says. "Let's go over to Bailey's so we can all talk."

Marlon is pouring himself a rum, neat, when they knock.

He walks over to the door and peaks through the peephole. He turns his head toward Bailey. "Hey, they're back," he shouts.

He swings open the door and Daniel says, "Just me. Dee's with the FBI."

Marlon swings his head back around. "Never mind, Dee's with the Feds. It's just Danny Boy!"

They all congregate in the living room when Sara starts talking. "Bailey, I need your help. I know Dee was a bit dismissive, but I have this feeling that the real estate agent is involved with this somehow."

Bailey shoots her a smile. "Sure, baby girl. Get me the info and I'll see what I can dig up on her."

Sara smiles. "Thank you! Maybe in the meantime, Daniel and Marlon can—"

Marlon cuts her off. "Daniel and Marlon nothin'! I can't be involved with this. I'm actually flying out tomorrow morning. I changed my flight."

Sara throws her hands up. "What? You're not going to help us?"

Marlon sets his drink down. "As much as I love the heat, I don't like it this much. I've helped Dee before and he still owes me a favor for that, but I cannot have the Feds looking into my business now. Especially having the connections I have."

Bailey agrees. "He's right, Sara. If they start looking into him, they'll find JJ and that would be a whole bigger mess."

Sara puts her head in her hands and starts to sob.

Daniel sets his hand on her shoulder. "Sara, they're right. We can't get Marlon involved with this."

Marlon picks his drink up and takes a swig and walks out of the room.

Sara sits down and pulls her phone out of her pocket. She sends Bailey a text message and sets her phone down. "There's the info I have on the real estate agent." She folds her arms and gives a little pout.

Bailey pulls out his phone and wheels over to his computer.

Daniel walks over to Bailey's desk and grabs a pencil and a sheet of paper.

Bailey looks up at him and asks, "What are you doing?"

Daniel says, "I'm writing down some facts we know and I am going to start a murder-board thing."

Bailey picks up a remote control and presses a button. A smart board lowers from the ceiling and he hands him a tablet.

"Draw it up on the tablet and it will display on the smart board," Bailey says with a smile.

With a surprised look, Daniel asks, "When did you get this?"

Bailey scoffs, "I always had this. Why do you think Dee always comes over here to solve cases? I got the tech, baby!"

* * *

After a few hours, Daniel has the board filled out with a barrage of information. Including the two killers (female and male), the real estate agent, Kevin, Badger, and gun-running overseas.

He steps back and takes a look. "Anything I left out?"

Sara and Bailey look over and think for a moment. Sara says, "Put the church in D.C. in there and the thing with the bible."

Daniel jots it down and it appears on the board.

Bailey says, "Dark Fenix. Something was up with him, too."

Minutes turn to hours. Feeling bored and helpless, Marlon pours himself another drink. He meanders into the den where the trio's trying to grasp at any straw they can and start pulling.

Taking a huge swig of rum, Marlon looks at the board filled with information and shakes his head.

Daniel is laying on the settee-style couch with his feet up on an ottoman starting to fall asleep.

Sara and Bailey are at the computer digging into files and reading cryptic documents.

"None of this makes any sense!" Sara blurts, breaking the silence.

Marlon walks over and peers over her shoulder.

"What are you working on?" he asks.

Sara rolls her eyes. "I thought you couldn't get involved?"

Marlon leans back. "I'm not. I was just wondering."

Bailey rolls his shoulders back to stretch and says, "We found this file we believe is connected somehow. I was investigating this music fraud and found this on Dark Fenix's system with JFP's music. To make a long story short, Fenix dropped his tour and admitted that the music was given to him and wasn't his. He released the tracks back to JFP and then went radio silent. It's weird as fuck. After that happened, Clifford was attacked twice. So, we think something in this file must be the reason, but it's all numbers and codes and shit. I can't make sense of any of it."

Marlon laughs as he looks at the file on the screen.

"What?" Bailey asks.

"Those really look like books, man," Marlon says, taking another swig.

Bailey looks back at the file, "What? You mean like financial books?"

Marlon finishes his swig and continues, "I'm surprised that you didn't get it. Your cousin uses a similar format."

Bailey shakes his head. "Of course. Dammit! I didn't get into that side of the business. But yeah. It makes sense now."

Marlon continues, pointing at the different sets of numbers, "Those numbers are locations or clients. They're probably for quantity. I bet that's a product code of some sort. That's the cost." Marlon takes another swig as Sara and Bailey are following along as he points to different areas of the file. "At least that's my guess," he continues after a hard swallow.

Marlon looks back over at the board. "I bet your real estate lady is dealing something and using Fenix as a front. He goes on tour and delivers the product. At least that's what it seems to me."

The rum is starting to hit Marlon at this point and he begins to slur his words a bit. He cocks his head to one side. "Not sure how Kevin fits into this," he says.

Marlon starts to rub his head.

Bailey asks, "What about the assassins?"

"Those two up there? How do you know they're assassins?" Marlon asks.

Bailey pulls up another file. "Here, look."

Marlon saunters over. He blinks a few times and stares at the screen for a moment to make out the words.

"So the landscaper is the guy that chased you and you shot up, right?" he says looking over at Daniel, who he forgot was asleep on the couch.

"Oh right," he says, seeing him fast asleep. "Who are the other two?" Marlon asks Sara and Bailey.

Bailey says, "Tofana and Dorothy. We think one of them is the female assassin that killed Senator Reeves."

Marlon nods, "Oh, yeah. I remember hearing about that. He was poisoned, right?"

Sara looks over and has an epiphany, "Tofana! Duh!"

Bailey and Marlon both look at Sara.

"Aqua Tofana was a poison for women to use to kill their husbands or something in Italy..." Sara blurts out.

Bailey shakes his head. "What? Really?"

Sara nods. "Yeah. I watched this documentary on it one night when I couldn't sleep. It was like in the sixteen hundreds and women couldn't divorce their horrible husbands, so a lady named Julia something Tofana, like Julie Ann. Or..."

"Who cares?! What about her?" Bailey interrupts to keep her on track.

Sara continues, "Yeah, whatever. She would sell a makeup called Aqua Tofana to her female clients, but it was really a poison so they could kill their husbands."

Marlon stumbles backward for a moment. "Morbid," he blurts out.

Sara looks at him and says, "Don't be an ass to your partner."

Marlon sets his empty glass down after taking his final swig and says, "Okay, I'm gonna hit the sack. Good luck wit da rest odda case. I have a flane to catch in the morning."

Sara and Bailey look at each other. "Flane?" Sara asks.

"I was gonna say flight and my brain was thinking about plane," Marlon says as he stumbles out of the room.

Sara looks back at Bailey, "I think he might miss his flane."

*　*　*

The sun wasn't even up when Clifford was shuffled out of his quiet holding cell. The agent escorting him smells of old coffee and cheap cologne. His hair was out of order and his tie was loosened. Clifford could tell he was nearing the end of his shift.

They leave the back-office area and into a side hall. He can hear chattering down the hall which connects to a main artery of the building. The early bird rush was starting to pick up and workers were beginning to trickle in through the hallways.

The agent swipes a security badge and opens a heavy door into another hallway.

This hall was less aesthetically pleasing to the eye.

The walls are a dull gray color and there are no windows. He could see other smaller cells that looked like short-term holding.

They continue past the cells and venture around the corner to a small office area with other officers and cubicles. He taps on the glass window to another room and an officer buzzes them in. He swings open the door and he and Clifford go into the room.

The agent slides a file under the glass and says, "Clifford Dee to interrogations," and continues on without skipping a beat.

They continue down the hall and open the door to a dank interrogation room. Clifford notices it's much darker and colder than the room at the police station. He's familiar with tactics to make people uncomfortable enough to want them to get out of the room as quickly as possible. This makes him think the state of the room is a tactic for just that reason.

The cold dim room actually brings a slight comfort to him for some reason he cannot explain. It just seems familiar. He even chuckles to himself thinking these were military tactics.

Sims walks into the room and shivers, "Jesus, did they not turn on the heat in here? It's cold."

Clifford laughs and says, "I thought this was a tactic to make me uncomfortable."

"Well, yeah, but I don't think it's supposed to be this cold. Damn!" Sims says.

He sets a file on the table where Clifford was sitting and starts fanning though. He stops on a page and begins reading. Clifford rubs his face and begins to rub his hands together. Sims mentioning how cold the room is made his body remember. Clifford thinks, Well played, Sims.

Sims looks up from the file, then sets it on the table. "You went to the hospital yesterday?"

Clifford perks up. "Yeah. I was drugged. Doctor said by injection. Some sort of roofie or something."

Sims looked confused. "The date rape drug?"

Clifford nods. "Yep. GHB or BHG or GBH or something like that. I'm not at all familiar with a lot of drugs."

Sims nods. "That's fair, but you did go to the hospital?"

Clifford unfolds his hands. "Yeah, I think Daniel drove me. I thought I was missing my gun. I went to Daniel about it. I wasn't feeling really well so he came over to help me look for it and I passed out."

Sims holds his hand out. "Okay, let's back up. You woke up and went to Dan's because you knew you were missing your gun? How?"

Clifford exhales quickly. "Okay, the previous night I had a vivid dream that someone was in my bedroom. I first thought it was a man and I tried to fight him, but now I am not sure if it was a man."

Sims asks, "They took your gun?"

Clifford shakes his head. "Yeah, I was half asleep and I remember waking up to someone next to me. I felt the prick and burn but wasn't sure at the time that I was injected with something. It was all really weird."

Sims nods, "Sounds like it. So okay, you woke up, someone injected you with something, and you just watched as they took a gun from you? Do you make a habit of leaving guns lying around?" he asks.

Clifford scoffed and shook his head. "No, nothing like that. I have a gun safe, but I always have a sidearm to protect myself in an emergency. I've had the occasional bad guy break into my place before."

Nodding, Sims circles back. "Enough about the gun, I'm confused about the dream thing. So, you were awake when they injected you? When you woke up, was it dream-like or did you get all loopy later?"

Clifford rubs his face. "I'm not sure anymore. Both, maybe? Neither?"

Sims starts writing notes. "Just start from the top again. I want to hear everything."

"Sure," Clifford says, pausing before he continues, "So, in the dream, I fought the guy off, but he pulled my own gun on me and pushed me back into my bed and ran off. I have no idea how long I was out for, but I woke up dizzy with a headache and a bit sick to my stomach. That's when I went to Daniel. He came back to my place with me, and I passed out. Next thing I know I was in the hospital."

Sims finishes writing and then taps the pencil on his lip.

"Did Daniel drive you?" Sims asks.

"I have no idea. I passed out," Clifford responds.

"What time was this?"

Clifford thinks for a moment, "Eight-ish, Maybe nine. I didn't look at the clock, honestly."

Sims furrows his brow for a moment and says, "I need to check on something, but you said that you originally thought it was a man you were fighting with, but now not so sure. Why is that?"

Clifford scoffs because he thinks this is a bit out there. "Well, I had another dream on the way here from the police station last night and this time it was a woman, first in a dress, then in that black hoodie. I grabbed her and I could feel slender feminine arms."

Sims narrows his eyes, "In your dream?"

"Yeah, in my dream," Clifford says.

Sims taps the pencil on his lip again and then stands up. "Okay, I have to check something. As far as that dream shit, I am sure your subconscious knows more than you think it does. Something happened to you for sure."

He grabs the file and promptly leaves the room, leaving Clifford alone in his thoughts.

A few minutes later Clifford notices that the heat in the room kicked on and the fans were blowing warm air into the room. He smiles and lets out a little chuckle as the air starts to circulate. He instinctively starts rubbing his hands together and he stands up from his chair. He stretches his legs and back and sits back down again.

Thinking about the dream again, he tries to remember more but his brain won't let him. He glances over toward the two-way mirror and can see his face. He stands up and walks over and rubs circles around his eyes. He imagines that there is some hard-nosed supervisor watching him so he starts checking his teeth and looking up his nose, just for fun.

Sims walks back into the room and Clifford smiles a bit. He walks past Clifford and sets the file down and sits. He looks over at Clifford and says, "No one's in there."

Clifford shrugs and walks back over to the desk and sits.

Sims folds his arms and leans back with a smile.

"What?" Clifford asks.

"You're innocent."

The smile on Clifford's face gets noticeably bigger. "Yeah, I know, but how do you know?"

Sims leans in and says, "Daniel did not take you to the hospital. He called 911. This is an official record. The ambulance arrived at your home at 8:47 am and arrived at the hospital at 9:02 am. According to the autopsy and witnesses that heard the gunshots, the murder of Mr. Hamilton took place at 8:52 am when he was on his way to a morning meeting. You were in transit to the hospital."

Clifford drops his hands to his sides in relief. "Am I free to go?"

Sims shakes his head. "Not yet. I have a lot more questions."

"Like what?" Clifford asks.

Sims rubs his brow. "Like who would frame you, for starters."

CHAPTER SEVENTEEN

The evening turns to morning and Daniel shakes Marlon awake.

"What the actual fuck are you doing?" Marlon asks in a drunken sleep-induced daze.

"Your flight's in two hours. The cab is probably on the way to pick you up," Daniel says.

"What time is it?" Marlon asks.

"Six-thirty," Daniel replies.

"Why are you here so fucking early?"

Daniel scoffs, "I never went home."

Marlon sits up and rubs his temples. He has a slight headache from the drinks the night before. Stretching as he stands, he spots Sara asleep on the settee with a blanket. Bailey is rubbing his face. He looks over at Daniel who has dark circles around his eyes.

"You didn't sleep long, did you?" Marlon says.

Daniel shakes his head. "Nope. Just a nap. Then Bailey and I stayed up reviewing the case. Sara passed out a few hours ago. We decided that Kevin is the common piece. We need to know how he's involved in all this."

Marlon nods. "Yeah, he is too clean. Speaking of clean, I need a shower."
Marlon walks into the bathroom and shuts the door.

Daniel talks through the door and says, "Dude, the cab is supposed to be here in like twenty minutes!"

He scoffs and walks back toward the den where Bailey is tapping his head.

Bailey turns to Daniel, "We need more information. Maybe we get eyes and ears on Kevin for a while."

Daniel nods. "Yeah, if we are going to do it, we should do it this morning while Clifford is still in custody. He wouldn't expect that."

Bailey agrees. "Yeah, you're right. Help me get the van together."

"What about Sara?" Daniel asks.

Bailey smiles. "We will need her, too, but let her sleep for now. She's peaceful."

* * *

Clifford and Sims leave the interrogation room and head out of that ward back toward the nicer, more pleasing area of the building. They head down the same side hallway, which was now booming with people, and into an elevator.

They go up a few floors and Clifford turns toward Sims and says, "You know it's much more colorful up here. Maybe you should get some artwork down there, you know, across from the short-term holding cells. Maybe a Danica Original or Jackson Pollock."

Sims smiles, looks over at Clifford, then at the ceiling of the elevator to avoid the awkward eye contact. "Yeah, a Jackson Pollock would be nice."

Clifford smiles back. "It would spruce some things up."

The elevator dings and the doors slide open to another hallway. They step out and walk toward Sims' office suite.

The desks were configured in low-cut cubicles which sacrificed privacy to optimize communications with each other. In the back were small conference rooms and glass-walled offices. They walk back to one of the offices and Sims picks up more files. He steps out and says, "Hey Johnson, we're going to set up in the conference room, bring all the files regarding Hamilton's death in here."

The glass conference room door slowly swings shut after they enter.

Clifford shakes his head. "Wow, so this is your office?"

Sims smiles and says, "This is a conference room. My office is that little desk in the corner next to the water jug over there. The division lead sits in the big office in the corner. We won't see him until ten-ish or eleven. He's a late owl."

Sims sits and begins filling out a form while Clifford moves toward the window and looks to the busy D.C. street below. Opening a folder, Sims pulls the USB drive he got from Clifford a few weeks before from a pocket inside and plugs it into a laptop. He goes back to writing on the form and then sets it aside.

Staring out the window, Clifford shakes his head. "So busy here. So many people." He sighs and continues, "It was nothing like this in Kentucky."

Sims looks up and nods.

Clifford continues, "I had a friend that worked at the Broward Valley department. Martin DiPietro."

"I read about that. Tragic," Sims says.

"Yeah. I still think about him," Clifford says.

"You always will." Sims continues, "I had a partner. Lopez. She was a firecracker. We were working a case that involved a drug dealer. She waltzes into this room, leaping behind furniture, dodging bullets, and laying down cover fire. It was like a scene out of an action movie. She was moving in slow motion shooting people left and right. Extreme badass style. We caught the dealer and it turned out that he was working with this hot-shot investment banker."

Clifford nods as he listens along.

Sims continues, "We went to go pick him up in his office the next day. We step in and she tells him he's under arrest. Next thing I know, the banker picks up a pistol from his desk, and boom, she was shot in the head. Dead."

Clifford's eyes widened. "Holy shit! Really?"

"Yeah," Sims says, pausing to reflect.

"I was a junior agent then. No one expected an investment banker to be a threat, so we were under-prepared. I'm never making that mistake again."

Clifford shakes his head. "Wow, man. I heard about Martin on the news. I wasn't there to witness it. That must have been rough."

Sims nods. "Yeah. I was in therapy for a while. I took it pretty hard."

He looks over at Clifford and smiles. "You know, I almost went to Kentucky?"

"Really?" Clifford asks.

"Yeah, a training buddy of mine got his orders just before I did and he ended up going to the field office there and I got D.C."

Clifford nods. "Cool."

Sims smiles again. "Yeah, Forrester is his name. He got this weird anonymous tip about a mob boss named Bandoni. Then, next thing you know he was delivered to the front step of his office building with a bow and all the incriminating evidence on a USB drive around his neck."

Clifford stretches and lets out a very suspicious yawn. "Wow, weird!"

"Yeah, really weird. He got promoted after that bust," Sims says with a smile.

Clifford peaks around the laptop Sims was typing on and says, "Not to change the topic, but have you found anything yet?"

"Yeah, actually. Check this out," Sims says as he turns the computer for Clifford to see.

Clifford looks on as Sims starts explaining the files.

"Remember you pointed out that there were logs going to a different server?

"Yeah," Clifford says.

"I did a domain lookup and the server is a dot-gov server."

Clifford asks, "Dot-gov, as in a government server?"

Sims nods. "Yep. They were being transferred to an unclassified DOD server."

"Do you know why?" Clifford asks.

Sims shakes his head, "Not yet. We were able to view the file names that were transferred, but not the contents. These look like records for accounts. We can't verify just yet, because the contents are encrypted, so we can only assume. It would be easier if we had the decryption file to view these. It literally could be anything."

Clifford looks over his shoulder. "So they aren't really hiding business. Just what the business is?"

Sims nods. "Yeah, we know they're doing something illegal, but we can't exactly prove what until we get proof of what this is. We can tell money is exchanging hands, but it won't hold up in court without proof."

"How are you going to get the proof if everything is encrypted?" Clifford asks.

Sims smiles. "We have a whole department whose job it is to figure out the encryption algorithms of files. Ya know, it's almost like we know what we are doing here at the FBI."

Clifford thinks for a moment. "Maybe I can get Bailey to look at this again. He could probably help."

Sims shakes his head. "You guys shouldn't get involved. We have our guys running with this and we don't need any hiccups."

Clifford smiles. "Yeah but Bailey is good. If there's something to find, he'll find it."

* * *

Bailey rushes Marlon to the door as the cab has been waiting for a few minutes already. Daniel is outside talking to the driver trying to stall him. Marlon walks outside and Bailey wheels up beside him.

"Hey, tell JJ I miss her, wouldja?" Bailey asks.

Marlon turns around. "Of course, but you know it would be nice if you guys came out to visit her. She really doesn't have the luxury of a vacation right now. She's a busy woman."

Bailey nods. "Yeah, I get that."

The cab driver gets out of the car and yells, "Hey! One of you get in the car now or I'm driving off!"

Marlon looks over. "I'm comin' tiny, calm your tits!"

He leans down to give Bailey a hug and then shakes his hand. He picks up his bag and tosses it into the back of the car and slides in. Bailey and Daniel walk up to the door as Marlon closes it behind him.

"Safe travels, buddy!" Daniel says as the car starts to pull away. Marlon doesn't speak, only waves goodbye.

Daniel and Bailey head back inside where Sara meets them in the hallway. Bailey spots that a worry has drawn up onto her face. He asks, "What's going on, baby girl? You look upset."

She bites her lip for a moment, "You need to see the news."

Bailey rolls into the other room and his eyes laser focus on the breaking news.

"A rising star in the rap scene, James Goldman, also known as Jimmi from Philly is in critical condition this morning after what officials believe was a gang-related shooting. Jimmi, or JFP as he is called by his fans, has no known gang ties but there were rumors of legal disputes that may have sparked action from angry gang members."

Bailey's face drops. "Oh my God!" he says, staring at the TV.

Sara drapes her arm around him and says, "I don't buy it. I don't think this was gang-related."

Bailey shakes his head. "Nope. Not Jimmi. He'd never." An angry look falls onto Bailey's face. He hates that the media would even speculate about gang relations.

Sara sits down in a chair and Daniel walks over to grab the remote as the news station changed the topic to local D.C. sports. He flicks off the TV and Bailey's phone rings.

"It's Ray, Jimmi's Agent!" he says while answering. "Hey! I saw the news." Bailey says.

"Shh, they're after me, too. I don't know what to do." Ray continues, "I went to visit Jimmi in the hospital and I was followed."

Bailey asks, "By who?"

"I don't know. He was shot last night in front of the studio. They made it look like a drive-by."

"Wait, what do you mean they made it *look like* a drive-by?" Bailey asks.

"Like, they fired three times and all three hit perfectly. But then they sprayed more shots after he fell."

Bailey says, "Oh, that ain't gang shit!"

Ray agrees. "Nope, it isn't. So anyway, I went to the hospital, but he was still in the I.C.U. and they turned me away. I parked in a lot across the street and when I was crossing, I saw a guy near my car, messing with it. I literally caught someone who was screwing with my car that watched me walk into the hospital. I freaked out so I ran. I left my car there and went to the nearest police station, and they said I was paranoid."

Bailey sighs. "Calm down, Ray. Is there somewhere you can go to lay low?"

"No, my closest relative is in New York, and she's got kids. I ain't gonna put them in jeopardy."

"Okay, listen," Bailey says, "Stay in public and around people as much as you can, we will come up there and bring you down here to D.C. It will be easier for us to protect you."

Ray is quiet for a moment. "Okay, sure," he says.

"Is there a park or a busy public place near you? We are going to leave now. Three, maybe four hours, tops and we will be there!" Bailey says.

Ray exhales. "Yeah, I'll be in Mifflin Square Park. It's pretty busy during the day and it'll be easy for you to get to. I can walk there from here. I'll be near Wolf Street."

* * *

Traffic was smooth all the way up I-95. The only hiccup was leaving the Baltimore Metro area and heading north toward Delaware. They reach the city limits of Philadelphia in a little over three hours and Bailey pulls up a map for Mifflin Square Park.

He navigates as Sara drives. Daniel is in the back looking at his phone.

"Okay, two blocks up and make a right. That should take you right to the park," Bailey says.

Sara pulls into a space diagonal to the park. "This is Wolf street," she says.

Bailey smiles. "Cool, he said he would be at a bench near Wolf."

"He should have said he'd be at a wall on Wolf Street," Daniel says, trying to ease the tension with a pun. Bailey looks over with side-eye in disapproval as he picks up his phone and calls Ray.

Daniel shrugs. "I thought it was funny."

After a few seconds Bailey says, "No answer. I got his voicemail."

Sara and Daniel look at each other with a little worry in their eyes.

They get out of the van and stretch. Daniel walks over to the side and helps Bailey get out.

Sara sees a man sitting on a park bench and says, "Hey, I think that's him."

They pick up the pace, dodging people left and right to get to him.

Approaching the bench Bailey says, "Hey, Ray!"

There was no answer back.

They walk to the front of the bench and see Ray with a warm cup of soda next to him clutching a cold burger, still in the wrapper, with his eyes open.

"Ray?" Bailey questions as he reaches over to touch his arm. As he places his hand on his arm, Ray drops the burger and slumps over.

"Aw shit!" Bailey exclaims.

CHAPTER EIGHTEEN

Sara, Bailey, and Daniel spent the next hour answering questions from police at the station. They filed a report and were granted permission to review some of the security tapes around the local area. Sergeant Ferrell points at one of the videos.

"Here he's seen walking into Big John's burgers and shakes. Fast forward eleven minutes, he's leaving with his food," she says.

The three watch the screen as Ferrell continues, "Here, he tosses a napkin and misses the trash can, and this is where we lose him on this video."

She pulls up another video on the screen.

"Okay, here we can see him walking onto Wolf Street, jaywalks across the street, and heads into the park. It looks like he sits on the same bench where he was found dead."

Sara scratches her head. "Can you rewind to the part where he jaywalks?"

Sergeant Ferrell turns and says, "I've got one more thing for you to see." as she un-pauses the video.

After a few more seconds of watching the video, Sara's eyes widen, "Pause it," she says.

"Okay, now what?" Ferrell asks.

"Look at that person there. The woman," Sara says.

Daniel laughs, "Always looking at some hot woman, amirite?" He suddenly perks up. "Oh wait!"

Sara looks over at Daniel, "Right?!"

Bailey and Sergeant Ferrell look at each other and Bailey speaks up. "Care to let us in on your little eureka moment?"

Sara says, "That's the woman that killed Senator Reeves!"

Bailey's mouth drops, "For real?"

Sergeant Ferrell asks, "That was in D.C. a bit ago. What's she doing in Philadelphia?"

"Follow her on the camera," Bailey said.

Ferrell says, "You're in for a treat! Let's focus on her." She rewinds the video, highlights her on the screen, which places a circle around her, and plays the video.

The woman walked into a shop across the street and waited until Ray crossed into the park. Slinking out of the shop, she stayed twenty yards behind him. He sat on a park bench and set his drink and bag down next to him. She stopped for a moment and then sat on a park bench a few yards away and waited. After a few moments, Ray placed a napkin over his lap to avoid getting any grease or food on his suit. He pulled some fries out of the paper bag and started eating them while he sipped on his drink.

She stood and slowly walked toward Ray and dropped her purse. All of her items fell out and onto the ground. Ray stood up and set his lunch down on the bench and began to help her pick up her things.

The woman set her purse on the bench next to Ray's food and they started conversing as they picked up her things together. She smiled and placed her things back into the purse. She thanked him as she picked up her purse. She leaned in and gave Ray a hug and then walked away. Ray admires her as she continues on and sits down to continue to eat.

Bailey says, "Wait, go back."

Ferrell rewinds the video again to the part where her bag fell, and she dropped her things. She sets her purse on the bench and Bailey says, "There. Look!"

They look closely at the grainy video.

As she is placing items back into her purse, she waved something over top of his drink just before putting it into her bag. After Ray watched as she walked away, he sat down to resume his meal. He took a huge swig from his soda and pulled out the hamburger from the grease-stained white bag. His body let out a little shake and went limp, still grasping what would have been his last meal.

They replay the video again.

Ferrell zooms in and she says, "It's blurry, but this is the best angle we have. And she definitely put something in his drink."

She turns her head and calls out to a coworker, "Hey Clemente, have them run a tox screen on the drink. Something was put in his cup."

She smiles and turns back toward Bailey. "Good eye! All of you! I can get you the results within the hour if you want!"

*   *   *

Sims gets a call. "Hold on a sec," he says to Clifford as he answers his phone.

"Okay. Yeah, okay. We'll meet him downstairs."

Clifford looks over toward Sims.

"Your lawyer is demanding your release," Sims says with a smile.

Clifford smiles back. "Aw shit! I probably shoulda called him."

Sims nods. "I'm going to release you to him."

The two walk into a conference area where Lipschitz is waiting.

"You had your time for questions, and I am here for- Oh, Mr. Dee!" he says as he spots Clifford walking in behind Sims.

Sims nods and says, "Your client has been very cooperative and we have cleared him off our suspect list at this time. He's free to go with you."

"Excellent news!" Lipschitz says, "See Cliffy, I told you I'd take care of you."

Clifford shakes his head. "Please call me Dee."

Lipschitz shrugs. "Dee? Why do you want to be called that? Sounds like a dog's name. Clifford is much better."

Sims chuckles as Clifford looks over and rolls his eyes.

"If we have any more questions, we'll be in touch, Cliffy!" Sims says, mocking, as the two men head out of the room.

Lipschitz hunches over the steering wheel, driving slower than normal for the traffic around him.

"This town is so busy these days," he says, "I remember when it would take a full day to get out to Leesburg. Now, it's like an hour from D.C. to there. When they finished Route 7 the firm moved from Tysons to Leesburg."

Clifford nods as Lipschitz continues to ramble on about random facts about the area and sighs as he drags on about how traffic is so much worse now.

He pulls into Clifford's condo parking lot and says, "This is a nice area for you. In about twenty years your place will be three times the value of what you paid for it. Good investment, good investment," he says.

Clifford thanks Lipschitz and waves as he drives off, turning the wrong way down a one-way alley. Clifford shakes his head and walks inside. He sets his things down and finds a cellphone with a note from Bailey:

New phone for you. Call me when you get this.

He calls Bailey.

No answer.

He walks across the hall and knocks on the door to Bailey's condo, but there was no answer there, either.

Clifford, now concerned, calls Sara.

"Hey, Dee! Are you out of jail?" Sara asks.

"Yeah, where are you? Is Bailey with you, he didn't answer his phone."

"Philly!" Sara says excitedly.

Clifford starts to smile as hears Sara whispering to Bailey to check his phone.

Sara gets back onto the phone and says, "Yeah, Bailey is here. Phone was on silent."

"Huh, ok, so, Philadelphia? What's in Philadelphia?"

Sara, being a smartass, says, "Cheesesteaks and a decent football team, for starters."

Sara could hear the sigh through the phone as she continues. "We're actually leaving now. I guess you didn't hear. JFP was shot and is in the hospital. His manager, Ray, called us scared he was next. We came up to get him but found him dead."

Clifford asks, "So what's with the jokes? This is terrible!"

Sara says, "Right, yeah. That's bad. Sorry, I'm just a bit excited. We got a huge break in the case. The person who killed Ray is from D.C. She's the same one who killed Senator Reeves."

Clifford is quiet for a moment.

"You still there, Dee?" Sara asks.

"Yeah. Just thinking."

"Okay," Sara says, "Just keep thinking, we'll be home in about an hour or so."

Clifford hangs up the phone and heads back into his condo. He opens his laptop but cannot connect to the internet. After a few attempts, he gives up and grabs his copy of the keys for Bailey's and goes inside. He's impressed with the crime board that the crew put together. He jumps over onto Bailey's computer, but it's locked. He picks up his phone and calls Bailey.

"Hey, I'm at your place. My internet is screwy. Nice crime board you guys set up. I want to look at those files you got off that server again but your computer is locked. What's your password?"

"The reason your internet is messed up is the same reason your phone is messed up and your cameras are not working. Someone destroyed them with a small electro-magnetic pulse. That's what I wanted to talk to you about. That crime board was all Daniel. He did a great job. It kinda reminded me of you and how you think. Oh, and uh, I'm not giving you my password, Dee," Bailey says.

"EMP huh? I thought that stuff was only in the movies?" Clifford says.

"Nope, they exist, and that is what I suspect happened. I can't prove it though. If you need to get on the web, you have your own account on my network and all that stuff is shared with you. Just grab the laptop off the desk and log in as yourself."

Clifford looks around for a moment and spots the laptop. "Got it! Thanks! Let's talk more about that EMP later." he says, hanging up the phone.

Clifford opens the laptop and logs in. He starts poking around at the files and finds the shared folder. He opens the folder that has the coded file and the music they took from JFP. He closes the music file and starts looking at the code. He shakes his head because he still doesn't get it. After opening the text file, Clifford stares at the three names: Landscaper, Tofana, and Dorothy.

"What am I missing?" he says to himself.

Clifford hears a noise outside the front door and it's quickly followed by a loud thud and smashing sound. He jumps up and runs over to Bailey's door and looks through the peephole. He can see his door wide open and the frame is splintered.

Someone kicked it in.

He heads around the corner to Bailey's elevator. It's on a common wall with his condo.

He opens the door and walks in.

After the door closes, he flips the elevator from running to maintenance mode, climbs through the roof, shimmies over to the edge, and climbs down a ladder to an open area in the back.

This secret room between the units was accessible through Clifford's linen closet as well as Bailey's elevator. He silently navigates through the room trying not to make any noise that would attract attention. He turns on a monitor that he had hooked up to hidden cameras in his condo. He watches as The Landscaper rummages through his things. Clifford notices a bandage on his left shoulder. It was clean and neatly dressed but impeding his arm movement. This is where he was shot when he was chasing them.

Thinking back to his dream, the intruder was not hindered by anything. He was now convinced it was not The Landscaper. It must have been one of the women. The Landscaper heads into Clifford's bedroom and looks in his closet.

He walks over toward his desk area and looks over his things. He reaches into his pocket and pulls out his phone. He snags a few photos around the room and walks into his bathroom. He continues to take pictures as he tours his condo. Finally, he places a phone call, but Clifford can only hear his side of the conversation:

"He's not here. I took a few pictures of his place so we know the layout. When will Tofana be back in town? I see. I don't think we should wait until after the funeral. Let me kill him now. He's starting to figure things out. Okay. Okay. Understood. See you in an hour."

He shoves the phone back into his pocket and heads toward the front door. He stops and looks around one more time and steps through the busted doorway, jumps into his truck, and drives off.

Clifford enters his condo through the false wall in his linen closet and begins to pick up some of the things he tossed around.

Just over an hour later, the group pulls up to see a maintenance crew working on Clifford's door.

Sara jumps out and runs over to Clifford, who has a drink in his hand. "What happened?"

Clifford looks over at the men working and then back at Sara. "B&E," he says just before taking a swig of his bourbon and coke.

"B&E? Who would burst into your place?" Sara asks.

Clifford raises his brow to confirm as he pulls the glass from his lips. He swallows and says, "The Landscaper paid a visit."

Daniel and Bailey, now joining the conversation, look over and Daniel says, "Shit. He came back?"

Clifford smiles and says, "I don't think it was him the other night when I was drugged. I think it was one of the women. Dorothy or Tofana. My money is on Tofana. She deals in poisons, right?"

Sara rolls her eyes, "Duh! Yes! That makes total sense. I think she was the one in Philly, too. She poisoned Ray."

Clifford nods, "She was. The Landscaper was talking to someone on the phone and mentioned she was out of town."

Daniel looks confused, "Wait, you were home when he was here?"

"Kinda. I was in the walls."

"In the walls?" Daniel asks.

Clifford nods, "Go get yourself situated and come back over in an hour or so when this guy is done fixing my door. I'll show you what I'm talking about."

A little more than an hour goes by and Bailey is sitting in the hallway in front of Clifford's linen closet with an annoyed look on his face. "You know it's bullshit that you didn't make the door big enough for me to go in, right?"

Inside the secret room, Clifford yells back, "It was an afterthought, man. This was the only place to put the door where it wouldn't be noticed."

Bailey crosses his arms. "It's still bullshit! And why didn't you tell anyone about this?"

Inside the room, Clifford shows Sara and Daniel where he watched The Landscaper rummage through everything. Behind them on the wall was a gun rack with several rifles, handguns, and drawers full of ammunition.

"Jesus, Dee. Are you planning for anarchy or something?" Daniel asks.

"You can never be over-prepared," Clifford says in a quip.

The three head out of the room and back through the linen closet. Bailey looks over at them and says, "Welcome back. How was Narnia?"

"Ha-ha!" Clifford mockingly laughs.

"Did you enjoy tea with Mr. Tumnus?" Bailey continues in an English accent.

Sara snickers, "Yeah, he had poison drinks too, like Tofana."

The crew continues into the living room and Daniel plops himself onto the sofa.

"So, you said he mentioned a funeral. Whose funeral?" he asks.

Clifford looks over and says, "My only guess is Badger's. I have no idea why they want to wait. I guess they're taking orders from someone else."

Clifford turns to Bailey. "Let's go back over to your place. I need to check the info you guys put together the other day. I have some thoughts."

* * *

It's quiet in Bailey's condo. Clifford sits and stares at the board filled with information.

"Daniel, you did this?" he asks.

"Yeah, I started filling it out and it just all came out. Sara and Bailey helped, too."

Impressed, Clifford nods in approval. "Great job."

Clifford stands and places his hands on his hips. "Let's start with Sara's hunch. We need to look into the real estate agent. According to the listing, her name is Kelly Singer and we have her agent ID and license number. Can we look up the houses she's sold?" He turns toward Bailey to ask.

Bailey nods. "Sure can. On it now," he says as he starts clicking away on his keyboard.

Clifford turns back toward the board and says, "Okay, while we wait for Bailey to find...."

"Done!" Bailey says, cutting Clifford off, with much accomplishment in his voice.

"Done? Like, done-done?"

Bailey nods. "Done."

The team gathers and Bailey starts reading off what he found.

"Okay, so in the last three years, she has sold two homes, both for multi-millions, including Rodney Brown's house she sold this week.

Sara bursts in, "That was Danica's home and I'm still not over it."

Bailey looks over at Sara. "Okay, fine! Danica's home. But still, she's only sold two houses in 36 months. It looks like she's never helped anyone buy a home. Prior to three years ago, she was selling close to a house a month. There is another account linked to hers."

"Like a partner?" Clifford asks.

"Like a partner," Bailey says. "John Singer, her husband."

Clifford ponders for a moment. "He must be the breadwinner, right?"

"Glad you asked, nope. He has not sold or bought anything under his license. This agent's business has to be a front for something else," Bailey says.

Clifford glances over toward Sara standing with her hands on her hips and raised brows. She cocks her head to one side. Clifford shoots Sara an apologizing half-smile while she sends a flurry of blinks his way in an I-told-you-so manner. He walks over and gives her a hug. Sara wraps her hands around him and says, "Apology accepted."

He pulls away and says, "Okay, so can we dig into their finances? Find out how they make money?"

Bailey shakes his head, "I can try, but we would need a lot more information. Financial data is super secure and we would need a reason to access it."

Clifford raises his brow. "Maybe a federal query?" he says, picking up his phone.

* * *

"Absolutely not!" Sims says in a confirming tone over the phone with Clifford. "We would never be able to get a warrant to search their financial records on a hunch such as this. For all we know, her real estate business is a side gig. She could be independently wealthy or have another job. It would be way too much and a judge would never sign off on this. Sorry, Dee. Can't help."

"Thanks, Sims," Clifford says, hanging up the phone.

"Welp!" Clifford says, "Feds can't help. Not enough to go on for a warrant."

"Damn!" Bailey says, smacking his lips.

Clifford looks at the board, "Okay. Kelly, the real estate agent, we think is engaged in some sort of illegal activity. Why was she meeting with Kevin?"

"We don't know yet," Sara says.

"Okay. Let's put a pin in that for now." Clifford says.

"Jimmi was gunned down and his manager was killed by Tofana. We know this because of the phone call made in my condo," Clifford says. "Who was he talking to?"

Daniel pipes in, "The real estate agent?"

Clifford looks over at Daniel and back at the board.

"Of course! Oh my God, she's a contract manager!" Clifford says, smacking his head. "Why didn't I see that before?"

"Why would you have?" Daniel asks.

"I sorta lived that lifestyle for a bit."

"Oh, right!" Daniel says, remembering.

"This all makes sense now, but we don't really have the proof. If she is a contract manager, then The Landscaper, Tofana, and Dorothy must be her muscle. Kevin was probably paying a contract," Clifford says.

"Like putting a hit out on someone?" Sara asks.

"Yup. That's exactly what it is," Bailey says. "While you guys were talking, I did some digging on Senator Reeves and check this out. He was drafting a new bill to crack down on weapons dealing. There is a dark web theory that Reeves was going to expose a ring on drugs and weapons trafficking in Africa, and that's why he was drafting this bill and probably why he was taken out."

Clifford steps over to Bailey's computer. "Oh son of a bitch! Are you serious?" he says as he turns to Bailey's monitor to get a better look.

Bailey looks over, "Yeah, Why?"

Clifford says, "Remember what the killer said to Reeves as he was dying? This is for Molly?"

Bailey replies, "Yeah, Molly, something like that."

Not even a split second passed before Bailey connected the dots. "Oh, Mali! Damn!"

Bailey continues as Clifford is reading over his shoulder, "Now, I don't make it a habit to trust the conspiracy theorists, but they do base a lot of their stories on kernels of truth. Also, knowing what we know about what was said to Reeves, this completely tracks."

After reading, Clifford rolls his eyes. "Yeah, a lot of this is bullshit, but the part on Reeves blowing the cover on the trafficking ring is pretty spot on. The three lobbyists that were killed a few days later were supporting him. It looks like someone offed Reeves because his bill was a threat and then they started covering tracks."

Bailey nods, "Yep."

Sara smacks Daniel on his shoulder, "You guys gave Badger a copy of those files. The encrypted files were probably the proof!"

You could see it in Clifford's face that his heart sank.

He turns toward Sara and says, "Shit, I got him killed."

"No, no, no, no. That's not what I was saying," Sara says with heartfelt emotion.

"I know, but it's true. But no one knew I gave that to him," Clifford says.

Daniel looks over at Clifford. "Kevin probably knew. He was inside the restroom while we were talking to Badger. Badger could have easily told him in an effort to get him to work with you."

Clifford swallows hard, "Fuck. You're right."

Bailey puts his hand on Clifford's. "This is not on you, Dee! It's on the guy who put the hit out. Not you! Just remember that!"

"Yeah, I know. It still feels shitty, though," Clifford says.

Sara looks over. "Dee, that makes you human, not responsible."

Clifford tears up a bit. "Too many people," Clifford shakes his head, "You're right. This isn't on me. We need proof that this is Kevin. Hard proof. I have an idea, but it's going to be risky."

CHAPTER NINETEEN

The next morning, Clifford places a call to Kevin.

It goes to voicemail, again.

Sitting in the van with Bailey he turns to him and says, "Shit! Voicemail. I'll leave a message."

"No, hang up," Bailey says.

"Why?" Clifford asks, hanging up the phone.

"Text him. People don't listen to voicemails for, I dunno, hours. But people do glance at texts, even if they don't respond right away."

Clifford smiles. "You're right."

Kevin is walking up the steps to his office building when he glances down at a new text message. He stops for a moment and reads. He drops his arm down and stands still for a few seconds, then continues into the building.

Bailey looks on through binoculars. "Shit. He looked like he did a hard reboot. What did you send?" Clifford shows Bailey his phone. "Damn, that will get his attention!"

Bailey and Clifford continue to monitor the building for over an hour when they spot Kevin walking out and heading toward the curb.

"Eyes on Kevin," Clifford says into a walkie.

Around the corner from the office, Daniel sits on a bicycle with a helmet, and sunglasses, and is dressed in neon-colored cyclist shorts and a matching top with zipper pockets.

He places his hands on an earpiece in his ear. "I see him. Sara, do you have eyes?"

Sara is sitting on a park bench across the street and is watching him walk toward her. She lowers a newspaper and says, "I got him. He's standing on the corner. Looks like he's waiting for something."

She turns her head to see a town car approaching. "Shit, car, guys. There's a car."

Clifford talks into the walkie, "Daniel can you tag the car?"

"On it!" Daniel says as he starts pedaling toward Kevin and the car.

Kevin gets in and the car starts to drive away. Daniel is pedaling as fast as he can, as he tries to keep up. The car rounds the corner and speeds away. Daniel cuts through a small park. Dodging pedestrians he pedals faster, wheeling down some concrete stairs.

"Sorry!" he belts out as he passes them.

He glides through an alleyway and out onto another street.

"I got 'em!" he says as he spots the car at a stoplight.

He slowly approaches, unzips the pocket on his top, and fishes out a tracker. He pulls the tape from the underside of the tracker with his teeth, exposing the adhesive. He wheels past the car, palming the device, and lightly slaps the tracker on the right-side door as he cycles ahead, slowing down to meet the flow of traffic. "The tracker is on. You should be able to follow." Daniel says.

Bailey links the tracker and says, "Signal is strong. We're good."

They drive the van past the park and spot Sara on the corner. She hops in and says, "Hello boys! Let's go catch a bad guy!"

Daniel calls over the radio, "I am going to stay on the bike and try to follow."

The car pulls away and starts to gain distance from Daniel. He pedals faster as he sees them take another turn. He goes through another side alley to try to get a bit closer but as he turns back onto the street, he sees that the traffic thinned out and the car was able to pick up a lot of speed and was too far ahead of him to follow.

"I lost him," Daniel says into the radio.

"Turn around," Clifford replies.

Daniel looks behind him as the van pulls up.

They open the back and Daniel slides the bicycle in and climbs in, closing the doors behind him.

They track Kevin to the lot of an abandoned warehouse. They pull up along the fence line of a neighboring property about a hundred yards away on a dirt road. They continue driving past an opening and into the tree line. Following the dirt road around, they find a spot where they can record him, but not be seen. They stop the van and Clifford jumps out.

He climbs to the top of the van and Daniel pops out, handing Clifford a telescoping pole with a camera and a long-distance audio recorder on it.

Clifford fixes it to the roof of the van.

They raise the poll so the equipment is just peeking above the tree line.

Another car swiftly approaches and stops next to Kevin's car. The real estate agent, Kelly, steps out and walks over toward the back of the car where Kevin is waiting.

Clifford adjusts the settings of the audio and video equipment to capture their conversation.

"We have a problem," Kevin starts.

"Wait!" She exclaims, stopping Kevin from saying anything. "Not yet!"

She pulls a device out of her pocket and sets it on top of the trunk of her car. She flips a switch, and the device emits a white noise that would distort their voices on any recording equipment.

Clifford rips off his earphones, "Shit! We lost audio!"

Sara leans in to watch the video. "Keep recording, I can read their lips."

She focuses intently on the video.

"Kevin's talking. He is saying that you're onto them. Clifford Dee is a problem. He knows Reeves was killed by your assassins and it will only be a matter of time before he finds out it was me who hired you. He knows that I'm running weapons into Mali."

Sara nods after hearing Mali.

"Kevin said, 'We need to kill Dee now.' Now she's saying, 'Don't panic. He's under control. We will get him soon. After Hamilton's funeral, he'll be taken out. I have my best two on call for this but the other can't be pulled in right now.' Kevin asked, 'Why?' She's saying, 'The third assassin has been off her radar.'"

She looks over at the guys and says, "Whatever that means."

Sara continues to read their lips. "Kevin said he wants it done before the funeral and she said it's too risky for them. Kevin said fine but he wants the whole crew done."

She turns to Clifford. "Shit Dee, he wants us all killed."

Clifford scoffs, "Figures, that weasel. What else are they saying?"

"She said, 'consider it done but I will need an extra thirty thousand to cover the crew. He said, 'Deal, you'll get the extra money tomorrow.'"

Kevin hands Kelly an envelope full of cash and returns to his car. The car drives off leaving a cloud of dust behind. Kelly stands outside her car and watches Kevin drive away. After a moment she pulls her phone out of her jacket pocket, dials a number, and places the phone to her ear."

Still watching the video, Sara says, "Gah! She turned away. I was trying to see what she was saying on the phone."

Clifford says, "It's okay. We have plenty to go on. Let's go."

They head back to their place after dropping the van off at the office.

"I can't believe he wants to have all of us killed," Sara says.

"Oh, I can," Bailey chimes in. "He's supporting ISIS by running guns over in Mali. They do all sorts of nasty stuff over there. Kevin will be in deep shit if Uncle Sam finds out what he's doing."

"Yeah, I bet," she says.

Bailey looks over and sees Clifford shaking his head.

"What's up, boss?"

Clifford smirks at the term 'Boss.' "I just find it hard to believe this is who Badger turned the department over to."

Bailey nods, "Yeah. I get it, but you can't think for one moment that Badger knew what was going on. That's what got him killed, ya know. If he was in on this or cool with it, he'd still be alive."

Clifford scoffs, "Yeah, I know, but he should have had better judgment. I knew Kevin was bad news. He's always been bad news."

"Hey, just because you had some bad run-ins with the guy doesn't mean that Badger didn't see the good sides of him. Also, he was human. He wasn't perfect. Everyone has bad judgment every once in a while. Heck, you took jobs from the mafia, remember?"

Clifford nods. "Yeah, yeah. You're right. I'm glad I've got smart friends."

Bailey laughs. "See, more bad judgment. Thinking I'm smart!"

Clifford laughs. "You ARE smart, you ass!"

"Smart-ass! Yes. See you're getting it," Bailey said laughing.

After a brief moment, Daniel breaks the silence. "So, they said that they wouldn't do anything until after the funeral."

Clifford nods. "Yeah?"

"Why wait until then?"

"Killing someone running for public office creates a lot of heat. There are a lot of people investigating this and a whole bunch of eyes watching for signs that it might happen again. It's too hot right now.

We probably have a month before things calm down enough to where an accident would happen to a whole crew of people."

Daniel slowly nods with a half-smile. "Ah, got it."

Clifford continues, "At the FBI, they're already set up in shifts so they can work this case around the clock. Kevin knows, Kelly knows, we know, and this benefits us greatly."

Daniel gives Clifford a confused look. "How so?"

Clifford smiles. "Because we know when they're coming, and we can prepare for war."

CHAPTER TWENTY

It was a cooler than average afternoon in Arlington National Cemetery. The breeze was blowing in from the east, lightly rustling the leaves in the trees, and the smell of the freshly cut grass was looming in the air. Badger's casket was pulled by a horse-drawn cart, slowly down the path toward his final resting place. The military procession was quite the sight and the only thing that could be heard were the slight sobs and sniffs of those crying and the beat of the drum as the carriage wheels made contact with the stone path.

The carriage moves off the path onto the grass, and the procession follows as they approach the awaiting open grave. After the carriage stops, the mourners gradually assemble in the rows of chairs while the pallbearers stand in uniform beside the carriage.

Clifford is among them, dressed in his ceremonial Class-A uniform with white gloves.

They are called to attention.

They pick up the casket in unison and with military precision, march it over and place it on the casket-lowering device.

After a beautiful service, Badger receives an eleven-gun salute while "Taps" is playing. The flag is folded and presented by Clifford to Badger's oldest living relative, his daughter, Angelica. The casket descends into the grave as mourners line up to toss a rose onto the lid, watching it lower into the earth.

Clifford looks over and gives Sara, Daniel, and Bailey a slight smile.

Kevin is there but stays in the back, away from everyone. He occasionally glares over at Clifford, but Clifford keeps his composure. As people start to leave, Kevin follows and disappears into a small crowd. Clifford watches him break away from the others and get into his car.

Sara walks up and tosses her own rose followed closely behind by Daniel. They walk back and stand next to Bailey and wait for Clifford to finish with his duties.

Clifford suggests that they skip the repast and head back home.

Back at Clifford's place, Sara says, "It was a good service. I was glad they let you be a pallbearer."

Clifford lets out a noticeable sigh as he pours himself a drink.

"You okay?" Sara asks.

"Yeah, it...It's just setting in, you know?"

Sara puts her arm around Clifford. "Yeah. I know."

"Kevin was there."

Sara pulls away. "What! Really? I didn't see him."

Clifford nods. "Yeah, he was in the back, away from everyone. He left quickly. It was almost like he was there for us, not Badger."

"Do you think he might have sent someone here while we were out?" Sara asks.

Clifford shakes his head. "I checked. None of the alarms tripped here or over at the office."

"Okay, cool. So, I'm going to change out of my dress, but I will be back for a bourbon. Pour me one?" Sara smiles.

Clifford smiles back. "Sure. Rocks or neat?"

"Rocks. I need to hydrate a little," she says with a little laugh.

After Sara leaves, Clifford heads upstairs to change as well.

He hangs his uniform in a suit bag, places it in the closet, and closes the door. He walks back into his bar area and pours Sara her drink. He sends a text to Bailey and Daniel asking if they want to come over for drinks as well and plops on the couch with his scotch and soda.

He is almost finished with his drink when Bailey and Daniel knock on the door. Sara follows in shortly after. Clifford gets up and pours himself another scotch and soda when Bailey notices.

"Scotch? Since when are you a scotch drinker?"

Clifford raises his glass and looks into the golden-amber fluid at an angle. He looks back at Bailey and says, "I only had this bottle for when Badger would come by. This was his scotch."

Bailey sets down his bottle of crown royal and picks up the scotch. "Scotch today for Badger!" he says as he drops a bit into his glass.

Sara knocks back her diluted bourbon and says, "Scotch it is!"

Daniel picks up a glass, drops some scotch in it, and throws it back like a shot. He winces and lets out a hot breathy groan. "Scotch," he says with hot whiskey breath.

Clifford lets out a huge laugh and says, "Maybe you should cut it with some soda or add a splash of water next time."

Daniel says, "I thought that was against whiskey law?"

"Nah, drink it how you like it."

Daniel drops a little more into his glass and splashes a little bit of soda water into it. Sara leans over and asks him for some soda water in hers. All four raise their glasses and say, "For Badger!"

A few drinks and several stories later, Clifford begins telling a story.

"I remember one time I was pulling duty. This was about a week before I was captured by the Taliban. Badger was still a Captain, and he was up for promotion.

"He comes up to me and says, 'Sergeant Dee, I need you to go over to the Sergeant Major's office and take him this packet.' Of course, I said, 'Yes, Sir!' like a good soldier, but then I took the packet and asked what it was.

"He looks me dead in the eye and says, 'It's my promotion packet for Major.' I said, 'You're going to get promoted?' And he said, 'No. probably not.' And then laughed. He said, 'Captain Armenstead has a better packet and he's good friends with the Colonel. There's only one spot for Major so he'll probably get it.' I look over and say, 'Why put in a packet if you're not going to get promoted?'

"And he said that they told him to and we didn't know ' ' and patted me on the arm. I had no idea what he meant by that. I thought Paul Harvey was a detective like Dick Tracey or something. So anyway, I walk over to the Sergeant Major's office and drop off the packet. He called me into the room and said, 'Is this Badger's promotion packet?' I said, 'Sergent Major, this is Captain Hamilton's packet.'

He motioned that I place it on top of a pile of other packets. There were like six or seven. I went back and told him, I said, 'Sir, there are like seven promotion packets, oh and are you the badger?'

"He smiled and said yeah, that's what he calls me. He went to Minnesota and I went to Wisconsin. Rivals. So he calls me Badger and I call him Gopher. I said, 'Oh, Sergeant Major Gopher?' And Badger says, 'Don't call him that.'

"So anyway, the Colonel had a lot of packets to review. Kevin, who was the First Sergeant at the time, sent my squad to an outpost outside of Kandahar where the incident happened. Badger took responsibility for not doing the intel and offered to lead the rescue operation. When they got me back, I was hospitalized for a month. Badger came in with a shiny brass leaf on his collar. I said, 'Sir, I see you're Major Hamilton now.' He said, 'Call me Badger.'

"I asked about Kevin and he was reassigned to a different unit. He went into a strategic unit and got promoted to Sergeant Major and then retired. Badger went on to become Colonel and then got his star before retiring to government work. I didn't know all that until I talked to him back when we were in Kentucky."

Sara smiles and asks, "So you are the reason he got that promotion?"

Clifford swirls his drink and says, "He thought so. He saved me, so I let him think what he wanted."

Bailey says, "Sounds like Kevin was always an asshole, too."

Clifford nods, "Yeah. I don't know why Badger stuck up for him and took the bullet for his mistake."

Daniel swallows a swig of his diluted scotch, "I bet Badger felt bad that he let Kevin run the mission."

"Maybe… Probably," Clifford says.

Sara raises her glass and says, "Well, Kevin is going to start paying for his past mistakes."

CHAPTER TWENTY-ONE

The following morning, Kevin leaves his house in Great Falls and has his driver take him into the office. His town car pulls up in front of the office building. He steps out, and heads inside.

After his barrage of morning meetings and briefings, he goes into his office and shuts the door. He sits in his chair and rests his face in his hands. After a minute, he opens his desk drawer and pulls out a bottle of Jack Daniels, sets it on top of some paperwork, and unscrews the top. He pops the plastic lid of his coffee and pours a few ounces in, closes the bottle, and puts it away.

He opens the drawer again and pulls the bottle back out. He unscrews the lid and takes a huge gulping swig from the bottle. He recaps it and tosses it back into the drawer, and slams it shut. He puts the plastic lid back on the top of his coffee and opens his email. After typing furiously, he grabs his Irish coffee and heads to another meeting.

After the meeting, Kevin walks out of the conference room and heads outside. He types away on his phone, sending a text. He walks down the street and stops at a newsstand and buys a paper. He uses the cashless app on his phone to pay and continues down the block and heads into a small park on the corner.

He sits on a park bench and folds up the paper and sets it next to him.

A few minutes later a car pulls up and a thin, well-dressed, dark-skinned man steps out. He unbuttons his suit jacket and sits on the other side of the bench facing away from Kevin.

The man says, "I am hoping for good news. For your sake."

Kevin glances over and says, "I need a little more time."

The man says, "Your delivery is already late. There is no more time."

Kevin replies, "I know. There's a lot of heat on me right now. My delivery service was compromised, and they shut down. I need another month."

"That is unacceptable."

The man stands up, rebuttons his suit, and straightens his tie. "You have two days," He says as he starts to walk away.

"Two days!? I can't get new transportation in that short amount of time!" Kevin exclaims as he turns to see the man has left. He spots him as he gets into his car, and it drives away. He picks up his phone and texts another number. He begins to walk out of the park when his phone rings.

He stares at the caller ID, which says "UNKNOWN."

He answers.

"Hello?"

"Kevin, hello, it's Kelly. Sorry, I can't meet you today. I'm booked solid." The real estate agent says over the phone.

Kevin grits his teeth. "It's very important that we take care of that last purchase. NOW!"

Kelly is quiet for a moment. "So sorry. Like I told you before, the market is just not right to sell that house. You'll have to wait."

Furious, Kevin says, "If you don't, I will-"

"You'll what?" Kelly says in a stern tone, cutting him off.

"I can expose your selling methods," Kevin says.

The call is quiet for a moment.

"You know what, I'm so sorry, but I cannot sell you a home. However, I am more than happy to list your home for sale," Kelly says.

Kevin stammers for a moment and says, "My home isn't for sale." He pauses, realizing what she means. "You can't buy it. Got it, lady?!"

Kelly laughs. "Oh, you're funny. Don't worry. I have three buyers ready to pounce. They're always looking for a killer property. I'll send them your information. Goodbye, Kevin," Kelly says, ending the call.

Furious, Kevin throws his phone down onto the ground and stomps on it, yelling out profanities. Several people notice his outburst and begin looking at him in astonishment at his crazed behavior. He realizes he's creating a scene, so he calmly adjusts his suit, runs his hands through his hair, and continues to walk out of the park.

With no phone, he can't call for a car. He reaches into his pocket to fish out cash for a cab but doesn't have any. He can't even remember the last time he kept any cash on him. He pulls out his wallet to find there is nothing inside but receipts, a collection of business cards, and a metro pass.

Without access to money, Kevin decides to walk over to the metro. It's several blocks away but he has no choice. It gives him plenty of time to think about his options and his next move. He uses his pass to get into the station and heads down toward the platform. He's starting to come down from his whiskey-coffee buzz and decides to sit on the bench while waiting for the train to arrive.

A train comes and goes and Kevin still sits on the bench in deep thought. Finally, he stands and walks up to the platform where a few people are milling about. One guy is reading sports news on his phone. Kevin walks beside him and says, "When's the next train?"

The guy looks up briefly and says, "The next one should be in a few minutes."

Kevin walks past him and heads toward the end of the platform. He looks down at the yellow bumpy textured concrete rumble strip that prevents things from rolling onto the track. He rubs the bottom of his foot along the strip and pokes his head out to look for the train. He leans back in and steps fully onto the strip. He takes small steps and continues to rub his feet along the textured strip. The tips of his feet reach the edge of the platform, and he leans over and spots the train quickly approaching. The man looks up from his phone and calls over to him.

"Hey, buddy, don't get so close," he says as he turns to walk toward him. Kevin looks over and nods, gives him a quick smile, then takes a step back. The smile fades from his face and he blinks slowly in acceptance.

Kevin's body doesn't even hit the ground before the train strikes him. The screech of the emergency brakes of the train blend perfectly in tandem with the screams of the terrified witnesses. The platform and a few of the would-be passengers are sprayed with blood. They stand, shaking as the events of what just happened are still processing through their minds.

CHAPTER TWENTY-TWO

Clifford looks down at his vibrating phone. The caller ID reads Sims.

"Hey Sims, what's up?" he says

"Hey! Remember that Kevin guy you wanted me to look into, but I said there wasn't enough evidence to get a warrant?"

Puzzled, Clifford says, "Yeah, what about him?"

"Well, he's dead."

"What? Dead? How?" Clifford asks.

"The guy decided to catch the metro. Stepped off the platform headfirst into the train," Sims explains

"Holy shit!"

"Yeah, the metro hasn't released a statement yet, but they're going to say it was a suicide. I have a friend who's investigating it and he sent me the video. It's clear. No one was near him, and he clearly jumped," Sims says.

"I don't know what to say. It's crazy."

"Yeah, I know. Also, it's not the only reason I'm calling. You told me you were working that copyright case for JFP's manager, Ray Robinski, the one who was poisoned up there in Philly?"

"Yeah."

"Can you send me everything you got on that please?" Sims asks nicely.

"Sure, I sent you everything except one file, but it was an MP3," Clifford explains.

"Send it. We're onto something," Sims says.

"Sure, I'll have Bailey send it this afternoon," Clifford says.

"Cool, thanks."

"Are you going to clue me in on your sudden interest in this?" Clifford asks.

"Well, I don't have the liberties to talk about it, but we're doing a deep dive into Kevin. Since you suspected he was involved somehow with this, we took a look at the server information you provided, and it turns out it was an unclassified government server managed by Kevin's former team."

"I hate it when I'm right."

"Me too," Sims sighs. "We're supposed to be the good guys, you know? I just hate seeing a fellow government worker involved in these things."

"All people are corruptible. It just matters where their line is," Clifford says.

"So does that mean you're corruptible?" Sims asks.

Clifford paused for a moment. "I found my line. I decided to move it."

* * *

Sara is with some friends sitting at the Blend Coffee Bar. She smiles and says, "Sorry I missed the last meetup. It's been crazy at work."

Her friend Joy says, "Girl, you and me both. I just ended it with my girlfriend, Becca. She was just too much. Maybe I'll go back to dating guys again. Your friend Dan still single?" she asks in a joking manner.

Sara laughs, "He sure is and I am certain he would jump on the chance, because gurrrl, damn! You're smokin', but I am pretty sure Paul Michaels would kill me if he found out I set him up."

"Oh, you ain't lying. He was all over that white boy," Tianni says, jumping into the conversation.

The girls laugh it off, and Joy turns and says, "Seriously though, I am NOT going back to men. They exhaust me."

Denise walks up to the table with her latte, "Ugh, men. Don't get me started. My ex-boyfriend is still in my DM's trying to get back together. I left his ass on read."

Sara laughs, "Try working with all men. They have no idea how women think."

She sits to reflect for a moment and smiles, "But they do try sometimes."

Denise asks, "Speaking of Paul Michaels, does anyone know why he canceled his class this afternoon?"

Sara says, "I have no idea. I got the same email you all did."

Her phone buzzes as a text message arrives. She glances and sees it's from Clifford.

Huge development. Too much to text. When can you get back?

Sara looks over and says, "Hey, I have to cut this one short. It's a work thing."

* * *

Daniel grasps the bar and rests it on his trapezius muscle. He lifts up and rocks backward, lifting it from the rack, and takes a step back. He knocks out fifteen squats and places the bar back onto the rack. After resting a moment, he does it again, and again.

And one more time for good measure.

He unracks the weights and heads over to the leg press and loads it up. He pushes up four hundred pounds on the sled, rocking out fifteen reps. He rests and racks another fifty pounds on each side. He pushes up the five hundred pounds, but only ten reps this time.

He rests again and then racks up another fifty pounds on each side and pushes up the six hundred pounds five times. After resting he reverses his process. Six hundred, five times. Five hundred, ten times. Finally, four hundred, fifteen times. His legs burn with the last set, but he endures and pushes through the pain, completing his set.

He climbs off and his friend, Trev, greets him. Daniel instantly feels a rush of adrenaline. "Yeah!" Daniel says, feeling accomplished.

Trev smiles, "You're gonna feel that tomorrow."

Daniel laughs, "I'll be good. I feel great!"

He looks over toward his gym bag and sees his phone on top, displaying that he has a text and a missed call. Picking up the phone he sees it was from Clifford.

"Shit!" he says, fumbling to unlock it to read the message.

"What's up?" Trev asks.

"Missed a call from my boss."

Trev shrugs. "So? I ignore my boss all the time. He'll get over it."

Daniel opens the message and starts to scan it.

"I gotta go."

Daniel grabs his bag and towel. He walks out of the weight room and heads over toward the basketball courts and sees Bailey looking at his phone. Bailey grabs his bag and hooks it to the side of his chair. He turns to head toward the weight room when he makes eye contact with Daniel across the courts, who waves his phone in the air in acknowledgment of the text.

Daniel and Bailey knock on Clifford's door. Sara is already inside.

"Hey," Clifford says, answering the door.

They enter and Daniel instantly heads to the couch and plops down with dead weight.

Sara looks over with a concerned expression on her face.

"It was leg day," he says.

Clifford walks over and says, "Sorry I called you guys back in, but I got a call from Agent Sims about an hour ago. Kevin's dead."

"What?" Sara asks.

Bailey and Daniel look at each other and back at Clifford.

"Explain!" Bailey demands.

Daniel sits up in his chair as Clifford starts in.

"So, Sims called and told me that Kevin killed himself."

"That motherfucker offed himself?" Bailey asks.

"Yeah, he. Uh." Clifford stammers.

"What?" Daniel asks.

CHAPTER TWENTY-TWO

"He jumped in front of a metro train."

Sara gasps. Daniel grimaces, and Bailey shakes his head and says, "Coward."

Clifford nods, "Yeah, he must have been in some bad shit to do something like this. Sims is going over all of his files, servers, work and personal email, everything. I mentioned that we thought he was involved in the case that got Jimmi shot and Ray killed, so he wants all those files too."

Bailey nods, "Consider it done."

"Thanks," Clifford says, "He wants us to lay low on our cases involving Kevin, but I say we continue, silently, so we can help if they need anything."

The three collectively look at each other and all say, "Agreed."

Bailey uploads all of the files to an FBI secure portal and sends an email to Sims letting him know that it was delivered. Bailey looks over at Clifford and says, "FBI has everything now."

Clifford smiles and nods, "Good. We need to go up to Philly."

CHAPTER TWENTY-THREE

Sims is reviewing the files that they sent over and added them to the case files in the database. He rubs his brow and continues to write up his report on Kevin when Agent Gunter steps in. "Hey Tal, Director Sorren wants to see you in his office."

Sims looks up from his report. "Okay. Thanks, Darren. I'll head over in a few."

Sims finishes typing up the sentence and locks his screen. He heads over to the director's office and knocks on the door.

Director Sorren says, "Come!" and Sims pushes the door open.

"Sir, you wanted to see me?" Director Sorren motions for him to sit, and Sims does.

"Glad to have caught you before you left for the day," the director says.

"Yes sir, I have a lot to catch up on so I'll probably be here for a bit before calling it a day," Sims replies.

There is a brief silence and Sims starts to look around the room. His eyes land on some of the desk tchotchkes used as paperweights to hold down some of the important files the director was looking into. He looks up from the desk to admire the pictures from years ago when the director was in the academy, hung next to his framed accolades and awards.

The director picks up a file from his desk and opens it, glances inside, and shuts it.

"Agent Sims, I hear that you're starting to look into Kevin Burr's suicide," he says.

"Yes sir, I think there's more to it than just a suicide," Sims replies.

"I'm sure there is," the director says.

The director stands up and motions for Sims to join him at the window of his corner office. They stood beside each other looking at the brightly lit streets of Washington, D.C. Traffic has died down by this hour and the pedestrians are at a minimum. Sims can see the top of the Washington monument poking out from behind the museums across Pennsylvania Avenue.

"Do you know what this city stands for?" The director asks.

Sims looks over at him and stumbles a moment, then says, "My first thought is liberty and justice, but, with all due respect, sir, what are you getting at?"

Director Sorren looks over at Sims and smiles. "Short, sweet, and to the point. I like that."

He walks away from the window and sits behind his desk again and swivels towards Sims who is still standing with his hands clasped behind his back. Sims walks away from the window and sits in the chair across from the director.

The director says, "Kevin was a colleague. He was always a bit squirrely if you ask me, but he was determined and egotistic. If he committed suicide, which I think he did, it was because he wanted to go out on his own terms."

Sims looks across the desk at the director. "What do you mean, sir?"

The director smiles and says, "Sometimes people skip the hard work and get places they shouldn't be by cheating." The director thinks a moment before he continues. "I believe that Kevin was that type of person. If you dig too deeply, you could find some of those people that helped him cheat, and I can't protect you from what you find."

Sims nods, "This sounds like you're saying Kevin was corrupt."

The director's smile fades. "Sounds like it, huh?" he asks. "Just be careful, Sims. Declaring it a suicide makes a guaranteed messy situation a very easy thing to handle."

"What exactly do you know about this?" Sims asks.

The director smiles briefly and looks back at Sims, "I sit on the director's council who briefs the FBI Director, who in turn briefs the President and Congress. So, to answer your question, way too much. Like I said, be careful."

The next morning, Sergeant Ferrell is sitting at her desk typing away when Officer Clemente tells her that there are people there to see her. She walks over to the front of the station and recognizes Bailey, Sara, and Daniel. Next to them is Clifford.

Sara says, "Hey Sergeant Ferrell, this is our lead, Clifford Dee. He wanted to talk with you about the investigation of Jimmi from Philly and his Manager Ray."

Sergeant Ferrell looks over at Clifford and then back at Sara. "You know we have phones, right? You didn't have to drive up here."

Clifford smiles and says, "Yeah, but we were also hoping to visit Jimmi and talk with him about who shot him. We understand he's in a protected room at the hospital and wanted to see if we could be cleared to go in."

Ferrell smiles, "Ah, there it is. Yeah, we can process a request, but what do you want to ask? He's only been awake for twelve hours or so and we've already got a bunch of info."

"Can I take a look at your files?" Clifford asks.

"If you don't mind, who hired you to look into this?" Ferrell asks.

Clifford smiles, "Ray Robinski, actually."

"Clifford," Ferrell starts.

"Please, call me Dee," Clifford interrupts.

"Dee." She continues, "Ray is dead. I'm sure you know this."

"I do," Clifford says. "This is why it's important that I finish my investigation."

Ferrell sighs, "Yeah okay, I get it. It's a moral thing, right?"

"Exactly," Clifford says. "By the way," he continues, "Do you think there's a link relating the shooting with the poisoning?"

Ferrell smiles and says, "No. Honestly, we had to elevate Ray's case to the FBI. We were unable to identify the female in the video, but your team suspected that she was the same person who was involved in the killing of a US Senator, so we had to push the investigation up to the Feds."

She looks over at Sara and Daniel and says, "Thank you for that by the way."

Sara smiles awkwardly because she couldn't tell if the thank you was sincere or ironic. She continues, "Eyewitnesses in the Jimmi shooting all said that the shooter was male, late thirties to forties of Latin descent."

Clifford slowly looks over at his team and back at Ferrell.

"What?" she asks. "What is it?"

Collectively, Clifford and his team say, "It's related."

Ferrell throws her arms up, "For fuck's sake!"

Clifford looks over at her empty coffee cup on her desk and says, "Pour yourself another coffee. It's a story."

After about an hour, Clifford gives her the number of Agent Sims and asks that she loop him in on this investigation. Clifford says, "I'll call him now to let him know to expect you to reach out."

Just as he goes to pick up his phone, it rings.

"Oh, this is Sims now."

He answers the phone. "Hey Sims, I was just about to call you. The Jimmi from Philly shooting and Ray Robinski killing are linked. I'm going to have the sergeant in charge send the info."

"Cool, listen. We need to have a talk, in private. Where are you?" Sims asks.

"I'm up in Philly. Why?" Clifford asks in return.

Sims replies, "Okay, get back as soon as possible. I'll meet you at your place in a few hours."

Clifford looks back at Ferrell and says, "Thank you, We'll have to finish this later. We need to run back to D.C."

She replies, "Maybe you should call next time."

By the time they get back to town from Philadelphia, Sims was already waiting in front of Clifford's condo. He's alone, sitting on the hood of his car waiting for them to arrive.

CHAPTER TWENTY-THREE

Clifford pulls up in their van and parks next to him and rolls down the window.

"Hey," Clifford says as he throws the van in park.

Sims scoots off the hood and onto his feet. "Sup?" he says back.

Sara leans forward from the passenger seat. "So glad we hurried back from Philadelphia for this stunning dialog."

From the back of the van, you can hear Bailey shout, "Riiiight!"

Clifford looks over at Sara and back at Sims, then shrugs.

Sims shakes his head and smirks.

The team, including Sims, gather inside Clifford's house when Sims starts. "I'm glad you all were able to cut your trip in Philadelphia short and meet up with me."

Bailey cuts his eyes and slyly under his breath says, "Yeah, welcome."

Sara is returning from the kitchen with a few beers in her hands and begins passing them around. "Totally happy to help you out, Agent Sims," she says, then looks over toward Bailey and rolls her eyes.

Bailey smirks.

"I can hear the sarcasm, Sara," Sims says.

Sara turns around with a jerk. "Sorry. Beer?" she asks without making her apology sound sincere.

Sims slightly shakes his head, "You know what? Sure. I'd love a beer," he said, reaching out for a cold one.

He twists the cap and takes several huge guzzling swigs before letting out a satisfactory "Ahhhh!"

Daniel asks, "Aren't you not supposed to drink on duty?"

Clifford chimes in, "Something tells me he's not here on official business."

Sims takes another swig of his beer. "Nope, not official business, but it's important."

Clifford nods as he suspected as much. Sims continues, "I was told by my director that I needed to rule Kevin's death a suicide now and close the case."

"What?!" Clifford says in disbelief.

"Yeah," Sims says as he takes another swig of his beer.

Clifford sets down his beer. "Let me get this straight... Kevin, a guy we suspect was corrupt, a guy we think hired assassins to kill people, is going to be brushed under the carpet?"

Sims raises his beer to his lips and before taking another swig, says, "Yeah."

"Unbelievable!" Clifford says. "What about all the crap he was doing?"

"I dunno," Sims says, shaking a now empty bottle. "Apparently, it's too dangerous to unearth and the FBI directors don't want the headache that will come with it. It's politics."

"It's bullshit," Clifford says.

"Like I said, it's politics," Sims responds.

"So now what?" Clifford asks. "Where do we go from here?"

Sims sets his empty bottle down on the end table and starts to walk into the kitchen. "Forward," he says, opening the fridge to grab another beer.

Clifford lets out a little smile. "Are you saying what I think you're saying?"

Sims walks back into the living room. "I will close my FBI case, but I'm opening a new case with you guys."

Sara and Bailey smile at each other and look over at Clifford.

CHAPTER TWENTY-FOUR

Early in the morning, Sims finishes his report on Kevin's suicide and sends it off to the Directors. As usual, it was a very busy morning.

Everyone is running around to meet their deadlines. They are finalizing reports and drafts before the supervisors 8 a.m. meeting, which is briefed at the directors 10 a.m. meeting, which then gets reviewed and briefed in the afternoon 2 p.m. meetings, and then again at the COB (Close Of Business) meetings to sum up the day.

Each case, each report, had a blip that would be briefed depending on the importance to their respective directors.

Sims sneaks into Director Sorren's meeting a little late and sits in the back of the conference room. Sorren notices and says, "Agent Sims, do you have anything for us?"

Sims sits up in his chair and clears his throat. "Yes sir, actually, I finished my investigation and report on Kevin Burr's suicide."

Director Sorren sits with a blank facial expression. "And?"

Sims lets out a slight cough and continues, "And, it was indeed a suicide. We found that he had been drinking that morning as there were trace amounts of alcohol in his coffee cup and also in his system. We reviewed his finances and discovered that he was in debt and his standing medical prescriptions suggested that he was suffering from depression. We do not see any evidence of foul-play, and due to the suspected depression and alcohol abuse, debts, and the video evidence that he dropped and broke his phone, which left him without any usable finances or communications at that period of time, we feel that this was enough to trigger a momentary fleeting suicidal thought."

Sims swallows hard as he knows this is all bullshit. Most reports of this nature would need more than just feelings and suspicions, but the Director wants the case closed, and he did the best he could.

"Momentary fleeting suicidal thought?" the director asks.

"Yes sir," Sims responds.

Director Sorren smiles briefly and says, "Very well. Is your case closed?"

"As of this morning, sir, it is," Sims responds.

"Very good. I'll review and sign off on it after the meeting. Now onto the next item." Director Sorren says, moving the meeting along.

After the meeting, Sims walks back to his desk and slams his case files down onto the desktop. Agent Hibbard looks over and asks, "You okay?"

Frustrated, Sims says, "Yeah. It just sucks when you have to cut a case short to meet a deadline."

"You were working that suicide on that DOD division lead, right?" he says, walking over.

Sims nods, "Yeah. A suicide. There's more to it, but the brass doesn't want to hear it."

Agent Hibbard sets his hand on Sims' shoulder, "Let it go. You got an easy one. High visibility and you were able to close it in a few days. This is a good thing for you."

Sims rolls his eyes. "Yeah. It was an easy one."

He plops down at this desk and unlocks his computer and starts checking his email. He opens his pending case files and begins reviewing what is next on his agenda.

Hibbard starts to walk away from his computer when Sims asks, "Hey, where ya headed?"

"Rock a piss," he says back.

"Would you mind grabbing me a Coke?" Sims asks fishing in his pocket for a bill.

"Sure. I got it," he says, refusing payment.

"Thanks Rob," Sims says, holding the bill in his hand.

As Agent Hibbard rounds the corner, Sims takes the opportunity to open the closed case file to review it for something he might have missed. The files that were all named after weapons were still encrypted and could not be opened. He begins browsing through the folder and reviewing all the files inside. After a moment, he opens a file encryption program on his computer and adds the encrypted files to it and clicks decrypt.

A message pops up.

Add decryption file one.

Sims opens up and looks through the folder that Bailey sent over but there was nothing there that indicated a decryption file.

Sims shakes his head and says to himself, "What am I missing?"

Just then Agent Hibbard waves his Coke in front of his face. "You were missing this tasty beverage, but not anymore."

Sims closes the folder and says, "Thanks," as he takes the Coke from his hand.

"What are you working on now?" he asks.

Sims smiles, "Nothing. Just an old case that stumped me."

*   *   *

Bailey is on his laptop looking at the files while listening to music. His phone buzzes and he looks over.

He hits a button on his laptop which instantly mutes the music and puts the call on speaker.

"Hey Sims, you're on speaker," he says.

"Hey, got a question for you," Sims says.

"What's up?"

Sims sighs, "So I had to close the case on Kevin. Once the directors review it and sign off on it, it will be filed away and will log everyone who looks into it. It'll be super noticeable if I continue to work on it here at work. I need you to look at the encrypted weapons files and find a decryption key. It could literally be anything. Most of the time they're stored separately, so they may have been in a different file location than the weapons files. You know, for security reasons. Can you take care of that for me?"

"Bet," Bailey says. "Want me to call you later?"

"Nah, I'll swing by your place in a few hours, and we can look at it together if you want."

"Cool. I'll take a look at it in the meantime."

"Sounds good. Thanks," Sims says just before hanging up the phone.

Bailey opens up his copy of the files and starts poking around. He turns his music on and goes to work.

Minutes turned to hours and the unreleased MP3 from Jimmi from Philly started playing from his playlist. He starts bobbing his head to the song and singing along until he realizes that he moved the MP3 file from the encrypted folder.

"Damnit!" He says out loud as he scrambles to put the MP3 file back in the encrypted folder. He plugs the encrypted folder into the file encryption software, adds the MP3 file, and then clicks decrypt.

A message pops up.

50% Complete. Add File 2

"Fuck!" Bailey says, "There's a second key!"

Bailey picks up his phone and shoots Sims a text.

About an hour later, Sims arrives at Bailey's.

"You said you got something?" he asks as Bailey answers the door.

"Yeah, check this out," he says, wheeling into his office.

Bailey continues, "So, I was playing around with that encryption tool you were telling me about. I got the folder loaded in there, but nothing was decrypting it. I even tried hack-...Uh, checking the source server where I got it, but it's offline."

Sims smiles at the slight slip-up in the verbiage. "Go on," he says, showing he doesn't care.

"So anyway, the server was offline so I couldn't get in. I had some music playing in the background, and then when the JFP song hit, the one that was stolen, I remembered it was unreleased. So, I thought, 'Hey, I got that from this folder because it was the song that Fenix stole.' So, I loaded it in the program and okay, watch this."

Bailey clicks the decrypt button and gets the same message.

Sims looked over his shoulder. "There's another key. Shit!"

Bailey smiled, "Yep, I said the same thing."

Sims looks at the files and asks, "Did you find anything else?"

Bailey shakes his head, "Nah. I've been looking but this is the only song from JFP that was on here."

Sims shakes his head and stands up. "Okay, what other files are on here?"

Bailey starts going over the list of files.

"These are all encrypted. We got the JFP MP3 file. Uh, the server signature file, which I tried and it doesn't work. We have these temp log files and I tried all those. There's this Dark Fenix logo JPEG file, I got this weird configuration file."

Sims cuts him off, "JPEG file? Have you tried that?"

"No, it's a picture. It's not code." Bailey says.

Sims smiles, "Try it."

Bailey moves the JPEG picture file over to the decryption program and a message pops up.

100% Complete. File decryption in process, please wait....

"Oh shit!" Bailey says. "It worked!"

Sims moves over toward Bailey, "Lemme see."

"Hold on. Wait," Bailey says, "I'll put it up on the big screen."

Bailey clicks a few buttons and projects his laptop onto the smart board TV screen.

Sims walks over and starts looking at the files.

"OH damn! This isn't just a few weapons, It's thousands! All military grade! Holy shit! It looks like Kevin was arming troops for war."

CHAPTER TWENTY-FIVE

The team gathers in Bailey's office and begins reviewing the files. Clifford shakes his head.

"Hundreds of millions of dollars' worth of weaponry already delivered, and they were expecting another shipment. This is ridiculous."

Sims says, "Yeah, and look at this here. The financials. Funds in and funds out. He kept all sorts of notes on here."

Bailey shakes his head, "Fenix is in some shit."

Clifford turns around and says, "Okay, so if Dark Fenix is involved in this, that means they were using his tour as a cover. They must have loaded up the guns and moved them with his equipment. They crate up his DJ equipment, props, cabling, and all the other stuff he needs, and then load up the guns and ammo within and deliver it when they get there. Security will be more relaxed and if they do get caught, they pay off the security to look the other way. It's genius."

Bailey clicks on another file and says, "Hey guys. Look at this."

Clifford and Sims turn around and look at the smart board.

"These files here have people's names in them. Senator Reeves is one. Look, there are two more senators, Christiana Laurence and Phyllis Cummings."

Clifford runs his hand through this hair. "I knew it! My gut instincts were right! But why would Kevin have these people killed?"

Sims nods, "The AGTPA."

Clifford looks over. "The what?"

Sims smiles. "Three senators joined together. Reeves, Cummings, and Laurence made this huge deal to cross party lines and work together to stop weapons trafficking. They called it the AGTPA. Anti-Gun Trafficking Protection Act. I remember listening to them talk about it after Senator Reeves's death. He was the main writer of the bill and both Senators Cummings and Laurence were going to be the underwriters and co-signers of it. It was a huge deal because it was the first Tri-Partisan effort."

Clifford looks over at Sims, confused. "Tri-Partisan?"

"Yeah, Laurence is a Libertarian," Sims says.

Sara chimes in, "Okay, gentlemen, time out, please. I want to ask the obvious question here. If these ladies are on a list, does that mean there is an active hit out on their lives?"

Sims' eyes widened. "Shit, maybe. We need to call this in. Wait, shit. I'm not supposed to be working on this case."

Clifford puts his hand on Sims' shoulder, "Easy fella, I'll call this in. Besides, we know for a fact that the assassins are already being investigated by the Philly P.D. Maybe we can get them to do the leg work on this."

Sims sighs, "Brilliant idea."

* * *

Sergeant Ferrell from the Philadelphia Police Department looks over at her phone as it rings. The caller ID says "Clifford Dee."

She ignores it.

A few minutes later, the phone at the station rings and it's patched through to her desk

"Sergeant Ferrell, can I help you?" she says in haste as she answers the phone.

Clifford sighs. "Are you ignoring my calls? See, this is why I prefer to swing by."

"Jesus Christ!" she says when she realizes who it is.

"No, it's me, Clifford Dee, but we have been confused before," Clifford says.

"Dee, what do you want? You already cost me two of my big cases."

Clifford laughs, "I can't apologize enough for that. Really, but I need a favor and this could make up for the cases I lost you."

"Okay, I'll bite, what is it?"

"We've uncovered a plot to assassinate two US senators and we need you to run with it."

The phone is silent for a moment.

"What?" Ferrell asks.

Clifford sighs. "Okay, long story short. My buddy, Agent Sims, can't work this case."

Sims yells from across the room at the phone, "Hello."

Clifford continues, "That was him. He's continuing to work the case, on the down-low, with us to solve it. We came across a file. It's related to the Jimmi from Philly shooting and the Ray Robinski murder, so this is right up your alley. We found this file that has a hit list, and it had their names on it and some US senators' names on it. We'd like you to deliver it to whoever you gave it to at the studio. so it gets linked to that case, not the case that we're on...the case that we're not supposed to be investigating. Tracking?"

Ferrell ponders for a moment. "Okay, let me get this straight. You have a file that belongs to JFP. It has the names of US senators on it that are supposed to be killed."

Clifford thinks for a moment. "Yeah. That's true."

"By whom?"

"Hitmen. Like the one who killed Ray and shot Jimmi," Clifford says.

Ferrell sighs, "Wow, you're in some nasty shit, Dee."

Clifford says, "Yeah, it seems to follow me around."

Ferrell sighs, "Okay. Send me what you got. I'll move it up to the FBI. But I get to take full credit for this."

"Exactly. Please run with it and I hope it gets you a promotion or something," Clifford says as he hangs up the phone.

He turns toward Bailey with a smile, "Okay, send the files to Ferrell."

Clifford turns to Sims. "So, you're off the hook for this, but what are we going to do about the assassins?"

Sims smiles. "Well, there were more than just the senators on that hit list. I have a plan."

CHAPTER TWENTY-SIX

The next morning agent Sims calls out sick and travels with Clifford up to Philadelphia. They head up to the hospital and visit with Jimmi from Philly.

There was a guard, still posted at the door. Sims flashes his badge and says "Agent Sims, FBI. We need to have a moment with Jimmi."

The officer at the door says, "Yeah, of course, Agent. Whatever you need," and steps aside.

Sims walks into the room and Clifford walks in behind him and glances back at the officer.

The rhythmic beeping of the machines is a very familiar sound for Clifford. He's been hospitalized enough to be able to relax, if not relate, to the sound of the machines.

Jimmi is awake but sedated.

"Hey man," he says weakly.

Sims waves off Clifford.

"Hey Jimmi, I heard you were feeling better. I wanted to ask you a few questions."

Jimmi mumbles something and dozes off.

Sims shrugs and looks over toward Clifford.

Clifford steps in and says, "Hey Jimmi? Jimmi!"

Jimmi wakes up and starts to come to.

"What up, man?" he says.

"My name's Dee. I'm a friend of Bailey, the guy in the wheelchair that came to see you about your stolen song. I want to ask you something."

Jimmi looks at him for a second. "Yeah Dee, what's up man?"

"Did you know that you were on a hitlist?"

Jimmi thinks for a moment. "I have a few hits. My OG track JFP was poppin', yo."

Clifford corrects himself, "No, no, no, That's not what I meant. Did you know someone wanted you killed?"

Jimmi nodded, "Yeah, man, I was shot man. Twice in the chest man."

Clifford asks, "Who shot you?"

Jimmi says, "Some Mexican dude. He had a scar on his cheek like he was in a war or something. Real scary lookin' fucker."

Clifford smiles. "That's good man, hang onto that. Why did he shoot you?"

Jimmi says, "Man, I don't know. I was walking down the street. He called out my name so I looked up and he shot me. Sped off."

Sims steps in and says, "Why do you think he shot you?"

Jimmi shakes his head. "I dunno man. Can I talk to Ray? Ray might know."

Clifford pats Jimmi on the shoulder. "No Jimmi. You can't talk to Ray. Not anymore."

Jimmi says, "Talk to Ray, he knows everything."

Clifford looks over to Sims and nods toward the door. Both men walk out and Clifford says, "I don't think he knows anything. This is a dead end."

Sims says, "He was shot and Ray was killed probably due to their involvement."

Clifford nods, "Yeah, Bailey told me that Ray mentioned that they reached out to Dark Fenix about them stealing their songs. I guess since it was used as an encryption key for Kevin's files, they decided to have them killed to cover tracks."

Sims says, "That sounds like as good of an excuse as any. Jimmi's obviously clueless. Ray probably knew a lot more than he let on, and he's dead. We're not going to get anything from Jimmi."

Clifford nods in agreement. "You're right. We should probably check out the studio."

Sims nods. "Yeah. Good call."

At the studio, the receptionist is juggling calls on the phone.

She looks up and gives a stressed half-smile. "Thank you for calling J-Rock Studios, this is Shari, please hold." After placing a call on hold, Shari looks up at the gentlemen and asks, "What can I do for you two?"

Clifford says, "You look really busy."

She smiles and says, "It's been a bit of a nightmare around here lately."

Sims flashes his badge. "I'm Agent Sims and this is my associate, Clifford Dee. We'd like to ask a few questions."

She lets out a slight laugh, "Of course you have questions. Everyone has questions."

Clifford leans in and says, "Take a deep breath. Seriously."

He waits a moment for her to finish her breath. She closes her eyes and shakes her hair out. "Thank you for that," she says. "It's been non-stop since Ray was killed and..."

Clifford cuts in, "Since you're handling the phones and I assume it's all press and fans wanting an update on Jimmi, is there someone else we can talk with?"

She takes another deep breath. "Yeah, John's in the back. He is, well, was Ray's assistant. He's kinda just taken over everything, but he's so disorganized. Maybe he can help."

Sims taps on John's office door.

"Yeah," John says as they push the door open.

"Who are you?"

"Agent Sims from the FBI and this is Clifford Dee. We have a few questions."

John shakes his head, "Dude, I'm incredibly busy right now. Trying to get all Ray's other clients in order, deal with his affairs, and now take questions from the Feds."

Sims laughs, "Yeah, I guess you are busy. This shouldn't take too long."

John scoots back from his computer, folds his arms, and says, "Okay sure. What can I do for you?"

Sims asks, "Do you know who would want to shoot Jimmi?"

John rolls his eyes, "Jesus, I've answered all these questions already and no. I have no idea who shot Jimmi or why."

Clifford pulls out his phone and asks, "Hey John, do you have a computer I can use to send an email? I am not getting a signal here in the office."

"Use Ray's on his desk over there. I haven't touched it since he died."

Clifford walks behind the big desk and says, "It's locked."

John stands up and walks behind Ray's desk. He taps on the mouse and then uses an admin login to open the computer. He browses real quick and says. "Okay, you're good. I just wanted to make sure he wasn't logged into anything."

He walks around and sits on the edge of his desk and continues his conversation with Sims.

Clifford sends a text to Bailey.

Dee: *What do I do now?*

Bailey: *Click on windows icon and in the search bar type cmd*

Dee: *k*

Bailey: *in the black window type ipconfig and send me the ip address*

Clifford texts the IP address of Ray's computer back to Bailey.

Bailey's next text tells Clifford to search for a program called Windows quick assist.

Clifford opens the program and then sees a prompt to give remote access.

Clifford clicks on it to give Bailey control of the computer.

Bailey: *OK don't lock the computer, just turn off the screen*

Clifford reaches over and turns off the screen and rejoins the conversation.

"Thanks, all done," Clifford says.

John looks around the desk and sees the screen off and says, "Oh, cool, thanks," as an assumption that Clifford turned off the computer.

Clifford just nods.

As Sims and Clifford are wrapping up the conversation with John, Bailey is behind the scenes with admin access to Ray's computer. He is taking his time going through the files. He looks at log files with user IDs and time stamps. He has access to Ray's calendar and is looking at dates and appointments when he makes a discovery that John, being Ray's assistant, was logging all of his appointments. He finds John's login ID and starts to search on all the files that he modified. Most of the files were for bookings and appointments and only one file he modified was a music file. It was the MP3 file that was used for the digital key to unlock the encrypted files on Dark Fenix's server.

Within the hour, Bailey sends the evidence to Sergeant Ferrell of the Philadelphia Police Department, who in turn sends it to the FBI Philadelphia field office, who then processes a warrant to search the computer systems.

Sims and Clifford sit in the parking lot eating cheesesteaks while the FBI raids the office.

Clifford looks over at Sims and says, "Shari's gonna be pissed."

Sims laughs a bit, "Yeah, that receptionist's day didn't get any easier, did it? A deep breath isn't gonna help now."

Clifford smiles and lets out a slight laugh.

A few hours later John is sitting in an interrogation room at the Philadelphia Police Department.

Sergeant Ferrell, Sims, and Clifford are all behind the two way mirror watching John, terrified, as the field agent starts asking questions about what they found.

John asks for a lawyer and Sims shakes his head. "This is gonna take forever."

Ferrell glances at her watch. "I can send you guys a recording if you want to get on the road. We digitally record everything in the room."

Clifford nods, "Yeah, shoot it to Bailey when you can."

She smiles, "Will do."

CHAPTER TWENTY-SEVEN

The next morning Sims gets called into Director Sorrens office.

He walks in and Sorren says, "Shut the door."

Sims closes the door and Sorren says, "I heard you called out sick yesterday."

Sims nods as he is pretty sure he knows where this is going. "Yes, sir, I did."

Sorren smiles and says, "I also heard that there was an Agent Sims poking around up in Philadelphia yesterday. Odd coincidence."

Sims swallows hard, "Yes sir, that was me."

"Why?"

Sims takes a breath, "Sir, you asked me to quickly close the case on Kevin, so I did. I know he was high profile and they wanted it to be resolved quickly and quietly, so I understand. However, when I looked further, I noticed that there were two senators whose lives could be in danger, and I knew that I needed to do something."

Sorren gives Sims a confused look, "Which two senators?"

"Laurence and Cummings. They worked with Senator Reeves on the gun trafficking bill. Kevin was involved with that somehow and had their names on a recently discovered hit-list. Reeves was the first, Ray Robinski and Jimmi from Philly were both on that list, and now I believe that Laurence and Cummings are the next targets. That's why I took this information up to Philadelphia where Ray's murder was being investigated."

Director Sorren rubs his chin and says, "You're smart, I'll give you that. You're also right. I was wrong to try to hurry Kevin's investigation along. I'm glad you did what you did. However, I still stand by keeping Kevin's investigation closed. But, this angle you're using to investigate this? It's working."

Sims allows himself to smile, "Thank you, sir."

Director Sorren continues, "But, there is the case of you misusing your sick leave."

Sims smile fades, "What?"

Sorren explains, "You misused leave and I feel that you need to think about your actions. One week of administrative leave should do it."

"Sir?" Sims questions.

"Your punishment for misusing your sick leave is one week admin leave. Go home and think about what you've done. And don't get caught investigating anything. I repeat, don't get caught," Sorren says with a smile.

"Understood, sir," Sims replies.

From his car, Sims calls Clifford to explain what happened.

Clifford answers the phone, "Hey, we just got the video from Ferrell on John's interrogation."

"Okay, cool. We have a week to figure this out. I was put on admin leave for a week and was given direct orders to not get caught investigating anything," Sims explains.

"So, you won't get caught. Get your ass over here so we can watch this video."

Sims arrives at Clifford's house and knocks on the door.

Clifford walks to the door and opens it. Sims is standing across the hall and Clifford says, "Hey, we're in Bailey's."

Sims turns around and walks into Bailey's house and follows Clifford into the office where they are set up.

Daniel is working on his crime board and Sara and Bailey are by the computer.

"Okay, Sims is here, let's catch him up," Clifford says.

Bailey swivels around and says, "Okay, we got the video from Ferrell, and she said we would love it. Basically, he is confessing to selling Jimmi's song to Kevin to avoid getting murder pinned on him."

Sims nods, "Cool."

Bailey smiles, "Get some popcorn, I'm-a put it on the big screen."

The group watch the video of John and his lawyer talking to the FBI field agent in charge.

John says, "I didn't kill anyone. And I didn't want anyone killed. Especially Ray, he was my best friend."

The agent asks, "Your login ID was all over these files that were found on the same servers as the hit list."

John looks over at his lawyer, "Look, this guy came to us wanting to buy the rights to one song. Jimmi was a nobody then, so I recommended one of his songs. Ray said, 'No.' I thought it was a mistake. The guy, Kevin, I think, was offering five hundred grand just for one song. It's easy money. But Ray had this feeling that JFP was about to pop so he said no."

"Then what happened?" The agent asks.

John lets out a sigh, "So I stole one song and sold it to the guy. I told him that we had to keep it on the down-low because Ray and Jimmi didn't know. The guy didn't care. He just said that he needed it for some project. Later that month, Ray noticed that the file was moved because he was right, and Jimmi did start to get hot. Ray did some investigation or something and found out that it was transferred over to Dark Fenix. I tried to hide it, but he found it. I denied that I did anything, and he believed me. Like I said, he was my best friend. We were friends for twenty years. I wouldn't do anything to hurt him. I just needed the money."

John starts to break down and cry and Bailey shuts off the video.

"So that's about it," Bailey says.

Sims scratches his head, "So, why use Jimmi's song and not something from Fenix? What am I not getting here?"

Bailey smiles, "I got this one. Fenix is international. If they used one of his songs as a key, it might get noticed that he has a song not in rotation. Jimmi was underground for a bit and was mostly unknown. Kevin just picked an artist he thought wouldn't get known. So, Jimmi's success was his downfall."

Sims nods, "That makes sense."

Bailey continues, "Using music to cover-up a gun running operation is just foul in my opinion. It sullies the art."

Sims sits back in his chair, "Okay, where do we go next?"

Daniel chimes in, "I would like to call your attention to my board."

Everyone turns around and watches as Daniel is moving pieces around.

Sara stands next to Clifford and folds her arms in wait.

"Okay!" Daniel starts in, "Let's start from the beginning. Sara and I were investigating Reeves' infidelity case. His wife suspected that he was seeing other women, and he was. He had a thing for sex workers. We set up some cameras which happened to catch his murder.

"Now, Bailey investigated the copyright case for JFP and this led to the discovery of a group of, I can't believe I'm saying this, assassins. One of which was hired to kill Reeves. The copyright case also uncovered an illegal gun-running operation that was being spearheaded by Kevin.

"We took this information to Badger which got him killed and exposed Kevin as the lead of the operation. One of the assassins tried to kill me and Dee but failed. They also tried to pin Badger's murder on Dee by drugging him and planting evidence to take the focus off Kevin. They shot Jimmi and killed Ray.

"After investigating, and thanks to Sara, we were able to find out, without actual proof, that the assassins were being managed by a high-end real estate agent named Kelly. Kevin decided to kill himself, for reasons unknown at this time, but I assume that it was because there was too much being uncovered by us and I'm sure his sparkling personality wasn't winning him any favors with the bad guys.

"Now, John has confessed to sending the music files per Kevin's request to Dark Fenix to use as an encryption key to hide the details, receipts, and files of the smuggling operation. Fenix was supposed to go on tour last month, but it was canceled. The assumption is that he was going to be the delivery vessel for Kevin."

Clifford looks over to Sara as Daniel is explaining the details of the case and says, "This is really good."

CHAPTER TWENTY-SEVEN

Sara smiles, "He did this all himself."

Clifford smiles.

Finishing up, Daniel says, "The only big piece missing is why, exactly, did Kevin kill himself and getting proof that Kelly is running a group of assassins."

Clifford steps in, nodding. "Well done, Dan. This is great. I agree, we need to find out why Kevin killed himself. Dan, Sara, and I can drive into the city and poke around. Bailey, you and Sims stay here and see what you can dig up remotely."

Sims chimes in, "I know the city, I should come with you."

Clifford says, "You're on leave, remember? The last thing we need is your director squashing our investigation because you were caught. You work behind the scenes with Bailey. No more flashing your badge and no more FBI help. We got this."

CHAPTER TWENTY-EIGHT

Clifford parks the car in street parking and drops some quarters in the meter. Sara and Daniel join him on the sidewalk. Clifford looks beyond the trees on the sidewalk and says, "Okay, Kevin's office is there. The report says he walked to a park down the street before going to the metro. The closest park is about two blocks this way."

They cross the street and walk down the sidewalk to the park.

Daniel asks, "Why do you think he went to the park?"

Clifford replies, I bet he was meeting someone. Look over here. The benches. He probably called someone to meet. It's secluded and conversations would be muffled by the sound of the fountain on the main path. It's perfect for a secret meeting."

Clifford starts to walk away when he spots small pieces of Kevin's phone that were not cleaned up. "Looks like he smashed it here. These are internal pieces of the phone. He must have been really angry." Clifford says while analyzing the debris.

Sara says, "If he's the type to use his phone for everything, he couldn't call or pay for anything. He probably had no choice but to walk to the metro."

"I think you're right," Clifford says. "You two head back to the car and meet me at the metro. I am going to walk it."

As Daniel and Sara walk back toward the car, Clifford takes a moment to look around. He notices a traffic camera on the corner.

Bailey's phone rings.

"Hey Dee, what's up?'

Clifford says, "Hey, how difficult would it be to get traffic camera footage from D.C.? I can text you the street locations of the cameras I would need."

Bailey looks over at Sims and smiles. "Yeah, I can do that, but I don't know if I should."

"What does that mean?" Clifford wonders.

Bailey lets out a little laugh and whispers, "Did you forget that I'm sitting with a member of the FBI?"

"Oh, right." Clifford says. "Try and be discreet."

"Discreet!?" Bailey angrily asks in a whisper.

"Thanks, you're the best," Clifford says as he ends the call.

Bailey rolls his eyes and looks over at Sims who asks, "Everything okay?"

Bailey sighs and says, "Yeah, everything's peachy."

Clifford continues down the sidewalk and begins texting Bailey each street corner he spots a camera on.

The walk from the park to the metro station was almost three times the distance between the park and Kevin's office. Clifford crosses an intersection to the other side of the street and starts down the sidewalk when he suddenly comes to a stop.

He turns to his left and sees a store called "Vintage Video Electronics." In the storefront window there is a recording display hooked up to a TV which captures footage from the entire corner, including the crosswalk to a few yards from the other side of the store.

He walks over to the door, watching himself on the TV the whole time.

Inside the store was filled from floor to ceiling with video equipment that stretches three decades, beginning from the eighties.

A voice rings out from behind a beaded curtain leading to the back of the store, "Be right with you, Champ!"

Clifford stands at the glass display looking at pagers, walkie-talkies, and camera accessories when the man finishes his task in the back and walks to the front, wringing his hands.

"What can I do you for?" he asks in a quirky manner with a cheesy smile.

Clifford smiles briefly and says, "I was admiring your set up in the window and wanted to know if it was for sale."

"Everything's for sale. Which piece are you looking at?"

Clifford walks over to the wide angled camera in the window and says, "This puppy here. I was wondering, is this recording or just displaying?" He asks

The man walks around and says, "Oh yeah, that is actually a great video camera, it's from nineteen-ninety-six and it's actually recording to a VHS tape in the VCR just below it.

I can get about a half-day's worth of video on one tape. I usually switch it out after lunch. I use it for security as well. You know, just in case."

Clifford nods as if he was interested. He looks over at the VCR and taps it with his finger.

"Hmmm, do you use the same tape, like, record over it every day?"

"Nah, but I do rotate them for a week and then buy a new set each month. They wear out after a while," He says.

"Can I buy them off of you?"

"The tapes? No, I don't think so," the man says.

"But you said everything was for sale."

"You're right, I did."

"So, how much for the tapes?" Clifford asks.

The man sits quiet for a moment. "I'll tell you what, if you buy that VCR over there in the corner, I will toss in those tapes. I was going to rotate them out after this week anyway."

Clifford looks over to the corner of the store he was pointing to and sees an old VCR. He walks over and picks it up and brings it over to the counter. "Does it work?" he asks.

The man says, "I wouldn't sell anything that doesn't work."

Clifford smiles. "Deal!"

The man goes to work boxing up the VCR and putting it into a bag. He walks over to a cabinet and pulls out nine VHS tapes in plastic sleeve cases and places them into another bag.

He opens up a new tape and walks over to the VCR in the display. He ejects the tape and swaps it out for the new one, placing the display tape into the case.

He walks back over to the counter and starts punching keys on the register.

Clifford stood with a smile on his face thinking about Bailey's reaction to the old recording equipment.

"Okay, that will be two hundred and fifty dollars," the man says.

The smile quickly fades from Clifford's face. "I'm sorry," he says.

The man repeats himself, "Two hundred-fifty."

Clifford blinks slowly and asks, "This costs two hundred and fifty dollars?"

"Yes sir, it's vintage. You can't find that anywhere."

Clifford slowly reaches for his wallet and pulls out his credit card. "I guess the prices are vintage too, huh?"

The man smiles as he swipes Clifford's credit card. "Actually, Mr. uh, Dee," he starts as he looks at the name on the credit card, "this unit would have cost closer to a grand in nineteen eighty," he says, handing the card back to Clifford.

Clifford takes the card and says, "I would have been six."

Rounding a corner to the metro, Clifford sees Sara and Daniel parked on the street by a meter.

He walks up and taps on the window. "Pop the trunk," He says, holding up the bags. The two get out and Sara asks, "So, you stopped to go shopping?"

Clifford smiles and says, "Yeah. There's a vintage video store that was recording the street. I got the videos from this entire week. I bet Kevin's on one of them somewhere. He would've had to walk past it."

Sara says, "Oh wow, that's awesome."

Clifford smiles, "Yeah, just cost me an arm and leg."

Daniel asks, "Why? How much was it?"

Clifford scoffed, "Two-fifty."

Daniel's eyes widen and his mouth drops, "Two hundred and fifty dollars for that piece of crap?"

Clifford smiles. "It's vintage."

Bailey is reviewing the texts he got from Clifford with the intersections of traffic cameras. Sims is sitting next to him on a laptop reviewing files.

Bailey goes to the D.C. Department of Transportation website and finds that they provide real time traffic camera footage. He says to himself, "They have to store logs of this footage somewhere on their servers."

Sims looks up and asks, "What was that?"

Bailey shakes his head. "Nothin', I was talking to myself."

After another minute, Bailey looks over at Sims and says, "Hey would you mind grabbing us some drinks or something from the fridge?"

Sims smiles and asks, "Are you about to do something you don't want me to see?"

"What? No. C'mon man. I just wanted something to drink," Bailey responds.

Sims narrows his eyes and starts to stand up. "Okay, sure. I'll get something from the fridge."

He starts to leave the room when Bailey looks over and says, "Take your time."

As soon as Sims rounds the corner, Bailey goes to work. He spoofs an IP address and jumps into a VPN from Detroit to avoid being traced, hacks into the DDOT servers, and starts to review the logs. The operating system is Linux which Bailey knows like the back of his hand. He recognizes the file structure and is able to pull up the logs quickly. The files are sorted by date. He grabs all of the files from the date of Kevin's death and copies them over to a proxy server and then ports them over to his local server. He then jumps to the next traffic camera file and does the same.

Sims returns from the kitchen and Bailey powers off his screen. "What-ja get?" he asks.

Sims smiles and asks, "You're not done yet are you?"

Bailey smiles, blinks, and says nothing.

Sims sets the drinks down and says, "I think I gotta go to the bathroom."

Bailey, still smiling, says, "Okay."

As Sims leaves the room, Bailey turns on his screen and continues to pull the files off each traffic camera server and copies them onto his.

After he has all the footage for the day, Bailey is able to start reviewing the footage and piecing together, by time, where Kevin was and where he was walking to.

Starting in reverse order, from the metro to the park, he was able to string together his complete route and saved the video to a file.

Sims starts to walk into the room and asks, "Is it safe for me to come in now?"

Bailey, just finishing up removing the incriminating files he stole from the DDOT servers, turns and says, "Hey, you wouldn't believe what I found."

Sims smiles and says, "I can't wait to hear this."

Showing the video he pieced together, Sims shakes his head, "This is incredible. Where did you find this?"

Bailey smiles and says, "It's a secret."

Sims says, "Mm-hmm, right. And none of what you did was illegal?"

"That's a secret as well," Bailey responds.

Sims nods and says, "Right."

Bailey's phone rings. "Oh, it's Dee," he says. "Hey, Dee, glad you called," Bailey says.

"Hey, I got a present for you. We're heading back now."

Bailey says, "Cool. I also found some footage for you to review."

"Okay, sit tight and let's go over it together," Clifford says.

"Cool, cool! See you when you get back," Bailey says,

He turns to Sims, "Let's wait until Dee gets back and we'll go over this."

They all get back to the condos. Clifford, with bags in hand taps on Bailey's door with his foot.

Sara and Daniel are chatting while walking up slowly from the parking lot. Sims answers the door. "Hey," Clifford says.

"What the heck is all that?" Sims asks.

"Let me in and I'll show you," Clifford says with a smile.

Sims steps out of the way and Clifford walks in as Sara and Daniel reach the door.

They all step inside and Clifford makes his way into Bailey's office.

CHAPTER TWENTY-EIGHT

"Surprise, happy birthday," he says, holding up the bags.

Bailey laughs. "Man, shut up. My birthday isn't for another few months. What's that?"

Clifford sets the bag down and pulls out the VCR.

"Holy Shit!" Bailey says. "Is that a nineteen-eighty JVC HM-DH3000?"

Clifford pulls it out of the box, "Uh, sure, it's a VCR."

"Dude! Where the hell'd you find this?" Bailey asks.

Clifford says, "There is a vintage electronics store in D.C. They were taking video of the street. I got those too and this to watch them on."

Bailey sits with his mouth agape, "You must take me to this place, Clifford Dee!"

"I promise, as soon as we're done with this case," Clifford says.

Bailey and Daniel spend the next half hour setting up the VCR and connecting it to Bailey's equipment, with Sara sitting in a chair watching.

Clifford takes this time to explain to Sims the reasoning behind his idea of following Kevin's route. He also mentions getting the video footage might help them translate his body language, spot if he was being followed, or if he stopped to talk to anyone.

After everything is set up Clifford turns to Sara and says, "Hey, would you mind looking over the VCR footage to see if you can spot Kevin?"

Sara asks, "Dude, how many hours of that do I have to watch?"

Clifford holds up one tape. "It's most likely on this one."

Sara looks confused, "Then why did you buy all ten tapes?"

Clifford smiles, "He threw them in for free. I wanted to get the best deal for my money if I was spending two hundred and fifty dollars on a VCR."

Bailey looks over and asks, "That was two hundred and fifty dollars?"

Clifford nods, "Yeah."

Bailey smiles, "Good deal!"

He spins back around and pulls up the footage that he retrieved from the DDOT servers.

He says, "Okay, I...," he pauses and slowly looks over toward Sims before continuing. "I was able to procure some video footage from the DDOT servers and save them on our local server. I pieced the footage together to make this," he says, clicking the play button.

The group watches the video and views him entering the park.

They watch as a car pulls up and a Black man gets out and walks over toward the fountain.

A few minutes later, the same Black man walks out of the park and gets into the back of the car and it speeds away.

Sims says, "Pause it!"

Bailey pauses the video.

Sims asks, "Can you rewind it to the guy coming out of the park?"

Bailey does and pauses it.

Sims stares at the footage. "It's a bit grainy but I think I know that man. It looks like it might be Zuberi Amadou. He can't hide that crazy limp from his prosthetic."

Clifford looks over at Sims. "Who?" he asks.

Sims continues, "Zuberi Amadou is associated with an African warlord. He's on the FBI most wanted list for orchestrating illegal weapons dealing. If Kevin was meeting with him, it's not good. He is a bad, bad man."

Clifford nods, "That explains the gun parts in those files. Kevin was working with Zuberi and using the rapper Black Fenix as a delivery method."

Bailey rolls his eyes, "Dark Fenix… Hey, you know, it's kinda obvious now… most musicians don't tour Africa 'cause it doesn't pay well enough to do so. He was gettin' paid, though. Fucker," he says, annoyed.

Clifford says, continuing, "The list was probably a delivery invoice for Dark Fenix to use to drop off the weapons on each point in his African tour. Since they canceled the tour, I bet Zuberi is pissed he didn't get his delivery."

Sims nods his head, "Bingo!"

Bailey presses play to continue the video.

They watch as Kevin enters the frame talking on his cellphone. He looks at it and angrily smashes it onto the concrete path and kicks it into the gravel. He stood with his hands shaking.

Clifford says, "I guess that phone call did not go the way he expected."

Sims shakes his head. "Nope. Not at all."

Daniel asks, "Who would he be calling after talking to that African dude? Think it might be Kelly to see if he could get protection from her hitmen?"

Clifford and Sims look at each other and then over to Daniel. "That's probably exactly who he was calling," Clifford says continuing, "Sims, do you think you could get a copy of his cell phone records?"

"No way," Sims says, "I cannot look into that or open his case again, remember?"

Clifford asks, "You can't even call the phone company and ask them to pull it?"

"Nope, no way. I would get into so much trouble. You have to file a report and my name would be on it and my superiors would find out. I wou—"

Bailey cuts in, "Got it."

Clifford and Sims both look over. "What?"

Bailey says, "While you guys were bitching at each other, I was able to pull the report for his phone records."

Sims asks, "How the hell did you do that so fast?"

Bailey smiles.

Sims just rolls his eyes. "Lemme guess. It's a secret?"

Clifford leans over Bailey's computer, "What does it say?"

"This is the last number he called," Bailey replies.

Sara chimes in, "Hey guys!"

The group looks over as she had the video paused with Kevin's face on the screen, clear as day.

"I found Kevin on here," she says.

They all continue to watch the DDOT footage, and they spot two people following Kevin's same route. Most of the video was from too far away to do any facial recognition, so they played the video from the storefront and watched as two Black men came into frame a few minutes after Kevin passed.

Sims points at the video. "Those are some of Zuberi's soldiers following him."

Clifford asks, "Why do you think they're following him?"

Sims shakes his head, "I don't know for sure, but they're probably going to report back to what Kevin was doing. He was late on their shipment so I'm guessing they want to keep eyes on him to make sure he doesn't disappear."

Clifford says, "He was clearly upset by the phone call, and now he was being tailed by these guys? Yeah, I bet he was out of options."

Sims asks, "So what's next? I can't go to the FBI with this information without getting in trouble."

A smile grows on Clifford's face. "True, *you* can't."

* * *

Daniel walks down the street to an old gas station. Out front was a working, archaic payphone. He picks up the phone and puts two quarters into the slot and calls the FBI tip line.

"Hello, I was at the post office in D.C. the other day and I saw one of those FBI posters with the wanted people. I saw a guy that looked just like the African dude. The poster said his name was something like Zooberry Ama-doo, or something like that. Anyway, he was in the park yesterday talking to a white guy on D street. He got into a car and it drove away and the white guy got all mad and smashed his phone. It was really crazy."

Daniel hangs up the phone and walks away.

He gets back to the condo and gives Clifford a nod. "It's done."

Clifford says, "Hopefully they take it seriously."

"Oh, they will. The FBI has been looking for him for about four years. They'll definitely look into this tip," Sims assures.

Clifford nods, "Now we have to prepare to go after Kelly."

Bailey asks, "But how?"

Daniel smiles and leans over and whispers in Bailey's ear.

Smiling Bailey says, "No, no, no, how about wine!"

Daniel lets out a slight laugh and says, "Even better."

Clifford shakes his head, "You two going to share this with the group?"

Bailey says, "We have an idea."

* * *

That evening Bailey lets out a huge, accomplished sigh. "Okay, I'm all done. Check this out."

Sara stands up, stretches, and walks over toward Bailey's computer screen to see her picture on a news article in front of a winery.

"Ooh. What's that?" Sara asks.

Bailey smiles, "That is Jessica Bach Matthews and a little article I created by spoofing the Napa Valley Register."

Sara cocks her head, "The what?"

Bailey continues, "That's what they call their newspaper. The article talks about how you left your father's whiskey business for wine in California and now you're expanding your very successful wine operation to Loudoun County, Virginia. I even made a fake website for your winery, with the news of your expansion."

"Oh cool! But, Matthews? Ugh!"

Bailey asks, "Why? what's wrong?"

Sara says, "I just knew a guy named Matthew and he was a dick."

Bailey laughs and says, "Ok, moving along then. I also created and backdated an Instagram account, a Facebook account, and I spoofed a verified Twitter account for you."

Sara smiles, "This is good stuff! You got me verified on Twitter!"

Bailey says, "Yeah, but no. It's a spoof, it's not really there."

Sara winks, "But it's verified!"

CHAPTER TWENTY-NINE

Sara walks over to Bailey's that Saturday morning and says, "Guys, I don't think this is gonna work."

Bailey looks her up and down. "You're fine."

Clifford walks in and says, "Oh, snazzy."

Sara turns around and pouts, "Are you kidding? These are twenty-dollar pants and a fifteen-dollar blouse. I don't have any expensive stuff. How am I supposed to pretend to be a millionaire?"

Clifford walks up and hands her a box. She opens it and inside is a beautiful brooch. She shuts the box quickly and looks up at Clifford. "Really?" she asks, surprised.

"It's all yours," Clifford says.

"I can't, this is way too much," Sara says, holding it close to her heart.

"It's a mic."

"What?" Sara asks.

"It's a microphone. We're gonna be able to hear everything you and Kelly say."

Sara sighs, "It's not even real jewelry?"

Bailey chimes in. "All you need to do is remember your lines. You did read the entire packet this time, right?"

Sara rolls her eyes, "Yes! I did!"

Bailey slowly gives her side eye.

Sara reaffirms, "I did, twice."

"Okay. I just wanna make sure," Bailey says.

Clifford puts his arm around her, "We've got your back. It's just a meeting. Act like you don't care what she thinks, and you'll be fine. Besides, she won't care what you're wearing when she sees what you're driving."

Sara gives Clifford a confused look, "What are you saying to me right now?"

Clifford smiles, "We sprung for a rental car."

Daniel walks in and tosses Sara some keys, "Your ride is here."

* * *

Sara parks the 2021 Land Rover SUV in front of the real estate office and steps outside to meet Kelly.

She is wearing a blonde wig with a flowery red slouch hat and sunglasses. Along with the bright red lipstick and makeup, she looks like a completely different person than her everyday self.

She walks over and gives her a hug, "You must be Kelly, I'm Jessica."

"Jessica, so glad to meet you. Please come in. I have several properties that you might be interested in."

Sara follows Kelly into the office building. They walk through two sets of double glass doors and into a huge lobby. Kelly walks up to the elevator and presses the "UP" button.

She turns toward Sara and says, "So, Jessica, what's bringing you into this area?"

Sara smiles. She rehearsed the prepared answer to this specific question a thousand times in the mirror as if it were a role in a play.

She wasn't prepared for stage fright.

Her mind starts to blank out and she stands there nodding for a moment. Suddenly she realizes it has been too long, so she blurts something out. "Oh, wine."

Kelly smiles, "Wine?"

Sara smiles again and goes off the cuff, "My father is in the Tennessee Whiskey business. I left the family business because I just couldn't stand the taste of whiskey. Wine is my passion."

Kelly smiles and asks, "So you've been successful with your wine venture?"

Smiling, Sara says, "So far, yes. Napa has been very good to me, and I've heard such great things about the Loudoun Wine district. I feel it will be a good expansion. The distilleries are being handed down to my brothers anyway. They would have nudged me out eventually. But they can have the whiskey. Soon there will be a bottle of Jessica Bach Wine in every kitchen."

The elevator chimed as it reached the lobby.

Kelly smiles, "I thought your last name was Matthews?"

Sara smiles back, "Indeed. Bach is my middle name."

They get into the elevator and go to the third floor.

Sara steps out of the elevator and notices that the entire floor was pretty much empty.

No one was in the offices or cubicles. No one was in the lobby or in the halls.

She smiles and says, "Not very busy today, I see."

Kelly turns and says, "I own the whole building, not just the third floor. I'm renovating the second, fourth, and fifth to lease out. My entire staff started working from home due to the pandemic and I haven't called them back in."

Sara asks, "You decided not to work from home?"

Kelly smiles, "Everything I need is here. I only come in when I have clients."

They continue down the hall and into a corner office next to a huge conference room. Sara walks in and sits in a huge chair. Kelly follows and walks behind her desk and grabs a laptop. Behind her desk are several filing cabinets. Next to them is a lockbox hanging on the wall. The office is cold and stale. There were no pictures, posters, or tchotchkes on the desk. Everything was beige and void of any exciting color. Off to the side is a couch and a coffee table that Kelly starts walking toward.

"How about we sit here and look at some homes for you," she says.

Sara stands up and walks over to the couch.

After a few minutes, Kelly's phone rings and she excuses herself.

"I'm sorry," she says as she looks at her phone, "I have to take this."

She stands up and leaves the room.

Sara opens her purse, pulls out an earpiece and puts it in her ear.

"Guys, I don't know how much time I have," she says.

Clifford replies, "You're doing great. What's in the office?"

"Nothing really. Just cabinets, a desk with a desktop computer, her laptop, a lockbox on the wall, and some chairs and couches."

"Check the cabinets and see if you can get into the desktop computer."

Sara tries, but the filing cabinets are locked, and the computer needs a password.

"No go, guys. It's all locked up."

Clifford says, "Check the lockbox on the wall."

Sara walks over and opens the box. There were a few keys in there, two of which looked like they would fit the filing cabinet. The other keys looked like they would fit doors.

Hearing Kelly's heels on the raised flooring, walking toward the office, Sara pulls the earpiece out and tosses it back into her purse.

"Gotta go," she says as she heads over toward the window and peers out.

Kelly walks in and says, "It's a great view."

Sara looks over her shoulder and says, "It really is."

The two women sit back down on the couch and continue to look at some of the properties that Kelly was proposing.

Sara sees a listing that is twenty miles away and says, "That looks nice. Is it available to see in person?"

Kelly smiles, "Let me find out."

After a brief call to the other agent, Kelly says, "Okay, it looks like they can show it in an hour. I think this will be perfect for you. It's on the edge of wine country, and the price is right in your range."

Sara smiles and says, "Delightful. Should we grab a coffee and head over to the property?"

Kelly says, "Wonderful idea."

The two leave the rental office just before Clifford and Daniel pull up to the building. Clifford decides to park on the side near the fire lane in order to stay away from prying eyes. The building is fairly new and sits by itself with its own parking lot.

There's a small field next to it with a few groomed trees, benches, and a little bar-b-que pit that it shares with the building next to it. Little community parks like these were becoming very popular with the new buildings that were popping up all over town.

Clifford looks around at the property and Daniel looks over at him. "What's wrong?"

"This building is new. I wouldn't even say it's a year old," Clifford says.

"So?" Daniel asks

"Why would you have a new building renovated?" Clifford asks out loud.

Daniel nods in agreement. "She also said that she sent her staff home because of the pandemic."

Bailey chimes in on an earpiece, "The building is only a year old, guys. She was definitely lying about it."

Clifford shakes his head, "Doesn't matter. Let's go take a look."

Inside the office, Clifford spots the alarm panel, and talks with Bailey over the radio.

"Alright, I'm at the panel."

"Okay, open the cover and there should be a code inside," Bailey says.

Clifford slowly does as Bailey says, finds the code, and reads it to him.

Bailey says, "Okay, take out the remote transceiver and plug it into the auxiliary jack of the panel."

"Done!" Clifford says.

"Here goes nothin'," Bailey says while pressing a button on the keyboard.

The yellow flashing lights change to green, and the word "Disarmed" flashes across the LED display.

"Looks like we're good!" Clifford says.

Daniel and Clifford head to the elevator and go up to the third floor.

As they step out of the elevator, Clifford stops and spots a floor plan drawing on the wall.

He walks over and takes a quick look.

Daniel asks, "What's up?"

Clifford smiles, "Always brush up on the layout. It's good to know your exits," he says with a wink.

He continues down the hall and heads toward Kelly's office. Daniel follows behind.

As they close in on Kelly's office Clifford looks over at a blank area of the wall and slowly starts to approach it. Daniel asks, "What's wrong?"

Clifford shakes his head, "Nothing. Just a weird feeling. I figured there would be—You know what, let's just go."

They continue into the office and start looking around.

* * *

Kelly is excitedly showing who she thinks is Jessica Bach Matthews a huge bathroom with a walk-in shower, covered in stone tiles, when her phone starts buzzing.

Sara looks over and sees her facial expression change as she is checking her phone. "Is everything all right?" Sara asks.

Kelly shrugs off a scowl and puts on a fake smile. "Yes, but you must excuse me. I need to place a phone call."

Kelly storms out of the bathroom and through the primary bedroom with the vaulted ceiling into the hallway.

Sara watches as she places the phone to her ear.

Sara puts the earpiece into her ear and says, "Kelly's pissed about something. Did you disarm the alarm?"

Bailey replies, "Yeah, the one in the lobby."

Sara recalls her flipping a switch in her office before leaving. "I think she may have had a silent alarm or something in her office."

"Shit!" Bailey says.

Sara pulls the earpiece out when she hears Kelly walking back into the room.

CHAPTER TWENTY-NINE

"Everything okay?" Sara asks.

*　*　*

Clifford and Daniel are rummaging through files and taking a few photos of documents with their phones when Bailey tries to call over the radio. "Dee, you gotta go now."

Clifford cannot hear Bailey. Tripping the silent alarm also triggered an electromagnetic interference signal which is messing with their communications.

A slight rumble is heard by Daniel, and he perks up. "Did you hear that?"

Clifford looks over from his file, "I did."

Daniel shakes his head, "Maybe it was nothing?"

Clifford grabs his phone to take another photo when he notices the words, "No Network" displayed in the corner.

"Hey, do you have a signal on your phone?" He asks Daniel.

Daniel looks over, "Nope."

Clifford calls out for Bailey and gets nothing.

He looks over at Daniel and says, "We should go."

Another rumble, this time bigger and louder shakes the building. Clifford slams shut a folder and says, "We need to go now!"

They leave the office and hurry down the hallway when they see smoke billowing into the hallway from the elevators and stairwells. The floor is starting to fill with smoke when they hear a slight explosion and fire starts to erupt into the hall.

"Shit!" Clifford says. "Back to the office."

They start to run when Clifford stops at the strange wall from earlier.

Daniel runs back toward Clifford, "Let's GO!" he says in a panic.

Clifford smiles briefly. He runs over toward the wall and pounds on it. It was hollow.

He pushes a rolling cabinet through the wall to a staircase on the other side.

Coughing up smoke, the two climb down onto the cabinet and into the stairwell.

"Down?" Daniel asks.

"Down!" Clifford says.

The stairs were dimly lit with emergency lighting. There was dust covering the stairs and the air was musty and stale due to the lack of air circulation.

They travel down the staircase which seemingly has no exit. When they reach the bottom, it opens to a dank and musty hallway with a rusted metal gate that creaks when it opens.

"Are you getting a bad feeling about this?" Daniel asks.

"I had a bad feeling since we got here," Clifford says.

Daniel nods. "That's fair."

They follow the hall, which is long enough to extend past the park above them.

Daniel is using his cellphone as a flashlight, but it is barely helping. Clifford is running his hand along one of the walls to keep his baring. The brick was cold. The floor was concrete with portions of loose gravel that their shoes skid across as they shuffled their feet down the hallway.

Jokingly, Daniel asks, "You having fun yet?"

Clifford replies, "Too much fun."

On the other side of the hall is a bricked-over door frame. Clifford starts feeling the walls around him and finds a lever that unlocks and opens the brick doorway. The door opens and a flood of light shines into the hallway. They walk through, into a room with pipes and pumps. They climb from the concrete sub-floor onto a metal scaffolding walkway. The metal walkway lets out a clunking sound as they step up onto it. The walkway leads to a metal door that is, thankfully, unlocked.

Leaving this pump room, they enter a basement hallway and see a neon sign that reads "Exit."

They follow the sign and make their way to the main floor. They calmly find their way towards a building emergency exit without being noticed as everyone was watching the building across the park glowing in a fiery blaze.

Clifford and Daniel head outside. Daniel glances over and his eyes widen.

He taps Clifford on his shoulder and points over toward Clifford's car.

Clifford looks over and spots his car with the windows smashed and a fire hose running through it.

"Aw fuck," Clifford says.

Daniel says, "Maybe we shoulda just parked in the parking garage."

Clifford rolls his eyes and walks away.

Clifford spots Sims in his car near the side road of the building. He motions to them both.

Daniel and Clifford pick up a slight jog and climb in.

Sims smiles, "Need a lift?"

* * *

Kelly and Sara pull up to a fire-torn office building, still drenched from recently being extinguished. The firemen extinguished the flames, leaving the building intact but everything inside was destroyed. Kelly steps out of her car and looks on with an expressionless face as a member of the crew walks up.

"You own the building?" he asks.

Kelly nods as she looks on. "I do."

"Well, you're going to need to contact your insurance company. Whatever sparked the fire caused it to burn hot and fast. It was completely engulfed when we got here."

Kelly blinks and shakes her head, "The building was vacant when we left, and I have no idea what could have done this."

The fireman nodded, "Yeah, it's still empty. No signs of anyone that we can see. The investigator is going to give you a full report when they're finished, and you can turn that into your insurance company."

Kelly nods and turns to Sara. "Jessica, let me walk you to your car."

On the way to the car, Sara starts shaking her head, "I am so sorry that this happened. This is just plain awful."

Kelly pats her on the back. "It's quite alright. We can always rebuild."

Kelly's phone buzzes again and she pulls it from her pocket.

They reach the car and Sara starts to get in.

Kelly, still looking at her phone, holds the door open for Sara as she climbs in.

Sara looks over as Kelly is still holding the door.

"Is everything okay?"

Kelly looks up from the message on her phone and smiles. "You know, my former client, Kevin, wanted me to sell a home. I was going to ignore it because I didn't think there was any value."

Sara swallows hard as Kelly glares at her.

Kelly continues, "Now I understand why he desperately wanted it sold."

Sara smiles awkwardly. "That's nice. I should probably go," she says in desperation to end the conversation.

"Safe travels. But I must say, you're not as pretty as a blonde, Sara," Kelly says with confirmation, slamming the door shut.

CHAPTER THIRTY

Sara arrives back at the condos in a panic. Clifford meets her outside as she pulls up and jumps out of the car. He throws his arms around her, and she starts sobbing. "We're fucked, Dee."

Clifford rubs her back, trying to calm her. "We heard the conversation. It's okay. We're okay."

Clifford continues rubbing her back and says, "Let's get inside."

They join the rest of the crew in Bailey's condo.

Daniel walks up and throws his arms around her. "So, I guess she figured it out, huh?"

Sara nods in confirmation, "She got a message from someone who tipped her off."

Clifford rubs his brow, "I have a feeling it's my fault."

A confused look flashes across Sara's face. "How's it your fault?"

"I parked in a tow-away fire zone, and they probably ran my plates. I'm sure her lackey assassins came by to look when we triggered the alarms and they probably noticed my car, ran the plates, got our info, and pieced it all together. They probably set the fire, too. That or the alarm triggered a fire trap to destroy evidence."

Daniel chimed in, "Also if Kevin put a hit on us, she would have our info. She probably just didn't recognize you at first."

Clifford shakes his head. "If only I didn't trip that alarm."

"Hey man, no one expected the building to be booby-trapped to burn down," Bailey mentions. "We've dealt with worse.".

Sara says, "True, but there are three assassins that we know of, in the area who are going to come after us."

Clifford pats her on the back to ease her mind and says, "We have some time, but you're right. The only assassins we know about are the Landscaper, Tofana, and Dorothy. We have intel on Tofana and the Landscaper, but Dorothy's a ghost. We know nothing about her except a name. We also don't know how many others she has on her payroll."

Sims chimes in, "You might have more time than you think. You destroyed her office and there's an arson investigation pending. She'll probably lay low until the investigation's over."

Clifford smiles, "That's true. She wouldn't want any more attention on her right now."

Outside the window the group spots a landscaping truck pull up across the street in the parking lot. They all duck down.

"Shit!" Clifford says, "Stay down!"

Sara slowly pokes her head up and stares out the window at the truck.

"Guys!" She says, "It's the legit landscaping company for the condos. It's okay."

Daniel shakes his head. "Dammit. That got my heart going for a second."

Clifford says, "Yeah, me too."

Sims stands up and dusts his jacket with his hands. "Okay guys, I need to go back to the bureau. I'm going to report back with our findings on Kelly and beg that they let us use FBI resources to help with this investigation."

Clifford nods with a half-smile on his face. "Good luck, we need all the help we can get at this point."

Sims nods and turns to walk out of the room. He rounds the corner to the hallway and approaches the front door. Twisting the doorknob, he gives a tug and the door swings open. In front of him stood the Landscaper, just as surprised as Sims, holding a gun with a silencer. He quickly points and fires at Sims. Due to his haste the bullet was off center and hit Sims in the left shoulder. Sims slams the door shut and instinctively grabs his shoulder. He cries out, "LANDSCAPER!" and turns to run away from the door.

The Landscaper fires three more rounds through the door, one grazing Sims' ear and two hitting him in the upper back. Sims falls to the ground with a slight bounce as The Landscaper kicks the door in and enters the condo.

Daniel, already taking action after Sims' cry, is charging toward the door. The Landscaper is caught off guard again and tries to take aim at Daniel, but is too late. Daniel knocks the gun from his hand and throws a powerful left hook to his jaw, knocking him off balance.

Clifford grabs Sims and pulls him out of the line of fire and into the next room where Sara has pushed Bailey out of harm's way and is protecting him.

The Landscaper kicks his knee into Daniel's gut, briefly knocking the wind out of him.

Daniel gasps for a breath and is stunned for a moment. The Landscaper throws a fist, hitting Daniel square in his jaw, whipping his head back with a crack. Daniel shakes off the punch and grapples him with both hands and headbutts him on the bridge of his nose in an attempt to blur his vision.

The Landscaper muscles him off and pushes him back. Daniel stumbles and loses his balance. Charging at him again, the Landscaper, this time prepared, twists his body, grabbing his arm, and throws Daniel into the wall. Daniel hits with a thud, cracking the drywall. The Landscaper grabs him by the back of his shirt and throws Daniel to the ground. Hitting the back of his head on the wood floor, Daniel is slowed. The Landscaper kicks Daniel in his already sore stomach and walks over to his gun.

He picks it up and walks over toward Daniel, crawling on the ground. He kicks him again, knocking him on his back, and aims his gun at his face.

A shot rings out and blood splatters all over the wall and floor.

After having his eyes shut tight, Daniel looks up and sees Clifford with gun in hand and The Landscaper falling over after a bullet traveled through his skull, killing him instantly.

CHAPTER THIRTY-ONE

Sims eyes slowly open and after he can focus, he sees Clifford standing over him looking down.

"Don't try to talk," Clifford says.

"You have tubes in your lungs. One of the bullets in your back caused your lung to collapse. You're going to be okay although, it won't feel like that for a while. The doctor said that none of the bullets hit anything life threatening. You've got some recovering to do."

Sims nods slightly and blinks.

Clifford continues, "The Landscaper is dead, we got him. If it wasn't for you screaming out to us and Daniel jumping into action, we would probably all be dead. I gotta say, Daniel was like a warrior. A real berserker charging him like that. Crazy," Clifford says with a smile on his face but worry in his voice.

A doctor walks into the room and says, "Ah, he's up. Good! Agent Sims, you've been asleep for about two days now and your friend here hasn't left the hospital since you arrived. I just want to reassure you that you are going to be okay. We have to run some tests first, but we think that your lungs will be stable enough for us to remove the tubing tomorrow. Blink if you want a rundown of your injuries."

Sims blinks.

"Okay! Well, the first bullet entered your left shoulder and exited out of your back cleanly. It did some ligament damage and we'll have to go in and repair some slight damage to your rotator cuff.

"One of the bullets took a chunk from your right ear. You will have a scar but that's about it.

The two that entered your back were the most severe. One of them nicked your lung and caused it to collapse and the other was lodged in one of your right scapula. We successfully removed them and you will be fine in a few weeks. You'll probably need physical therapy for a bit."

Sims blinks twice to thank him.

Clifford thanks the doctor and he goes over the vitals on the charts. "Everything looks great. We will have the nursing staff do regular checks to be sure his comfort levels are perfect."

Clifford smiles. "Thank you."

As the doctor exits the room, Director Sorren walks in and looks down at Sims. "I heard you're doing well. Your friend, Clifford, told me what happened. I'll make sure that you're recognized for your heroics."

Sorren turns toward Clifford, "Mr. Dee, would you please follow me outside the room."

Clifford nods and looks down at Sims and smiles. "Rest up, buddy," he says while turning to follow Sorren into the hallway.

Sorren turns to Clifford and says, "Thank you for saving him. He mentioned this issue to me but because of the sensitivity of the matter, I couldn't allow him to use the FBI to investigate. I want you to know that I spoke to my superiors about this and because of the car accident and shooting, the attempted murder of a public figure, the murder of an innocent civilian, the fire, and various threats to public safety, they want this matter ended quickly."

Clifford starts to smile while Sorren continues, "However, they still do not want the FBI officially involved, so you have to run point on this, but you'll have our support at your disposal."

Clifford looks confused. "One of your best men was shot and almost killed. How can the FBI not get involved with this?"

Sorren says, "I'm not at liberty to discuss our reasoning to be anonymous with this investigation. We just cannot be visibly involved."

Clifford rolls his eyes, "Great. Thanks for your help."

Annoyed, he walks away from Sorren.

Back at the condo, there was a crew fixing the door and patching up the holes and cracks in the walls. Clifford walks in and stares at the blood stains on the wall. A tech taps him on the shoulder and says, "Excuse me. I have to clean."

Clifford steps out of the way, over old crime scene tape and walks over to Sara and Bailey in the other room.

"Where's Daniel?" Clifford asks.

Sara says, "He's back at his place, passed out. Between staying awake, then not allowed to have restful sleep, you shoulda seen how grumpy he got. Especially when they told him no physical activity until," she pauses to check her watch, "well, until tomorrow."

Clifford nods. "I bet. I was going to check on him, but I guess I'll let him sleep."

Bailey asks, "How's Sims doing?"

Clifford says, "He woke up. He just needs to recover from surgery and the collapsed lung, but the doctor said he should be up and about in a little while."

Bailey smiles. "Great news."

"Yeah." Clifford says, "If those bullets didn't travel through the door first before hitting him, he'd be much worse. Oh, I also talked to his director, Sorren."

"Oh yeah, are they going after Kelly?" Sara asks.

Clifford shakes his head. "Nope, they want us to, with support from them. He said the FBI can't be officially involved but wants them taken out."

"WHAT?" Sara asks, furious. "Why the hell aren't they doing anything?"

Clifford shrugs. "He said he isn't at liberty to discuss it."

Bailey shakes his head. "Unreal!"

Clifford nods in agreement. "I thought so, too."

Sara looks up and asks. "So, what's next?"

Clifford says, "Well, since we have the FBI backing us, I thought that we could talk with the fire department to see what they found in their arson investigation and ask if we could get access to the building again. I want to see if everything was destroyed. We can also talk with some people in the building across the park to see if they noticed anything suspicious."

Sara smiles. "Do you want me to tag along?"

"Sure," Clifford says with a nod.

Bailey smiles and says, "While you guys go out, I'll start doing research on Kelly's real estate properties to see if she has any other places where she would set up."

Clifford says, "Sounds like a plan. It's getting late so let's head out first thing in the morning."

Bailey asks, "You takin' Daniel with you. too?"

Clifford shakes his head, "Nah, let him sleep in. He needs a day off that isn't forced upon him."

CHAPTER THIRTY-TWO

Clifford is awake at first light. He pours himself a cup of coffee into a "World's Best Investigator" travel mug and heads over toward Sara's condo.

It was an eerily quiet and chilly morning. He could clearly hear the slight hum of traffic from the Greenway toll road which was a few miles away. Clifford stops at the front stairs of Sara's condo and peers into the wood line to his right. He can see a deer foraging in the distance. He takes a moment to admire the wildlife then takes a swig from his mug and continues up the stairs.

He taps on Sara's door and waits, sipping his coffee. After a few minutes, she answers.

"Why are you up so early?" Sara asks.

"I just thought we would get an early start," Clifford explains.

"Jesus, Dee. Okay. Let me get dressed," she says, inviting him in.

Clifford continues sipping and finishes his coffee by the time Sara is done changing.

She bounces down the stairs into the living room and Clifford holds up his empty cup of coffee.

"I need more fuel."

Sara yawns and says, "Yeah, me too."

Clifford looks at his watch and says, "I'll tell you what. Let's get some breakfast and then we'll head to the fire department."

A smile grows on Sara's face.

About an hour later the two are finishing up their meal when Sara pulls out a bottle of ibuprofen from her purse.

"Headache?" Clifford asks.

"Now that I have a full belly and appropriately caffeinated, I'm going to tackle this small hangover."

"Oh? Party a little too hard last night?"

"Not really. Denise came over for a bit and we had a few."

"Did Denise stay over?" Clifford asks, unsure how to approach the topic he wants to really address, but also curious if Sara's starting a new relationship.

"Subtle." Sara swallows the pills with what's left of her coffee before continuing, "She's one of my best friends and she's very straight."

"Ah. Sorry to assume, it's just you haven't really hung out with any of your friends one-on-one before that I know of."

Sara's quiet for a moment. "Yeah, I'm not really looking for anything more than friendship."

"Really, why not?" Clifford asks, already knowing why, but feeling that Sara needs to acknowledge it.

Sara shrugs and looks out the window.

Clifford reaches to touch her hand, but she pulls away.

"I want to keep doing what we're doing. Taking down bad people. I love it. I love working with and hanging around you guys. I can't have a relationship, too. It's just too dangerous." Her voice trails off.

"Have you thought about talking to someone? A professional?"

"What, like therapy?"

Clifford nods.

A few long, silent seconds pass.

"Sara, you're drinking to the point of hangovers a little too often. I-"

"Are you seriously doing this to me right now?" Sara says, feeling defensive.

Clifford goes quiet again giving her time to process that he's noticed her change since Kentucky.

Sara swallows hard and bites her lip. "You know how in the movies; people say that drinking numbs them? How it helps them not feel anything?" Sara says, breaking the silence.

Clifford nods.

"All it's changed for me is that I'm waking up with a different type of headache."

Clifford leans in. "So, let's help you find a way to wake up without one."

"If I tell you I'll think about it, can we drop this and go do our job today?"

"Deal!" Clifford says, reaching his hand over the table to shake hers.

Sara smiles and says, "Want me to drive again?"

Clifford nods and says, "Sure. I rented it for you, or Jessica. Let's head over to the fire marshals and talk with them. I also want to know where my car is."

After parking in the fire department parking lot, Clifford and Sara walk up to the station front office and head inside.

A woman at a desk asks, "Can I help you?"

Clifford walks up and says, "Hi, yes. My name is Clifford Dee and I'm working with the local police and FBI with an investigation on the real estate office building that caught fire yesterday."

Clifford flashes his private investigator credentials as well as his government ID that was given to him from Badger to enter the government building where he and Kevin used to work.

Seeing the government credentials as well as an investigator badge, the woman behind the desk had no reason to doubt Clifford's story.

"Yes, Mr. Dee, how can I help?"

Clifford continues, "An associate and myself were looking into the fire and we were told that there was an arson investigation being done. Is that correct?"

She types away on the computer.

"As a matter of fact, there is. They still have the case open and probably still going through the building as we speak."

Clifford nods, "Great, can we head over to the building?"

"I don't see why not. I can call over, so they know to expect you."

Clifford smiles, "Thank you. Oh, one more question. There was a vehicle that was parked in front of the hydrant. Do you know what happened to it?"

The woman begins typing away again and after a minute she says, "It was towed. We work with Hebb's Dragon Wagon Towing company. They're in Leesburg."

She hands Clifford a card with the towing company's information on it. He looks at the name and says, "Cute. Thank you."

Sara and Clifford walk back to the rental car. Clifford asks, "Do you want to go up to Leesburg first and pick up my car, or should we hit the office building?"

Sara thinks for a moment. "Office building. If the fire marshals are there now, we want to catch them."

Clifford nods, "Good call."

Sara drives past the office building and notices the parking lot is roped off. She heads toward the building across the park and slowly cruises through the parking lot to find it completely full. "Ugh! There is nowhere to park around here," she says, frustrated.

Clifford spots a sign that says, "Overflow parking on Lee Street. Parking garage."

He points at the sign, "Hey, that's the garage Daniel spotted. Let's just park there."

Sara loops around in the parking lot and heads two blocks over toward Lee Street.

They find the garage and turn in. Sara looks over at Clifford and says, "I'm parking on top. It's a nice day."

Clifford narrows his eyes, "Why?"

Sara repeats herself, "It's a nice day. And besides, not many people drive all the way up. I think it would be best to stay away from other cars in case of dings."

"Dings?" Clifford asks.

"Uh-huh, this is a rental. I don't want you guys to get charged for chipped paint," Sara says.

An awkward smile crawls across Clifford's face, "How thoughtful."

They continue driving around in circles, up the ramps until the sunlight breaks the darkness of the parking garage as they reach the ramp leading to the top of the building.

Sara parks the car and the two get out. She walks over toward the waist-high brick ledge and looks over. The building was situated on a slight incline for drainage purposes, making the five-story garage seem much higher than they were. "Woah, we're up here, aren't we?" Sara asks.

Clifford walks over, looks out and has a bit of a dizzy spell, "Oh Jesus, we didn't have to be, but yeah, we are up here."

Sara sees the distressed look on Clifford's face and asks, "Wait, are you afraid of heights?"

Shrugging it off, Clifford says, "No, I'm fine."

A slow smile creeps on Sara's face. "Okay."

Clifford smiles uneasily and turns away to walk toward the elevator.

Sara takes a moment, breathes deeply, and admires the view of the town below before following Clifford.

The elevator reaches the top of the parking garage, and the doors open. Clifford and Sara walk in and hit the ground floor button.

The elevator ride seemingly takes forever. Once the doors open, Clifford belts out, "Finally! That had to be the slowest elevator in all of Virginia!"

Sara nods her head. "That was a small eternity."

Clifford smiles briefly and says, "Had to park on the tippy top."

Sara narrows her eyes and turns toward Clifford. "Shuddup."

It was about a fifteen-minute walk from the garage to the office building. They spot a member of the fire marshal's team outside by the truck smoking a cigarette.

He butts it out on the bottom of his shoe when he spots Clifford and Sara walking toward him.

"Sorry, this area is closed off for an investigation," he says as they approach.

Clifford pulls out his identification, "That's why we're here. I need to ask you guys a few questions."

Clifford hands him the same government and private credentials that he showed the woman at the fire hall.

The investigator reaches his hand out to shake Clifford's, "I'm Will. You're with the government?" he asks.

Clifford says, "Not exactly, I'm a private investigator that was contracted out by the FBI to look into the matter."

Will narrows his eyes, "Why isn't an agent with you? Shouldn't you be working with an agent?"

Clifford nods, "I was. He was shot in connection with the person who owns this building and is in the hospital right now."

"Oh, wow. Did it have anything to do with the fire?" Will asks.

Clifford looks over at Sara and back at Will. "That's what we're trying to find out."

"Sure, sure. Let me call up the Marshal," he says, picking up a walkie-talkie.

The radio squawks and Will talks into it, "Hey, Roger, we have a detective out here who wants to talk to you. He's working with the FBI."

Clifford hears him call back over the radio, "Okay, I'll be out in a minute."

After a few minutes they spot two men walking out of the building and heading over towards them.

One was a bit older and portly; the other was tall and thinner.

The portly man extends his hand to Clifford, "Roger McDuffie, FPS. How can I help you?"

Clifford shakes his hand, "Clifford Dee, private investigation services. What's FPS?"

"Fire Protection Services. It's the department I'm with. Fire investigations fall under our branch. What can I do for you, Mr. Dee?"

Clifford nods, "Ah, that makes sense. Well, I'm working with the FBI, and they asked that we come here to see if we could do a walkthrough with you."

Roger asks, "Walkthrough?"

"Yeah, in the building. To see if there's any evidence of a crime," Clifford explains.

Roger shakes his head, "No, but you can request a copy of our report when we're done."

Clifford clenches his jaw in frustration. "Please, sir. My partner, FBI Agent Sims, was shot by a man who was employed here. The fire happened moments before he was shot, and we would really like to take a peek around to see if we can find anything that can help with our investigation.

Roger lets out a huge audible sigh, "Fine, but only you. The missus stays here. It's way too dangerous for a woman in there."

Clifford slowly looks over at Sara, preparing himself for what he thinks she's about to say, but is surprised to see her smiling.

"Oh, thank you for your thoughtfulness, Rog." Her smile still firmly planted, but not reaching her eyes, "My female brain and body can't possibly handle such a place."

Will turns his head before Roger catches his smile.

Clifford smiles and turns toward Roger, "I guess my most observant colleague can wait for me out here."

As they walk away, Will gives Sara a fist bump.

Clifford's phone dings and he pulls it out to see a text from Sara: *Can I throw Roger off the top of the parking garage?*

He looks over at Sara who's still smiling.

"Have fun inside," she says.

Clifford smiles back and turns to follow the Fire Marshal into the building.

Sara sits on the bumper of the fire department's paramedic truck and Will walks over and asks, "Wanna see the inside of the truck?"

Sara smiles, "Sure, but before you try too hard, I'm gay."

Will laughs and says, "I'm cool with that. So's my sister."

Sara jumps up and raises her hand for a high five and says, "Let's check out the truck."

Clifford follows Roger and the other investigative team members into the building. He's handed an N95 mask, and they head toward the stairs.

The smell of burnt wood and the stench of melted plastic fills the air. Clifford's nose twitches behind his mask.

Roger turns and says, "They had security cameras that were closed circuit. You can see there, and there," he says as he points to the corners of the lobby at the melted cameras.

"And over here," he continues, "check this out."

He walks over to a compartment in the wall that was blown out.

"This is a gas lever that failed. This is where the fire started. It went up the elevator shaft and spread through the floors like a fireball."

He motions Clifford to follow him up the stairs.

Clifford asks, "So was this like a controlled burn or-"

Roger cut him off, "Yeah, it was a controlled burn. That's the weird thing. The gas line ruptured but then the fire acted as if it were controlled. The blast hit the third floor and spread. It destroyed that floor completely."

Clifford asks, "How does that happen?"

"We're not sure right now. There was no other accelerant other than the ruptured gas line. It looks like an accident, but the fire didn't behave that way."

They walk out onto the third floor. The stench of the burnt plastic was stronger than ever, the desks had a plastic laminate covering that curled up and burnt from the heat. Some desks had melted pens sitting in a soot covered metal mesh pen holder. The floor was raised and was covered with what was once a synthetic carpet, now a slick mess.

Clifford steps into the hall and looks down toward Kelly's office.

"Damage like this on the entire floor?" Clifford asks.

Roger nods, "Yessir, it actually gets worse all the way down, but check this out."

He points down the hall and shows Clifford the secret staircase he discovered previously.

"The damage to this wall was done before the fire. I think someone knew it was here and used it to escape."

Clifford nods. "Oh yeah? So, are you thinking this was arson?"

He starts walking away from the stairs and toward the office to get a look.

"Arson? Maybe, but I don't think the person who knocked down this wall set the fire. I think they were trying to escape the fire."

Clifford let out a sigh of relief internally.

"Who do you think they were?" he asks.

Roger says, "Not really my department to guess. This stairwell goes to a sub-basement that leads to the neighboring building across the park. I haven't been over there yet, but I plan to take a look at their security cameras to see if we can see anything. If anything looks odd, I'll share it with the police"

Trying to change the topic, Clifford blurts out, "So this office looks like it took some damage."

"Yeah, it festered in the office, and everything's gone."

"Everything?"

"Yessir, everything."

Clifford grits his teeth and peeks his head into the office to see that even the file cabinets were warped and everything inside it was destroyed. He shakes his head knowing that he is going to walk away with nothing.

Clifford realizes that the entire building was built to be a giant failsafe. The fire was designed to destroy everything, her files, her computer, her backup server, everything that could be used to incriminate her.

Letting out a sigh, Clifford says, "Well, I guess that's all to see, huh?"

Roger nods, "That stairwell and the way it burned are worth looking into. I hope you catch your shooter."

"I appreciate it. Thanks for your time."

"Did you still want a copy of the report?" Roger asks.

"Sure, can you send that in the care of Agent Sims? He's the agent in charge. The one who was shot. I want him to get the credit."

Roger smiles, "You got it. I'll walk you out."

Stepping outside, the fresh air hits Clifford's lungs as he disposes of his mask in the garbage. He lets out a little cough and inhales deeply.

Roger says, "Makes you appreciate the clean air, doesn't it?"

Clifford smiles. "Sure does."

Roger waves goodbye, and heads back inside the building.

Approaching the truck, he spots Sara sitting and chatting with Will on the bumper of the fire paramedic truck. She's giving her number to him as he puts it in his phone.

Clifford shakes his head with a smile on his face.

"Will was showing me the truck. He wouldn't do an I.V. for me, though."

Clifford laughs. "How is the hangover?"

"Better, actually. So, did you find anything useful?"

Clifford's smile fades. "Nothing. Everything's gone in the fire."

Sara kicks a rock and then looks up at Clifford. "What now?"

Clifford shrugs, "Get my car. Then we can head back to Bailey's and see if he found any info on other properties owned by Kelly."

Sara says, "Alrighty then."

Clifford puts his arm around her as they both turn and start walking back toward the parking garage.

Clifford and Sara get closer to the office building across from the park and Clifford says, "You know what, let's head inside."

In the lobby is a security guard. He looks up from his computer screen as they approach, "How can I help you?"

Clifford smiles and says, "Hey there, I'm a private detective working with the FBI." He hands the guard his government and private investigator credentials, "I'm helping with the investigation of the fire across the way and the bureau wanted me to see if you had any footage caught on your cameras. Can I take a look at your videos from that day?"

The guard hands the IDs back to Clifford and says, "I have to call this in."

Clifford nods, "Sure, no problem. I'll be over here," he says, walking away and taking a seat. Sara smiles and sits next to Clifford and picks up a magazine that has her favorite local artist, Danica, on the cover. She flips through and starts reading an article about her and how she was inspired to paint by another local artist, Jenny Wilson, who later became her mentor.

Sara nods along reading the article while Clifford looks around, scoping out the lobby for cameras.

The guard hangs up the phone. "Mr. Dee, someone will be with you shortly."

Clifford smiles, "Thanks."

Moments later a burly man walks into the lobby and says, "Mr. Dee, please follow me."

Clifford and Sara stand up and follow the man into a side hallway and then into a small office.

The man sits behind a desk that has several monitors on the desktop and even more affixed to the wall behind it.

"I have the day of the fire keyed up. This is the video from outside, pointing toward our parking lot near the park. You can see the building in the background."

The flames blew out the windows on the third floor first, followed by the second floor, then the fourth.

Clifford asks, "Can you see anyone entering the building?"

"Not from our angle," the man says.

Clifford looks at some of the other camera footage on a different monitor.

"Were there any unidentifiable people in your building on that day? I mean, can you check to see if anyone was walking around in your building that isn't supposed to be here?" He asks.

The man swivels around, "We only have cameras in the main lobby, and some in the loading dock. We don't have cameras in the halls, but all visitors have to check in with security."

Clifford nods, "Okay, good. I don't think these videos will work for us, but thank you."

The security officer stands up and says, "Sure thing. Anything we can do to help."

Leaving the building Sara turns and asks, "So, what was that about?"

Clifford says, "Daniel and I found a tunnel that leads to the basement of this building. I just wanted to know if we were caught on their security cameras."

Sara smiles and nods, "Ahh. Smart thinking."

Clifford winks, "Actually, it was Roger's idea."

"Ah, Rog, a man fit for the 1950's."

They continue up the sidewalk and finally reach the garage.

Clifford asks Sara, "Wanna take the slowest elevator in the world, or do you want to take the stairs?"

Sara looks over at Clifford, tilts her head, and says, "Stairs."

Clifford chuckles and holds the door for Sara. "Ladies first."

Sara looks behind her, "Oh, you mean me?" She says, jokingly.

Clifford grins and rolls his eyes. Sara skirts past Clifford and starts heading up the stairs. After rounding the second floor, she turns her head to see Clifford starting to limp up the stairs.

"You're slowing down, what's up?" She asks.

"It's my knee acting up again. I'll ice it when we get back. I'm fine."

She says, "Maybe I should've asked Will how to carry people on stairs instead of an I.V."

Clifford laughs, "Yeah right, I'd pay to see that. I'm twice your size. I'm good."

As Sara rounds the next set of stairs, she passes a man heading down. "Excuse me," she says.

The man squeezes to the side and smiles, "Excuse me," he says back. The first thing Clifford notices is the strange European accent the gentleman has. The second thing he notices is the handle of the Beretta 92FS sticking out when his jacket opens as he turns to maneuver past Sara.

Clifford moves his eyes in a downward direction as the man turns to face him. He looks up at him and the man straightens his jacket and then waves to invite Clifford up the stairs to the landing. "Please," he says with a smile. "After you."

As he reaches the landing Clifford says, "Thank you."

The man smiles and nods. He turns to head down the stairs when Clifford glances up to a corner mirror on the stairwell to keep his eye on him. He sees the man reaching inside his jacket, going for the gun. Instinct kicks in and Clifford, with the higher ground, turns and leaps down the stairs onto the man as he draws. A shot is fired, but the bullet hits the brick wall behind Clifford. They fumble with the gun and it gets knocked loose.

Sara comes running down the stairs and Clifford shouts, "I got him. Get to the car!"

She stares for a moment while Clifford lands two good punches. "Go now!" Clifford shouts.

Sara nods, still in shock, she turns and starts running up the steps.

At the tops she flings open the door to the roof of the garage.

Two shots ring out as she steps out onto the roof, both missing her by mere inches and hitting the door and brick wall behind her. Sara jumps to the ground and pushes backwards, sliding back into the stairwell.

She grabs her phone and turns on the camera. She pokes the top of the phone out, aiming the camera toward the shooter.

It's Tofana.

Sara watches on her phone as Tofana starts to walk toward her. She decides to go down a level.

Tofana reaches the entrance to the stairs and peeks down, seeing that it's empty.

CHAPTER THIRTY-TWO

"Where did you go, little rabbit?" Tofana sings out to Sara.

She heads down the stairs and enters the fourth floor. Sara, hiding behind a car, hears, "Run, rabbit, run!" echo through the garage as Tofana is searching for her.

Sara crawls under a Jeep and stays low on the other side. Crouching she moves between two other cars.

She can hear Tofana's calls getting closer and louder.

"It's raaaaaabbit season!" Tofana teases.

Sara looks to her left and sees a fire extinguisher hanging on the wall of the garage. She unlatches the metal straps holding it onto the wall and quietly removes it.

She crouches back down and pins her body against the wheel of the car next to her.

Tofana lays down to look under the cars, but at the angle she is in, she cannot see Sara's feet behind the wheel of the car.

"Where are you, rabbit!" she yells, getting annoyed. "Come out, come out, wherever you are."

Sara is starting to tremble, holding the extinguisher tight to her body. Her foot slips out from under her, scraping across the cement floor, giving up her position.

"Gotcha!" Tofana says to herself.

She starts walking with a quickened pace toward the car Sara is hiding behind. She springs around the corner but is met with the extinguisher powder sprayed to her face.

Sara then uses the butt of the metal cylinder to strike her jaw, dislodging two of her teeth.

Tofana falls backward and hits the ground in a thud.

Sara drops the extinguisher and takes off running. She rounds the corner and runs up the ramp to the top level.

She runs toward the car, pulling the keys from her pocket. She fumbles with the keys, and they leap from her hand, skidding across the ground, away from her.

"Shit!" she cries as she stops and turns to get the keys. She starts to run toward them when she notices Tofana coming up the ramp.

With a few teeth missing and a bloodied nose, she speaks with a slight lisp, "You fucking bitch! I'm going to skin you alive!"

Sara looks over at the keys a few feet from her. She knows that there is no way she can get the keys and then double back to the car in time to get away. She needs to fight.

"We don't have to do this," Sara pleads to her.

Tofana spits blood. "This is personal for me, now."

Sara mutters, "Fuck," under her breath.

CHAPTER THIRTY-THREE

Daniel wakes up in a daze. His face is still a bit swollen, and his neck still hurts a little. He grabs his phone and stares at the time.

"Oh shit. I must have been tired." he says to himself.

He notices the text icon and checks his messages.

The text was from Clifford.

"Hey bud hope you're feeling better. Went out with Sara. Check in with Bailey when you get up."

Daniel closes the message. He sits up, swings his legs off the edge of the bed, and with a huge yawn gives himself a nice stretch.

After a quick shower and getting dressed, Daniel heads down to the kitchen and whips up some scrambled eggs. He scarfs them down quickly and follows the eggs with a protein shake.

Popping a few ibuprofens, he heads to Bailey's to see what he's up to.

"Good morning, Sleeping Beauty. Was sleep any better for you this time?" Bailey asks.

"Yeah. My neck still hurts. What are Dee and Sara up to?"

"They went over to Kelly's crispy office to look around. See if they can get their hands on anything incrementing before the investigators give the all clear to its very pissed off owner."

"Your place is still wrecked from the other day," Daniel says, looking around.

"I've been a little too busy to clean, Dan."

"Can I clean?"

Bailey turns toward his friend. "You wanna clean my place?"

"I need something productive to do and I really don't feel like going to the gym."

* * *

Clifford hears two gunshots coming from the roof. "Sara!" He screams as he struggles with the gunman on the concrete floor.

He backhands Clifford in his face, knocking him off balance.

He rolls onto his feet and throws a swift kick into Clifford's gut. Attempting a second kick, Clifford grabs his boot, sweeps his plant leg, and twists his ankle, sending him to the ground.

He lands on his hip while Clifford rolls onto his feet, grunting, as he pushes off using his bad knee.

Hobbled, Clifford stands battle ready as the gunman pops up and faces him. Clifford goes to pull his gun, but it skirted out of the holster during the scrum and slid away.

The gunman glances down and spots the gun a few feet from Clifford. He begins to circle toward it. They both make a dash for it. Clifford kicks the gun away as the gunman lunges for it. He hits the ground with a bounce and Clifford lands a kick to his face. He rolls to his side as Clifford bends down to pick him up. As Clifford is pulling him to his feet, the gunman pulls a boot-knife and lodges it into Clifford's thigh.

On the roof, Sara can hear Clifford's scream. Tofana turns her head and smiles as his scream reaches their ears.

She looks back at Sara and says, "Sounds like your friend is having fun, little rabbit."

Tofana slowly starts walking toward Sara as she retreats, walking backward. Tofana pulls out her gun from her hip holster, removes the magazine, and tosses both on the ground. She slips her arms out, removing her jacket and tosses it aside. She momentarily stops, pulls a karambit-style knife from her leg holster, and starts twirling it around as she begins to pick up the pace toward Sara.

Sara starts to back up toward the roof's ledge. Her lower back rests against the half-wall's edge as Tofana reaches her, swinging the karambit toward her face. Sara dodges the swipe and Tofana throws a blow to her ribs.

Sara bends sideways and grunts as the punch lands hard against her side.

Tofana swings the karambit again. This time Sara raises her arm to deflect but the blade connects, slicing her arm.

Sara lets out a slight audible shriek as the blade cuts through her skin.

Tofana smiles and says, "Time to make rabbit stew out of you."

Sara looks up to see Tofana grinning.

"What's with you and rabbits?" Sara asks.

Tofana says, "You cower like one. Running away as I hunt you down."

Tofana throws another punch and again Sara quickly parries, throwing her arm up to block, and moves away from the roof's ledge.

Tofana whips around and slowly starts to circle Sara.

"See, you don't fight back. You're just food, like a good little rabbit," Tofana says as she slowly moves around.

Sara circles away, holding her freshly sliced arm.

Tofana, grinning, says, "Time to end you."

She lunges at Sara who falls backward, grabbing Tofana by her shirt and throwing a foot to her chest, using her momentum to kick her away. Sara pops back up as Tofana bounces off the ground, hitting her already beaten and bruised face.

She rolls over cussing, "You're fucking dead now."

Sara stands towering over her as their eyes connect. "I'm no fucking rabbit," she says as she starts to kick Tofana. She lands a kick in her ribs and another in her face, spraying blood across the concrete. Tofana starts to roll in a defensive ball as Sara lands kick after kick. Tofana starts to roll away when Sara lands a kick against her back. Tofana swings her arm around with her finger in the karambit loop, slicing across Sara's shin. Sara grimaces in pain as Tofana pops back up to her feet.

She wipes the blood from her chin and spits blood from her mouth.

Sara starts to limp backwards again keeping her eye on Tofana to gauge her next move.

Her fear has been replaced with rage and she is ready to take on any attack from the bloodied assassin. Tofana picks up on her body language and smirks. "So, you do have a bit of fight in you. I see it in your eyes."

Sara says, "If you want me dead, you'll have to work for it."

Tofana shrugs. "Fair enough."

She walks toward Sara who is limping backwards. She swings the karambit at her violently and Sara goes to block. Tofana spins and connects a kick to Sara's midsection, knocking her on her ass.

Tofana continues to walk toward Sara as she scoots backwards, furiously. She finds herself butting up against a parked car.

"Get up!" Tofana demands.

Sara climbs to her feet.

Tofana charges at Sara swinging the karambit in a downward motion. Sara moves and the blade strikes the hood of the car, lodging itself.

Tofana pulls, but the knife is stuck. Sara throws a punch, hitting Tofana in her jaw, adding to the severe damage to her face. Tofana lets out a painful shriek and let go of the knife.

Sara starts to run around the car, but Tofana reaches out and grabs a fist full of her hair and pulls her back toward her.

Still grasping her hair, she pulls her down against the hood of the car. Sara's head bounces off the hood and Tofana pulls her up by her hair and grasps her head with the other hand, throwing her into the side mirror of the car. The glass from the mirror shatters from the impact of Sara's shoulder and sprays across the ground as she tumbles and falls.

Tofana lands a kick on Sara's side.

Sara begins to crawl to her feet as Tofana kicks her again. She bends down and pulls Sara to her feet and throws her against the half wall of the parking garage.

Tofana picks an exhausted Sara up by her shirt and muscles her to her feet. She pushes Sara up against the wall and starts to push her over the top. "Goodbye, rabbit," Tofana says as she starts to push Sara over the ledge.

Sara hooks her leg around Tofana's planted leg to regain her balance. She twists her body to the side and swings her arm around Tofana, using her leverage against her, and elbowing her in the back of the head, knocking her against the ledge. Sara quickly swoops down and grabs Tofana's feet, lifting her over. Sara grunts and cries, "It's duck season, bitch!"

The momentum carries her quickly over the edge as Tofana whips her arm around wildly grabbing at Sara's arm.

The body weight of Tofana pulls on Sara and she begins to tumble over the edge with her.

Sara can feel her body being pulled back to safety as Tofana falls to her death, hitting her head against a dumpster in the alley below.

She turns her head as Clifford wraps his arms around her.

Sara buries her head in Clifford's chest and sobs.

Clifford pulls her tight and repeats the words, "I got you. I got you," over and over again.

CHAPTER THIRTY-FOUR

Nestled in Clifford's arms, Sara cries. Emotionally exhausted, beaten, bleeding, and bruised, the two hold each other.

Clifford soothes her by rubbing her back. In the distance he can hear the sounds of police sirens racing toward the garage. In what seems like a flash, officers surround them with guns drawn. Clifford does not let go.

* * *

Bailey and Daniel are almost finished cleaning the condo when they notice the time.

Bailey says, "Dee and Sara have been gone a long time."

Daniel asks, "What time did they head out?"

"Early," Bailey explains.

Daniel looks at his phone and says, "I got nothing from them, want me to call?"

Bailey nods. "Yeah. He would have checked in by now."

Clifford does not answer the phone.

"Voicemail," Daniel says. "I'll call Sara.".

Again, the call goes to voicemail.

Daniel looks over at Bailey and shakes his head.

Bailey gives Daniel a concerned look.

Outside, they hear Clifford talking to Sara. "We're here. We're home," he says.

Daniel takes off in a sprint, out the front door and out to the parking lot where Clifford is helping Sara out of the car.

"What happened?" Daniel asks.

"Help me get her inside. We can take her to her place later," Clifford says.

"No, I don't want to be alone," Sara says.

Clifford nods. "Okay, let's go inside Bailey's."

Daniel swoops her up off her feet and carries her like a baby.

"Careful!" Clifford says, "She has stitches in her arm and leg."

"I got her," Daniel says as he whisks her away.

Clifford stops for a moment, watching Daniel care for her like a concerned brother.

Limping, he follows behind into Bailey's place.

"What the fuck happened, Dee?" Bailey asks.

Clifford shakes his head. "Let's get Sara settled first."

Evening turns to night and Sara lays, passed out on the couch after eating the gummy Bailey gave her to calm her down.

Daniel sits in a chair next to her as Clifford recaps the events that took place.

"So, wait," Bailey interrupts, "how the hell did you get to her before she went over the ledge?"

"I heard the gunshots. I had no idea if Sara was okay or not. I couldn't get away from the guy. We wrestled for a bit, and he knocked my gun away and went for it. He ended up stabbing me in the leg," he says, pointing to his bloodied trousers.

"After that, I fell backwards, and he jumped on top of me. He pulled the knife out of my leg and tried to stab me with it. I head-butted him and was able to knock the knife away. He put his forearm against my neck and leaned down into it, using as much weight as he could and I...."

Clifford hesitates for a moment before continuing.

"I took a bite out of his ear."

Bailey leans back in his chair and Daniel's eyes grow to the size of saucers.

"You what?" Daniel asks.

"I was starting to blackout," Clifford explains.

"Damn dude!" Bailey says.

Clifford shakes his head and continues, "Okay so, yeah, I bit some ear off and spit it out."

"And that's when you went to Sara?" Daniel asks.

"Nope. He got away from me and found my gun. I dove between two cars just as he fired at me. I saw the knife at this point and picked it up. I don't know how he didn't see me. He walked right past me, so I popped up and rammed the blade through the back of his skull."

Daniel shakes his head. "Damn, man."

"Yeah," Clifford continues. "So, I tried the stairs, but my legs were too bad. I couldn't drag myself up the steps, so I walked the ramp which seemed like forever. One leg with a gaping hole in it and the other with a fucked-up knee. I got up there just in time, man. I yelled, but I don't think they could hear me. Sara did this swim-move thing and switched positions. It happened so fast, but they switched spots and Sara ducked down and flipped Tofana off the edge. I've never seen anything like it."

Bailey wipes his hands across his face. "Shit dude. That sounds fucking nuts."

Clifford nods. "I don't think she'll want to be alone for a while."

"No doubt," Bailey says.

Daniel rests his hand on Sara's side, and she lets out a little sleepy moan. "We got her. She's going to be okay."

CHAPTER THIRTY-FIVE

The next morning Sara awakes on the couch and spots Daniel sleeping in a recliner next to her, lightly snoring away. She sits up to stretch and spots Clifford sitting by the counter-island in the kitchen drinking coffee. She slowly walks over and says, "Good morning."

Clifford looks over and says, "Hey! How'd you sleep?"

"Good," she says, "Did everyone stay here last night?"

Clifford nods. "Yeah. We decided it was best to keep watch. Bailey took first watch. I don't want to freak you out, but we don't know how many more assassins Kelly has at her disposal."

Sara closes her eyes and shakes her head. "I don't even want to think about it."

Clifford shakes his head. "I don't either."

Clifford notices a tear roll down Sara's face. He leans over and wipes it with his thumb.

"Are you okay?"

Sara looks up and slowly shakes her head. "I'm scared. But that's not it."

"What is it?" Clifford asks.

Sara lets out a sob. "I've been scared before. Liam Stacey scared me. Bandoni scared me. Hell, you scared me when I first met you, but this time, I felt like I was going to die. I believed it."

Clifford wraps his arms around her.

Sara sniffles and smiles. "Sometimes I think about how scared Tracy must've been when Stacey-" Her speech is overcome with her sadness as she continues, "She was all alone, Dee. I wasn't there to help her."

Clifford squeezes her again and starts stroking her hair. "It's okay. We're going to get everything worked out," he whispers.

"Sorry. I'm a mess," Sara apologizes as she pulls away from him and reaches for tissues.

"No, you're not," Clifford says in an affirming tone. "You're shook. You're facing your trauma and yesterday was a really shitty day that just added onto it."

Collecting herself, Sara says, "But look at you, You're a rock. I never see you get emotional."

Clifford chuckles. "Trust me, I'm a fucking wreck."

"Really?" Sara asks.

"Yeah," he says, holding his smile, "I'm just really great at that macho-internalizing crap."

Sara gives a soft laugh. "And I've never been more jealous of you."

Clifford laughs.

Sara, wiping the last tear from her eye, asks with a smile, "Any coffee left?"

Clifford grins. "I'll pour you a cup."

He slides off the chair and walks around to the cupboard. She perks up and a smile slowly grows onto her face.

"Cream and sugar?" Clifford asks.

"Just cream, please," Sara replies.

Sara closes her eyes and takes another hit of the wonderful coffee smell in the air. Seconds later Clifford is sliding the coffee across the island to her.

After a little while, Daniel and Bailey join them in the kitchen. Clifford says, "Since we're all up, I have to type up and send off my report to the FBI. I say we take it easy for the rest of the day. No investigating, no going off to look at any buildings. We lay low."

Daniel nods. "Smart idea."

Bailey says, "I have a few irons in the fire. I'm doin' a web crawl. Should get results on Kelly's properties soon." He said, looking over at his computer, "There are gonna be a lot of files for me to go over, so I'm set with plenty to do. I agree with the laying low part."

Sara shakes her head. "I don't think anyone should leave the condo! We all need to stay put!"

Daniel perks up. "How about a movie night! We all stay up and watch some movies."

Sara's eyes light up, "Comedies!"

Daniel continues, "Yeah, we can all pick a good movie, some action-coms, funny shows, and we'll get snacks."

Clifford says, "I'll go for snacks," surprised that he likes the idea.

Daniel says, "I'll go too, if that's okay with Sara, of course." He looks over to Sara for approval.

Sara nods. "For snacks, I'll allow it."

CHAPTER THIRTY-SIX

Mid-morning became a bit busier. Clifford writes up his report to send as Bailey finishes up his web queries and reviews the results. Sara and Daniel play a video game on the big screen TV. Clifford looks over and smiles seeing Sara kicking back and enjoying herself. He stops for a moment and allows himself to think of what might have happened.

He wipes his hand over his face to regain his moment in the present. Bailey notices.

"You okay, Boss?"

Clifford smiles. "Never better, and don't call me 'Boss'."

Bailey smiles. "How 'bout 'Shirley?'" he quips. "Seriously, she's gonna be okay. Yesterday was a bit much for both of you."

Clifford nods. "Yeah, it's just, a few years ago, we did this in Kentucky. It was supposed to be different here."

Bailey wheels over closer to Clifford. "Did you think political corruption would have been much different? More gentlemanly?"

Clifford shrugs. "I didn't think any of your lives would be in this kind of danger again."

"Well," Bailey says, "You didn't drag us along with you. Each of us came willingly."

"Thanks," Clifford says, knowing his friend had a point, but still not feeling much better. "Since I joined the military, I feel like it's just one war after another, after another."

Bailey smiles, "Life's a war. A war without end, my friend. You have to fight to survive. You have to fight for rights and equal opportunities. You have to fight to make things better. I dare you to try being me for a day. A black male in a wheelchair."

Bailey continues, "When I go somewhere, people automatically look past me. They dismiss me. Not only am I considered second-class, but I'm also an inconvenience." He points over to Sara, "And that gorgeous, smart, funny, badass has to go through life, not only as a female, in this male-dominant world and profession, she's also gay. Then, Dan..." he looks over at Daniel and goes silent for a brief moment. "That fit and good-lookin', straight, white boy don't count."

Shaking his head and smiling, "Never mind. Bad example."

Clifford laughs and says, "Oh, for fuck's sake!"

Bailey laughs and says, "I'm not wrong!"

Clifford shakes his head with a smile and turns back to his report.

Another hour passes and Clifford hits send on the laptop. He walks over to Sara and Daniel.

"Report is on its way. When do you want to go out to get the snacks?"

Daniel looks over from the video game and says, "Whenever, but let me kick her butt real quick."

Just as he says that Sara strikes a death blow to his character. "No! I wasn't paying attention! Redo! Redo!!" Daniel demands.

Sara laughs and says, "Nope, I won fair and square. Now go get me snacks."

Daniel looks over toward Sara with a scowl. "You're lucky you're cute." Daniel looks at Clifford and says, "Black licorice and pretzels it is!"

Sara shakes her head and says, "If you don't get something with chocolate and peanut butter then don't come back!"

Clifford laughs and says, "I'll be in the car."

Stepping outside Clifford squints from the sun. He takes a moment to allow his eyes to adjust when he spots a figure to his left walking toward him with something in his hand. Clifford quickly places his hand on his gun and begins to draw.

"Woah! Woah!" The man shouts, "Package for you, guy!"

Clifford blinks hard to help his eyes adjust and slides his gun back into the holster. He gives the parcel delivery guy a half smile and says, "Sorry," as he reaches out to take the package.

It was for Bailey.

Clifford shakes his head and walks over to the door and sets it on the stoop. He returns and gets into the car, watching as Daniel picks up the package and slides it inside and continues toward the car.

Daniel opens the door and slinks into the passenger seat. "Bailey got a package," he explains to Clifford.

Clifford smiles and says, "Yeah, I almost drew my gun on the driver. Maybe we should also hit an ABC store."

At the store, Daniel picks up a hand basket and Clifford pushes a cart.

They pick up some beer and head over to the candy aisle. Clifford laughs every time Daniel lets out an audible, "Ooh," over some candy he hasn't had in a while.

Clifford walks past Daniel and says, "I'll be over gettin' some chips."

Clifford rounds the corner of the chip aisle and can feel his pulse quicken. He starts to sweat, and his breathing becomes rapid. His tinnitus flares up causing an unbearable ringing in his ears. He closes his eyes and counts to himself. "One, two, three, four, five, Clifford Dee is still alive."

He realizes Daniel followed him sooner than he thought he would.

Embarrassed, Clifford closes his eyes tight and opens them again. Seeing the look of concern on Daniel's face, "Yesterday kinda triggered my PTSD."

Daniel asks, "Are you okay?"

Clifford looks away for a moment and then back at Daniel again. "I think I need to make an appointment."

Daniel pats him on the back and says, "Whatever you need. Tonight's not just for Sara, it's for you too."

Clifford nods and says, "Thanks."

Daniel smiles and says, "Let's pick out some chips and get out of here."

Back at the condo, Sara walks over to Bailey who's going over his computer files.

She smiles at his focus and asks, "Almost done?"

Bailey smiles and says, "I'm almost done, I just have to concentrate a bit."

"What are you looking for?" she says, clearly not concerned if she was disturbing him.

Bailey turns to Sara and says, "Check it out. This is a web crawling program, similar to how google searches websites except my program doesn't ignore things. I plug in keywords and then I start to review what comes back. If I want to see more results focused on, like this," he starts as he points to a word on his screen, "then filter those results and it will tweak the output until I find exactly what I'm looking for."

Sara blinks rapidly and says, "Wow, that's like big brain stuff."

Bailey says, "I'll take that as a compliment."

"You should."

Bailey says, "I can't take all of the credit. I tweaked a program that was already out there and made it do what I needed it to do. I guess you could say that I perfected it."

Sara smiles, "Wow, so humble."

She turns and says, "I'm going to go back to playing those dumb video games while you do your smart stuff."

Bailey laughs, "Actually, I'll join you, if that's okay? I need to let this run a bit longer. I can pick it back up later."

He follows Sara over to the big screen and picks up a controller.

Moments later Daniel and Clifford walk in with several bags of groceries.

Bailey looks over and tosses the controller down, "Damn, that's a lot of shit!"

Clifford starts rattling off the snacks they got.

"I got four kinds of beer, chips, dip, chocolate, gummy bears, cookies, candy, you name it, we got it!"

Daniel and Clifford start unpacking the bags and laying things out on the counter.

Sara perks up, "Ooh, cheddar cheese popcorn! Milk duds! Reese's! Oh, you guys really do heart me!"

Clifford turns from the fridge and asks, "Should we order a pizza?"

Sara says, "I'm not feeling pizza, how about Chinese?"

Bailey says, "I could throw down some moo shu."

Daniel smiles. "Sounds good."

About forty minutes later the crew has a buffet of junk laid out. They put on a movie and settle in.

Hours go by and the snacks are plowed over. Clifford hands Bailey a beer and plops down in the chair. "I ate too much," Clifford says.

Bailey looks over, glassy eyed, "Me too."

Sara and Daniel are still munching away and laughing.

"I miss being able to eat like that," Clifford says.

Bailey scoffs. "I can when I'm high."

Clifford laughs and clinks beers with him and takes a swig.

A moment later, Bailey's computer pings. He looks over and sees an alert message.

"The hell is that?" Bailey asks as he starts to wheel over.

Clifford looks over at Bailey and takes another swig and looks back at the movie.

He turns back to Bailey and says, "C'mon man, no working right now. Look at it tomorrow." Bailey fixates on the screen and clicks and moves files in a rapid succession.

"No way. No. Way," Bailey says to himself.

Clifford stands up and starts to walk over toward Bailey. The beer is starting to kick in and he stumbles as he walks.

A woozy feeling comes over Clifford and he starts to shake his head a bit.

"Damn, this beer is kicking my ass. What did you find?" Clifford asks.

Bailey turns and says, "I found out who Dorothy is."

Clifford stares at Bailey for a moment.

Bailey looks back at Clifford and starts to get a dizzy spell. "Dee? Are you feeling woozy, too?"

He asks as Clifford starts to sway.

Bailey watches as Clifford falls and hits the ground.

He looks over to see Sara and Daniel lying, passed out, where they had just been sitting.   Bailey shakes the dizzy spell off for a moment and tries to go for his phone, but everything goes dark before he can call anyone.

CHAPTER THIRTY-SEVEN

Bailey is the first to awake. He looks around the unfamiliar, dark room. He can see Clifford tied to a pillar with Sara, and Daniel is in a chair tied to a pole.

His vision is blurred, and his head is throbbing. His hands are bound behind him. His body is bolted to the floor with a chain and padlock. As his eyes start to focus, he can see a door and a little bit of light shining underneath.

"Dee! Hey, Dee!" Bailey yells over to Clifford.

Clifford slowly starts to come to, recognizing Bailey's voice calling out to him. He looks around for a moment to gauge the room. He can't see Bailey from his angle, so he just yells back, "Bailey, are you okay?"

"Yeah, Dee, I'm tied down, but I can see everyone."

"Who am I tied with? I can feel someone."

"It's Sara, she's on the other side of the pillar."

Clifford pulls at the ropes a little and Sara jolts awake.

"What the fucking fuck?" she says, groaning.

Clifford says, "Bailey is to your left, my right. Can you see Daniel?"

Sara's eyes can barely focus.

She looks around and says, "Hold on. My eyes kinda hurt."

Clifford says, "I think we were gassed. Knockout gas will do that."

Sara's eyes begin to focus. "I see Bailey and Daniel. Dan's still passed out."

Clifford wiggles and moves around trying to find some slack, but there is none.

"Stop it, Dee, you're making it tighter," Sara says.

"Sorry, I'm trying to see if I can get free."

Daniel starts to groan.

Sara says, "Baby Bear's awake."

Clifford calls over, "Dan, what's your situation?"

Daniel, still a bit dazed, says, "It's hard to see, but I think I may be tied up."

Clifford says, "We were gassed."

Daniel asks, "Gassed?"

"Yeah, gassed. Knocked out."

Daniel says, "This doesn't look like Bailey's."

"Can you move?" Clifford asks.

"No. I'm tied to a chair."

Clifford starts looking around the room to see if he can spot anything to use.

A moment later he hears a sound coming from outside the door.

The group remains quiet as the sound of footsteps grows louder.

The door swings open and lets a flood of light into the room. Clifford grimaces and closes his eyes.

"Oh good, you're all awake! Kelly says, flipping on a light.

The fluorescent lights flicker a few times and slowly illuminate the dark room.

Clifford shakes his head and says, "Kelly."

"Mr. Dee," Kelly continues, "I've been doing this job for a very long time. I'm careful. Very careful I try not to attract attention, but you, Mr. Dee, you caught on. Caught on fast, and you don't give up, do you? You just won't go away."

Clifford smiles and says, "Sorry, for that. Toxic personality trait. I promise to work on it."

Kelly smiles briefly and says, "I'd like to give you the opportunity, Mr. Dee. However," She pauses for a moment before continuing, "I did some research and read up on what happened to your last employer."

Clifford smiles, "Ah, you read about that did ya?"

"I did, and it was impressive. A bunch of amateurs. A ragtag group of new, unlikely, buddies taking on a crime boss like Bandoni is pretty notable, adorable. A made-for-TV movie. It's also a fluke," Kelly says, with a demeaning tone in her voice.

She starts to pace the floor and look around at the team.

Kelly smiles. "I'm so glad you guys decided to have a little slumber party. Made my life a bit easier. Of course, you might consider that a fluke, as well," she says smugly.

"Mr. Bailey," she says, strolling over to him, "the street thug turned super geek."

Bailey rolls his eyes and demands, "Can you please spare us the evil supervillain monologue? It's a bit derivative, don't you think?"

Kelly laughs to herself. "Yes, indeed it is."

She looks over toward Sara and says, "Ah, Sara dear. *Cherchez la femme!*"

Sara, with a confused look on her face says, "Cher-what-la-what?"

Kelly continues, "You pretend to be the ditz and cute, but we all know you know what you're doing. You're crafty and smart. And who knew you could fight so well! I'll admit, I was impressed with how you took down my best killer. I mean, I'm still royally pissed, but impressed, nonetheless. And the real ditz," she says going towards Daniel, "is the boy. Life experience always tops youth. It's too bad you won't live long enough to figure that out on your own." She reaches to ruffle his hair as Daniel dodges her hand.

Turning her attention back to the leader of the group, she says, "You see him as your protégé, don't you?"

Clifford, beyond annoyed, says, "Okay! Yeah! You got us all figured out. So what? What's your plan? You don't seem like the type to get your hands dirty and by my count, you're pretty short on henchmen, am I right?"

Kelly smirks, "I have plenty of 'henchmen,' as you called it. How did you think I got you all out here? Your friend, Kevin, thought he was pretty smart by keeping track of some of the people he hired from me. Besides, it doesn't matter how many I have. No one will find you down here. No one knows you're here. Miles from any type of civilization and no one ever comes up here. I could just lock the door and leave you all here to starve to death."

Clifford narrows his eyes and says, "Why do I have the feeling that you're not gonna do that?"

"No," Kelly says quickly, "I'm not gonna do that. I hardly leave things to chance, and I don't want to chance that you'll escape somehow, despite my doubts that you could." She thinks for a moment while gazing at Clifford's face. "A good-looking man who isn't a weasel and matches wits with me." She sighs. "Too bad I didn't get to experience any *other* fields of expertise with you."

"Oh no, that's just gross," Sara blurts out.

"Yeah, real estate bitch, can we get some courtesy buckets for the rest of this speech?" Bailey chimes in.

"What I am going to do is have you watch," Kelly says, ignoring the others.

Clifford swallows hard. "Watch?"

"Oh, yes, Mr. Dee. I want you to watch your team die."

Clifford struggles with the ties and pulls on them hard but cannot get free. "No, I won't let you harm them."

"You have no choice. And I think I'm going to start with your youngest, your trainee, your apprentice. Then the cripple, then the girl."

Kelly pulls a handgun out of her purse and sets the purse down on an old cable spool in the corner.

"I usually don't get my hands dirty, you're right, but in this case, I'm going to take pleasure in watching you witness your entire team taken away from you before I put a bullet between your gorgeous eyes."

She clicks off the safety and walks up to Daniel and looks over at Clifford.

"Oh, wait a minute. You can't see from this angle." She hesitates for a moment and says, "Oh well, you'll just have to take my word for it."

Clifford can hear the hammer of the gun click as it's moving backward.

The loud explosion of a gun rings out and echoes through the room. Sara let's out a blood curdling scream and Bailey shouts "Oh SHIT!"

CHAPTER THIRTY-SEVEN

Clifford cries, "NO! You, bitch! You fucking bitch, No!"

"Dee!" Daniel screams, "Dee, I'm okay."

The body of Kelly lay near Daniel's feet, dead.

Panicked, Clifford looks over his shoulder and sees a man standing with a gun.

Sara's eyes focus on him through her tears, and she exclaims, "Paul Michaels!"

Clifford asks, "THAT's your art teacher?"

Daniel smiles, "Yeah, that's Paul Michaels!"

Clifford asks, "How?"

Paul looks at the crew and says, "Who the hell did you think Dorothy was?"

Bailey says, "Yeah, that's what I found out right before the gas got us."

Paul looks over at Bailey and says, "Do me a favor, Wheels, erase my name off that list."

He walks over and leans over Daniel in the chair and says, "I couldn't let her hurt my sweet Daniel. You're just too..." he pauses, "precious."

Daniel laughs nervously, "So, what now?"

Paul Michaels pulls a knife from a holster on his leg and leans forward, kissing Daniel on his forehead. "I'm going to help you escape."

He slips behind Daniel and places the knife in his hand.

As he starts to walk out of the room in haste, Clifford yells, "Hey, Paul Michaels," and waits for him to turn around, "Thank you!"

Paul Michaels winks, turns around, and leaves without saying a word.

Daniel slices through the ropes and finally frees himself.

He cuts Sara's ties and says, "Get Dee, I'll work on Bailey."

Before Sara cuts through Dee's hand ties, she runs over to Kelly's body and snags her gun, "I'm not taking any chances now, either."

Clifford slips out of the ropes with Sara's help. He jogs over toward the door and sees a long hallway and a metal staircase at the end. He turns back around and sees Sara and Daniel struggling to free Bailey.

Clifford finds a metal pipe on the ground and walks over to the group. "Stand back," he says as he inserts the pipe into the loop of the padlock on the chain to create tension on the locking mechanism. He pulls the pipe down and stomps on the lock, popping it open.

"Holy shit, how'd you know that would work?" Daniel asks.

Clifford laughs, "I saw it on YouTube."

Daniel throws Bailey over his shoulder and proceeds to walk out and up the metal stairs.

They reach the top where a large metal door is flung open.

Clifford looks over and sees two dead men on the ground next to the door.

They had guns that were never drawn.

He looks over at his teammates and can only muster out the sound, "Hm."

They continue to walk toward the door and out into the world.

They emerge on a hilltop looking down a wooded path. They were in some sort of abandoned bunker. Kelly wasn't lying about no one finding them. They were in the middle of nowhere.

CHAPTER THIRTY-EIGHT

"It's been two months," Daniel says.

"So what?" Clifford replies.

"Why did it take so long for them to do this? He should have gotten this a long time ago," Daniel says, perplexed.

Bailey tries to look over someone else's head, "Why did they put us in the back?"

"Would you guys be quiet?!" Sara demands.

The three men look at each other and back at Sara's glare.

"Sorry," they whisper in unison.

The room is full of colleagues and team members of Sims' from the bureau. Sims stands next to his superior, Director Sorren, as he is making a grand speech.

Director Sorren turns to the crowd, "With that, I have the honor of bestowing one of the bureau's highest awards, The FBI Star, to Agent Talmadge Sims."

The attendees erupt into applause and cheers. Sims smiles as Sorren places the medal around his neck. He shakes Sorren's hand and waves to his peers.

He nods at Clifford and Clifford nods back.

A few hours later Sims walks into a local brewery and spots Clifford, Sara, Bailey, and Daniel sitting at a table with a seat reserved for him.

The group cheers, "Hey!" as they see him walking toward them.

Sims sits down and Clifford says, "I'll get you a beer, stay here."

A few minutes later Clifford returns with a cold glass of their special brew.

Sims takes a huge swig and says, "Thank you! I am so happy you guys didn't die in that bunker."

Clifford laughs and says, "So are we, jackass."

Sims takes another swig and asks Bailey, "You get any pings on Dorothy yet?"

Bailey shakes his head, "Nah, he's gone. May have changed his codename. Hell, we don't even know if Paul Michaels is his real name."

Sara chimes in, "His art studio is a daycare now."

Sims almost chokes on his beer, "A daycare? Already?"

Sara says, "Crazy, I know. It didn't take long for another functioning business to spring up in its place."

Sims shakes his head, "That's crazy. This place is all go."

Sara nods.

Clifford asks, "So, does that star come with a bigger paycheck?"

Sims smiles, "Nope, it doesn't, but it looks good."

Sims takes a big swallow of his beer and says, "Damn is this good or what?! I'm going to grab a pitcher."

He stands and heads over to the bar.

Daniel walks up to Sara and asks, "Did you see the other room?"

Sara looks confused, "What other room?"

Daniel nods over his shoulder to a back room, "Over there."

"No, why?"

Daniels eyes get big, "Pinball."

"What?" Sara asks in surprise.

Daniel smiles, "And NES!"

Sara's mouth falls agape in shock, "Let's go!"

Sara grabs her beer, jumps up and rushes to the other room to play.

Bailey says, "Back to the good times." He raises his glass and Clifford raises his.

"Let's hope we don't get any surprises. I kinda wish I knew where Dorothy went off to."

Bailey smiles.

Clifford tilts his head, "You know, don't you?"

Bailey still smiling, says, "Let's just say it's good to keep tabs on people without the Feds knowing."

Clifford nods in agreement.

Sims comes back to the table with a pitcher and Clifford says, "Ooh, just in time."

He grabs the pitcher and tops off his beer. Bailey does the same.

Sims smiles and raises his glass. "Partners in crime?"

Clifford looks over at Bailey and they both look at Sims with their glasses raised. "Partners in crime!" they reply.

Sims takes a swig and asks, "What's next?"

Clifford nods and says, "Well, I'm refiling my security paperwork to renew my government consulting spot that Kevin ruined for me. Bailey's taking on the private-for-hire cases and will utilize Sara and Daniel as his main investigators. If all works out, I could become a full-blown agency and be able to hire a staff."

Sims nods with excitement. "Nice, nice!" he says, happy for his friend.

Clifford's phone starts to buzz. He picks it up and looks but does not recognize the number. He declines the call, places the phone back in his pocket, and continues to have celebratory drinks with his friends.

Sims looks up from his beer and motions toward the television in the corner. "Check it out."

Clifford and Bailey both look over and see a news story about an arrest being made. A man with a jacket over his head is being led in handcuffs by police and is accompanied by a team of lawyers, shooing away reporters.

"Police have arrested Eugene Gray, more famously known as the rap sensation Dark Fenix, on allegations of illegal weapons dealing. The details are still unfolding, but this is a shock to the music community."

Bailey smiles and says, "I hope Ferrell gets a promotion for this."

Clifford raises his glass, and the three gentlemen clink them together.

Evening turns to night, and everyone retreats to their condos. Clifford goes up to his room and pulls his phone out of his pocket. He sees the missed call notification on his phone and the voicemail light is illuminated. He sets his phone down and goes into the bathroom to brush his teeth.

When he returns to his room, he picks up the phone and looks at it again. Finally, he plays the voicemail. He can hear someone dragging on a cigarette and exhaling then immediately afterward, letting out a huge sigh before ending the message. Clifford listens to it again to confirm that the sigh sounds like it was coming from a woman.

He deletes the message.

He shakes his head and continues to get ready for bed. Moments later the phone rings again. Clifford picks up the phone and sees it's the same number.

"Hello?"

"Clifford Dee?" the woman's voice asks.

"This is. Who's this?" Clifford asks in return.

"You came to my house a few years back. My name is Grace." She drags on another cigarette and exhales into the phone.

Clifford thinks for a moment and says, "Husband named Raymond and a little girl."

"Bingo. My daughter's name is Hadley."

Clifford says, "It's been a while."

Grace says, "I need your help again. Hadley's missing."

Clifford asks, "Where can we meet?"

Grace takes another drag off her cigarette and is silent for a moment.

* * *

A short week later Clifford walks out of the airport and crosses the pickup and drop-off lanes. White snow caps are nestled on the jagged mountains in the distance.

He looks up at the night sky as snow pelts him in the face. A wind cuts through his clothes like cold steel, and he says, "I should have brought a bigger jacket."

ABOUT THE AUTHOR

J. Denison Reed was born in Trenton New Jersey, and grew up in a small town south of there called Carney's Point. He joined the Army after graduating high school and moved on to become a network engineer. He now owns a small candle business with his wife, living in Virginia with their children and two cats. He enjoys creative outlets like photography, making candles, and writing poetry. Other published works of J. Denison Reed include *Clifford's War: The Bluegrass Battleground*.

CPSIA information can be obtained
at www.ICGtesting.com
Printed in the USA
LVHW082023080822
725450LV00013B/482

9 781737 164043